PLEDGE
OF
ALLEGIANCE

BRAD FLINT

PAGE PUBLISHING, INC.
Conneaut Lake, PA

First originally published by Page Publishing 2020

ISBN 978-1-64628-961-5 (pbk)
ISBN 978-1-64628-962-2 (digital)

Printed in the United States of America

ONE

T he fear of death can come upon you suddenly—a rush of bile in one's throat—or it can build as your mind accelerates toward an expected peril. Either way, when it arrives with conscious embracement, the apprehension locks your body in a series of automatic reflexes.

Juan Carlos Sanchez, as he was called, could not see the fear, but he felt it expand around him in the fetid darkness, fed by those who began to mumble, curse, weep, and pray. It was a group emotion, a shared and reflected harmonious chorus in a single key.

They had been on the move for more than four hours with no light and diminishing air that thickened with every mile. The fear was tearing at all the men, except Juan Carlos, who had tasted it many times over the past ten years. He accepted its presence, for only he among the twelve men had irrevocably committed himself to an impending death. He prayed that he be permitted to meet that death at a time and place of his choosing, at a time and place which would witness destruction of the godless infidels, at his hands, the hands of HajI-Ahmed Ayazi.

Hell on earth would have conveyed an accurate description. Pitch-black, hot, and endless rolling and tossing. Packed as sardines in a can they sat without room to stand or lie flat, identifiable in the dark one from another only by their sounds and the odor of sweat. Just two hours out of San Fernando, several of them had passed out.

The one on Ayazi's right slumped against him and was gasping as the heat continued to rise in the cramped steel container. In front of him, somewhere in the dark, the sound of retching began again, then stopped, replaced by the putrid smell of vomit. The small plastic bottles of water distributed at the outset to each had long since been drained.

The jostling subsided as the truck inched ahead in the long line approaching the Laredo customs station at the Rio Grande. Each man held his breath, listening to the screech of the trailer's heavy rear doors as they swung open. Any movement or sound from the container could lead Ayazi to more than arrest and eventual expulsion back to Mexico. The Mexican driver's license in his pocket, while expertly fashioned, might not be enough to convince the American authorities that he was simply another wetback seeking economic survival north of the border. They could hear the Border Patrol agent entering the rear of the trailer. After a long and anxious ten minutes, the agent completed his inspection of the cargo in the identical steel container at the rear door, comparing its contents and the total number of containers with the truck driver's printed manifest. He waved the driver on with a listless nod of his head and returned the manifest to the driver's nervous hand.

Once again, the truck moved forward with the rear doors closed and locked. Someone on Ayazi's left muttered Gracias Dios and then called out to Chico with a laugh. The heavy tension evaporated and everyone broke into a rollicking song, a Mexican poem unknown to Ayazi, who remained silent. He was not ungrateful; his prayers to the Mighty One had been answered, but he simply kept his vigilance as he had been taught for almost two years to avoid any prolonged communication with those whose language, customs, and morality were so alien to him. Living in a world totally populated with *ferangi* was a constant strain, offset only by his faith in his holy jihad.

The relief of the successful border crossing ebbed hour by hour, depleted by the stifling heat and stale air. Rumbling north on I-35, the odors in the container became ever more nauseating and several of the men began pounding on the walls, willing to risk discovery should the Highway Patrol decide to check the truck and its cargo.

Ayazi felt the day should be nearing an end when the truck pulled off the highway and slowly bumped over a rutted road for another thirty minutes before grinding to a halt. Anticipation, smothered in silence, greeted the driver's efforts as he unlocked and opened the rear doors with the help of two grunting men. Not daring to speak, the weary men waited and squirmed while the rear containers were wrestled onto a loading dock and the door of their prison was swung wide by one of the driver's helpers. The heavy air flowed out of the open container door, and the man reeled as the stench assailed his nostrils. Shouting "Jesus Christo," he swung about and ran from the trailer.

Blinded by the low sun piercing the back of the trailer, a few were able to stand and walk out onto the dock, quickly glancing left and right, fearing the presence of any police or other authorities. The one that had slumped against Ayazi did not stir until a pail of water was dumped on his head and he was roughly dragged out by his feet.

Ayazi mouthed a silent prayer of thanksgiving, praising Allah that he had completed his long journey to America, the land of his country's tormentors, the killers who had wantonly defiled his native soil by killing innocent women and children for more than ten long years.

He walked onto the dock, clutching his small canvas bag to his chest, pulsating his clothing, razor, prayer rug, and worn Koran with his thumping heart. The wearisome months in Mexico taught him that a prayer rug carried by a Muslim was no surprise to many in the Western world. Still, he never displayed it except during prayers at his small room in San Fernando and at the mosque in Matamoros.

Looking around the dirty parking lot off the end of the dock, he was relieved to see the man as he had been described. Wearing blue jeans, a red long-sleeved shirt, and a straw cowboy hat, he stood next to the door of a shiny black Toyota pickup. The truck driver herded the other men into a large, worn van with tinted windows and seemed not to notice that Ayazi veered off toward the man in the red shirt. When Ayazi was a few feet from the man, he was tersely greeted.

"I am Ali. Get in."

They were the first words in Arabic Ayazi had heard since coming to the Western world. As he started to respond, Ali held up his hand and said in English, "Speak only in English or Spanish."

Inside the pickup, smelling of new leather and glittering with many gadgets on the dashboard, Ayazi recalled the old Toyota truck his father had driven in Khost while he clung to the large and deadly machine gun mounted in the truck's worn bed behind. They had driven many miles together in search of the American soldiers who had driven the Taliban into the high mountains.

TWO

Ayazi rode in silence, listening to the whine of the pickup's tires on the highway. The speed of the many cars and trucks mile after mile was both amazing and frightening. Nothing in Afghanistan and Pakistan had prepared him for such a rolling diorama. Not even the loud and diesel-choked highways in Mexico had produced such a feeling of dynamic force and impending doom.

Ayazi removed the worn baseball cap and wiped his brow. He was growing accustomed to the denim pants and cheap boots that were furnished to him in San Fernando on his arrival there months ago, but he still longed for baggy pants, long-tailed shirts, and colorful vests of his native country, which he would never wear again.

He glanced at the silent older man driving, staring straight ahead. Ali's brief direction that he should enter the black truck left him with no information about their destination. The chief in San Fernando had warned him he would be provided the barest instructions and then, only when he was assigned his mission, his destiny with martyrdom. Ayazi knew only that Ali was a Muslim who lived in Dallas and was to be his sole contact before his entry into the glorious afterlife before the presence of Allah and his own father and grandfather.

The countryside shone bright and clear in the fading sunlight.

Rolling green fields festooned with large rolled bales of hay and small villages sped by. So this was the land of the devil America, the home of the infidels who ravaged his own village, Afgh, in the Urgun tribal area of Southern Afghanistan. None of the homes in view were protected or obscured by the mud walls like he had helped build in Afgh to protect his parents, brothers, and sisters from the thieves who plagued the dark nights. How strange. How careless these Americans must be!

Thoughts of his village and his family raced through his mind, reminding him of the great distance his travels had carried him during the past several years, a trek to avenge the deaths of his father and grandfather who had given their lives in the centuries-old battle of the Afghan people against multiple invaders. His father's father, a respected mullah, had left their village in 1980 to join the mujahideen resistance to the hated Russians, armed with weapons from the American allies.

The mujahideen had finally succeeded in driving out the pagan horde from the north, just six months after his father brought news of his grandfather's death near Kandahar. Political chaos followed, and the old warlords reestablished their civil warfare. America's assistance vanished the moment the Russians were gone. Within a year, his father departed Afgh to join the Taliban to bring peace and true Islamic law out of the anarchy sweeping over the country. Thereafter, on his infrequent visits, his father carefully instructed Ayazi and his brothers in the ways of true Islam and the struggles of the Taliban to enforce Allah's divine will on the people. This history he had learned at his father's knee.

On his fifteenth birthday, he was permitted to leave Afgh and join his father's cadre high in the mountains bordering Pakistan. In six months, he became proficient in cleaning and firing the old machine gun mounted in his father's truck. Death soon became a daily experience as they together roamed the southern villages, enforcing the Taliban rules in the name of Allah.

He came back to the present, and as they passed through a town which straddled the highway, Ayazi stared at two young girls waving at the passing traffic. Both were blond headed, wearing only a small shirt and blue shorts. How disgraceful!

They were pagans who would have been beaten if such a showing of their bodies had occurred in his village. Traditional Chanderi were mandatory for any woman appearing outside a home in Afghanistan. Mexico had been no better, confirming that even those of Christian faith were shameless before God. Truly God's kingdom would not tolerate such apostasy forever. The wrath of Allah would be visited by his own hand none too soon.

Dusk was enveloping the flat fertile land when Ali slowed the pace, curving onto an exit ramp. It appeared to be another town like those they had seen the past hour, but the road paralleling the main highway soon led to a much larger community.

"We are here," Ali muttered in English. Ayazi had been instructed that neither he nor Ali were to speak in any other language even though Ayazi was proficient in Pasto, his native tongue, Arabic, and passable in Spanish. He had no doubt that utterances in Pasto or Arabic would only arouse suspicions in America. Quick-witted from the time he could walk, he exhibited little difficulty during his training in learning to speak and read Spanish and English although his English idiom remained sparse.

One of his instructors in Pakistan had been born in America and drilled him during those long days in the barren mountains, but still, the American language was complicated.

"Where are we?" Ayazi responded, relieved to finally hear a human voice.

"It is called Lamar. You will not be going to Dallas as you were told. It is wiser for you to remain here, away from the brothers in Dallas. We will contact you as necessary." With that terse comment, he held out a small cell phone and a short cord for recharging the phone's battery.

"A small apartment has been arranged for you. It is furnished with a bedroom and a kitchen. There is a TV, and you will learn from it more English and knowledge of the events in the area. A serviceable truck is waiting at the apartment."

Ali's words were short, direct and invited no response, question, or comment from *Juan Carlos*.

"On Monday, you will drive to the address on this paper I am handing you. It is the office of a small excavation business owned by an Hispanic man. You will be employed and will speak in Spanish or English as may be convenient."

Ayazi nodded silently. It was much like he had been told by his instructor in San Fernando, except he had believed that he would bring about a magnificent jihad in Dallas. Had he traveled around the world only to watch TV in some unknown village?

"What is excavation?" he asked when Ali fell into a long silence.

"It is the business of digging and moving dirt" came the curt reply as Ali stopped the truck by a small one-story duplex building, where one dim light over the front entry twinkled through a broken glass fixture.

The vow to give his life in an act of martyrdom, taken almost two years ago in Pakistan, was a moment of glory. Was that honor to be buried in a ditch with shovel in hand? Ayazi's mood was downcast as he stepped from the truck and carried his meager possessions to the door on the left, entering behind Ali. A sofa, a chair, and a small table occupied the first room.

"There is your bedroom," Ali gestured with a hand before entering the small alcove on the right containing an electric range top, refrigerator, sink, and a small table with two chairs. Opening several cabinet doors, Ali silently displayed cooking utensils, pots, pans, and canned and packaged foods. The refrigerator door remained closed.

"Oh yes, here is the key to the pickup that is behind the building. You do have your Texas driver's license, yes?"

Ayazi nodded, marveling at the spacious apartment which was larger than his family home where he and his three brothers and two sisters were reared. He knew he would enjoy his final days however few he might have remaining.

"Don't forget, you report for work on Monday. It was not easily arranged, so do not fail!" Not waiting a reply, Ali departed the front door and walked to the curb.

"When and where will I fulfill my mission?" Ayazi yearned to inquire, but it was clear that Ali had delivered all the information he wished to share. He had seemed almost hostile. Was he jealous that he had not been chosen for martyrdom, or was he suspicious of the fact that Ayazi was not an Arab but an Afghan?

Ayazi clutched the cell phone and cord in his hand, the only lifeline he could claim in this foreign land thousands of miles from his home. He did not even have a telephone number which might connect with those in Dallas who would one day direct him to his ultimate fate. He plunged his hand into his pocket to confirm that the five thousand dollars in American was still there. It would have to serve his needs until his new employment as a ditchdigger returned some unknown earnings.

Tomorrow he would explore the town in the waiting truck and purchase foods and other needs. Work clothing would have to wait until his employment was confirmed. Tonight the small bed beckoned.

THREE

T he warm and unusually clammy evening embraced the numerous cars and pickups in the parking lot next to Mac's BBQ Joint and Emporium. South of the town square and two blocks west of I-35, the single neon light near the entrance anchored Mac's thirty-plus years as Lamar's leading purveyor of barbecue and cold beer. Emporium sardonically referred to the Texas flags, sports-figure bobbleheads, T-shirts, and other paraphernalia which attracted more dust than dollars as they sat on the racks near the cash register.

Inside, a flat-screen television hung over the end of the long, battered bar, competing with the noise emanating from the fifty or sixty people who were regaling one another with tall stories, complaints about government, and occasional shrieks of laughter heightened by the free beer, wine, and *real* drinks.

Bobby Sanford just happened to glance at the rolling reports moving across the bottom of the TV screen when "Lamar City Council Place 3" appeared and finally confirmed he had been reelected to his third term by a 25 percent margin, with 90 percent of the precincts reporting. As the revelers noticed the report, a rousing cheer filled the walls.

The Dallas television had spent most of the evening predicting and reporting the results in Dallas and Fort Worth. The races in the numerous other cities and towns in Dallas County, Tarrant County, and surrounding areas were but fleeting scrolls across the screen. Few had doubted that Bobby would be representing Lamar's citizens for another two years, but the formal confirmation by the media was the catalyst to kick off a rapidly forming conga line through the bar and into the back room where the brisket and ribs were still being devoured by the usual patrons who wondered why their evening was disrupted by the noisy election workers who had descended upon them.

"Speech, speech, Bobby!" was shouted up and down the bar. Mac himself, a short balding Greek with dark brows and sagging face, confirmed the demand by pointing the controller at the TV and silencing the sound.

In khaki slacks and a bright blue shirt, Bobby held up his hands in a victory salute. His smile split a handsome face, sparked by bright blue eyes under his strong forehead, a face well-known to any fan who ever attended the Lamar High football games over twenty-five years ago.

"Let me thank all of you for being here tonight and for all your hard work over the past six weeks. I am so honored to be able to serve all of you, even those who did not vote for me!"

A loud chorus of boos erupted to express the displeasure directed at those who had not supported Lamar High's greatest quarterback.

"Well, I appreciate that," Bobby continued, "but you know we can't run a city government for just a part of the people. At least that's one thing I've learned in my four years on the council. We have a lot work to do yet to solve the challenges thrown at us by the growth we've see the last ten years. And that growth is not going to stop. The 2010 census reported that Lamar is home to more than fifty thousand people, with more coming. We must be doing something right! We need more police officers, firefighters, roads, schools, and that's only a start." He paused and inhaled, his eyes glowing.

Becky Sanford grimaced. Why was Bobby still giving his campaign speech? Her feet hurt, and she was ready to go home. She put her hand over Libby's hand, pleading, "Please go tell your dad that enough is enough. We've got to get up early if we don't want to be late at DFW."

Libby rose, flashing her long tanned legs under her skirt, grabbed Josh by the hand, and pulled him along for support in moving through the rollicking crowd. At six feet, three inches, Josh Powers presented a persuasive front in any setting.

Bobby smiled as he spotted the duo of his daughter and Josh approaching the bar. He had no doubt about their mission and who had sent them. He wound down with more thanks and appreciations before he worked back through the crowd toward Becky, his wife of twenty-one years.

The crowd was urging them to remain, but they quickly overcame their disappointment when Bobby assured them that the tab would remain open.

Bobby and Becky bid a happy farewell to Libby and Josh in the parking lot and got into Becky's new Ford sedan as Becky slid behind the steering wheel. She had insisted on driving her car to the election watch party. She studiously avoided riding in the councilman's carriage, as Libby branded Bobby's twelve-year-old Jeep Cherokee. In spite of Becky's pleas, he refused to buy a modern, respectable automobile.

"The voters in Lamar are not interested in seeing me parade around in a shiny new car," he repeated each time she mentioned it.

Becky turned down their street, lined with upper-middle-class McMansions, which populated the older and wealthier sections of the city.

"I hope those people don't continue the party into next week," Bobby said, smiling at Becky.

Becky smiled at his attempt at sarcasm. He ordinarily communicated in straightforward and honest prose, a trait which endeared him to most people who knew and lauded his four years of service on the council.

In the house, she turned to him.

"Before we turn in, don't you think you should call Mac to see if they are still running up your tab? The election is over, and they should go home."

"I don't know, Becky. They worked so hard. Tom Wegman ran a tough campaign. His cry to confine the gas drilling to industrial zones rang a bell with a lot people. I could have lost. The Barnett Shale boom has not been welcomed by a lot of people."

"Well, the world would not have ended if you had lost. Maybe we could have found time to enjoy a real vacation instead of a short four days in Colorado." Becky sighed wistfully.

"I know, I know. We'll do that, I promise," he soothed, lifting the bedside phone and dialing Mac's number.

FOUR

Buoyed by the bright sunshine on Friday morning and the memory of the brief Colorado visit, Bobby drove to the law office on Second Street. His three law partners, their two assistants, and four secretaries congratulated him once again on his victory. They had no doubt that the business coming in the front door to The Law Offices of Robert J. Sanford was, more often than not, boosted by the fact that one of the partners served on the city council. However, Bobby scrupulously insisted that they not represent any client whose business might be directly affected by the council's actions. They and their clients, of course, were taxpayers and their pocketbooks were impacted by the council's tax rate determinations. This was a nicety that even the *ethics hawks* seemed to understand as they railed about more obvious misdeeds, real or imagined.

In his spacious office, the antique desk discovered by Becky at a Dallas sale crouched in waiting, with mail and law-case reporters stacked on top, business that had been pushed aside the last two weeks of the campaign. At one corner sat the council agenda package for next Wednesday's meeting.

The agenda, prepared by the city staff, was distributed to the mayor, the four council members, the city manager, and the two assistant city managers five days before each council meeting on the first and third Wednesday of each month. Action was required on every resolution, contract, purchase agreement, land acquisition, land sale, and zoning change affecting the city's coffers, city property, or citizens' property. That was all in addition to any proposed ordinance which mandated or prohibited future actions by a citizen or anyone who might be acting or transacting in the city limits. In order to forestall meetings lasting half the night, many agenda items were put on the consent docket if deemed routine or noncontroversial by the city manager. With few exceptions, the consent agenda items were passed together in one routine vote at each meeting before launching into the remainder of the agenda.

Leafing through the agenda, Bobby sighed, noting once more how it continued to expand each time, reflecting the rapid growth of Lamar the past ten years. He remembered his recent suggestion to the city secretary that she consider acquiring larger notebooks to accommodate the increasing business coming to the council.

Once an early settlement of a few hundred in rural Johnson County, south of Fort Worth, Lamar boasted only 12,350 residents in 1998 when it incorporated as a home rule city under Texas law, but older citizens had continued to refer to it as our town. Even now, at 51,000 population, it remained largely a bedroom community where most slept but worked in Fort Worth, Arlington, Dallas, or in some of the other 100-plus municipalities in the DFW Metroplex.

The town aldermen were replaced by the council in 1998, consisting of the mayor and four district council members. Next meeting, seven would sit on the council as the two newest members were sworn in to represent the creation of two additional districts following the United States 2010 Census. A strong mayor city was an apt term for Lamar. J. D. "Dub" Fanning, once an alderman, had been elected as mayor in 1998 and still presided with no opposition in the past five elections.

Bobby knew little of this history until he began service as the District 3 Council member. Born in Lamar, he played quarterback as Bobby Joe at Lamar High, with scant knowledge of the local government.

The town center along Main Street, until recent years, was little more than a backwater stream of commerce, overshadowed by the franchise row which fronted on I-35. The flow of significant commerce traveled the interstate, and the citizens of Lamar drove its lanes in the mornings and evenings as they plied their jobs to the north. The phenomenal population growth in Fort Worth spilled over to Lamar, fueling a host of headaches for Bobby and the other council members. Country living had enticed large numbers of people from Fort Worth and beyond to seek property in Lamar, but the swelling head count had succeeded only in bringing with them most of the societal challenges they had hoped to escape.

Demands for new roads, fire stations, and parks underlay several of the upcoming agenda items which Bobby poured over. "And of course," he muttered to himself, viewing the drilling application on Wednesday's schedule. The council's drilling ordinance, patterned after the one in Fort Worth, required a council waiver if the drilling company wished to drill a gas well closer to a residence than the 600-foot setback limit in the hard-fought ordinance. Drilling in an urban area gave birth to numerous challenges and many protagonists. The ordinance, as Bobby and most council members appreciated, represented a compromise between those who wanted to drill and recover gas under their property and those who believed safety and public health should forestall any such industrial activity in the city limits. Each proposed action by the council under the ordinance served as a launching pad for those opposed to drilling, and Bobby sighed, wondering how many times they would have to hear the same arguments over and over during the next two years. Well, he was the one who chose to run for another term. He had asked for it!

FIVE

A light rain fell as Bobby parked the Jeep in the District 3 parking space, lined by faded white paint, one of the forty-plus spaces behind the city hall. All but two of the council spaces were filled as afternoon May showers wetted the city under a heavy gray sky. At seven that evening, the entire lot would probably be filled with the cars, trucks, and SUVs of citizens who drove through Main Street and turned at the south side of the hall to enter the lot behind. The agenda would be a long one.

Main Street ran to the west side of what passed for an old town square. Once the center of the early town, the square resembled those typically holding the county courthouse in most of Texas's 254 county seats. But in Johnson County, the seat of county government was in Cleburn, some miles to the southwest of Lamar. It was becoming a matter of consternation to those in Cleburn that Lamar was now the largest city in Johnson County, and the rivalry between the two football teams was growing more each passing year.

With the recent growth, the square was seeing the rebirth of commerce along Main and the other streets circumscribing the small park at the center of the square. The old feedstore and the dry goods emporium, abandoned for many years, now housed offices along with a local restaurant and several insurance agencies.

The new city hall, built in 1999, occupied a flat of land to the northwest of the square, facing on the park. Two stories high, the redbrick pillared house of government resembled a Neo-Georgian style, if one did not look too closely. It had provoked a band of critics among the older denizens of the square who complained of the increasing flow of traffic now jamming the streets that defined the square.

The main entrance into the hall faced on Main Street, which, at one time, served as the old north-south state highway leading to Fort Worth, Oklahoma, and beyond before the advent of I-35. The ground floor in the front housed a cluster of city departments and staff offices and a payment center for water, sewer, and trash services. At the rear were the offices for the police and fire chiefs, not far from the council chamber and pre-council chamber. On the second floor rested the offices of the mayor, council members, city manager, assistant city managers, and their respective staffs. Restrooms, conference rooms, and miscellaneous spaces completed the large second floor.

A 2005 pistol shot by a deranged citizen in the Fort Worth City Hall had prompted the Lamar Council to call for the installation of metal detectors and sentry duty by police officers at all public entrances. Mayor Fanning initially decried the need for such extravagance, but shortly thereafter, he promoted the addition of another rear entrance off the rear parking lot. Largely hidden by a maintenance building, the entrance was accessible by the use of hard card keys issued only to the mayor and council members. Once through the secure door and down a secluded hallway (the chute), the cardholder could access a small elevator up to the rear of the second floor. The chute route was not known to most city hall visitors who were required to run the metal detector gauntlet at the public entrances at the front and the parking lot.

With a swipe of the card, Bobby passed through the rear door and down the chute to the elevator, impatiently waiting for it to return from the second floor. Exiting on the nondescript carpet lining the hall, he proceeded past the council and mayor's offices, which occupied the south wall of the building, overlooking Wood Street. Two of the offices once housed two of the three council assistants, who were to be displaced by the two new incoming council members.

Still aglow from Saturday's election party, Bobby strolled up to Carl Jeffers's office and shot a "congratulations" to him for topping the polls along with all the other incumbent members.

Carl immediately responded, "Same to you, Bobby," and waved him in to take a seat. As usual, papers, books, and other paraphernalia populated the office, forcing Bobby to move a sheaf of papers from the guest chair before he flopped into it.

"Now that our wise citizens have returned us to our solemn duties, do you think we can finally get our budget on track?" Carl asked, smiling at his own query.

Carl always delighted in stirring the proverbial pot just to observe the reaction from Bobby when the budget was mentioned. He wasn't disappointed.

"I don't know," Bobby replied. "Two of our members represent some of those folks who feel the city should provide funds for every project on their wish list. They promised the voters they would make it happen. I guess they will express shock, as usual, when they are reminded there is not enough money to do everything for everybody."

Bobby paused and went on, "Alece Jackson and Estella keep harping about the *underfunded* and the *disadvantaged*. Hell, I think the council has done a very good job of caring for the entire city, and it upsets me when anyone wants to paint the issue as a battle between the haves and the have-nots. Look what that has done over in Dallas."

Bobby's years of law practice, in his opinion, had formed in him a genuine understanding that a democratic society demanded respect for the needs of all people yet required a vigilant oversight to maintain a sustainable budget. Even so, he was no Pollyanna and was acutely aware not everyone shared those sentiments no matter how much they appeared to profess their love of the country's mantra.

"You tell 'em, Counselor," Carl replied. "But you're right. I'm worried about where we are headed too." He gruffed, rising to pace the small area between his desk and the window. Known in the media as the hide-bound conservative of the council, Jeffers was more outspoken at the council dais than others. A native Texan and ex-Marine gunnery sergeant long returned from the Gulf War, he still carried a raspy voice from his time in the desert. He made no effort to hide his disdain for the many outstanding taboos imposed by the politically correct society that was, in his estimation, creeping into Lamar. He did not hesitate to call a black man a black man even though that term seemed to be replaced by African American.

"Hell, I'm an American and there is no need to call me an Irish American because my great-grandfather came to this country years ago from Ireland," he had proudly remarked to a *Lamar Tribune* reporter shortly after his first election. His stand not only reflected his views, but it also made him popular among the local customers who patronized the Auto Zone parts store he and his partner, Jim Grant, operated on the east side of I-35. He never referred to Jim as black or African American. They had served in the same Marine regiment and viewed each other only as gyrenes who loved and fought for their country.

Pausing to glance out the shade-draped window, Carl asked Bobby, "Have you seen that resolution on tonight's agenda? The one that declares the city's financial policy shall be amended to add a new goal."

He reached over to his desk, picked up the resolution, and read, "Consideration of the annual budget shall include a review and provision for enhancing city expenditures necessary to promote and benefit underdeveloped areas of the city."

He threw down the resolution, staring at Bobby.

"Where in hell did that come from? Is someone on the staff trying to codify Alece Jackson's campaign platform? Are we supposed to divide up the city into economic enclaves and keep a running total of which taxpayers' money is spent in which enclave? This is a sure recipe for disaster!"

A painful expression stole across Bobby's face as he envisioned the debate which might take place at the next council meeting, especially if the proposed resolution drew a significant public participation at the public speakers' stand. Estella Jiminez, a long-standing council member, made no secret of her belief that more economic assistance was due those who represented diversity in the city. She enjoyed a staunch comrade in arms with Alece Jackson, who raised the same entitlement cry during his campaign.

"You may be right, Carl," Bobby responded. "I think I'll visit with Dub about this. Maybe the proposed language can be tuned a little so that it doesn't turn every budget study into a dogfight. We don't need diversity to become another term for *division*."

Realizing that he and everyone else would hear more from Carl on the subject, Bobby rose and continued down the hall, offering congratulations to Estella, who was in her office, two doors down, the phone jammed to her ear.

SIX

The mayor, sitting in the largest office on the second floor south wall, looked up as Bobby rapped on the open door, and laid down the weekly edition of the *Lamar Tribune* which he was reading.

"Come in, Bobby. I'm happy you ran a successful campaign. You deserved to win."

"Thanks, Mayor. Your support was critical in getting the whole crew returned."

At age seventy-three, Dub Fanning was in his eighteenth year as mayor, knowing his term would continue as long as he chose to run and his health permitted. What few people knew was that his beloved Sue Lynn was in the early stage of breast cancer and her future health held the real story of when he might quit the political arena. His lean five foot eleven no longer reflected the six-foot stature that had marked his early days as a baseball player on the Texas Longhorn team, one of the best players to come out of Lamar. On his sixty-fifth birthday, he closed his small insurance agency office on the square. With a substantial savings investment, he decided that the city deserved more of his attention at the shining new city hall.

He was honest enough to admit, at least to himself, that he truly enjoyed the prestige of being the glue that held the council, and hence the city, on course for an ever-growing reputation as a livable community. He missed no opportunity to tout Lamar to the thousands of new people that were flocking to the Metroplex, believing more people and commerce were necessary if Lamar were to avoid the fate of many smaller towns in the rural areas where the youth sought the fastest way out of town the minute they finished school. He personally encouraged many of those employed in Fort Worth to come and enjoy the relatively quiet life in Lamar, including many of the police officers and firefighters who worked for Fort Worth.

The mayor waved Bobby to the sideboard, indicating that he should pour himself cup of coffee before lowering into the comfortable visitor's chair facing the large desk that had come from the insurance office. After two sips, Bobby smiled briefly before revealing the concern that had prompted him to stop by.

"Dub, Carl and I were discussing the resolution on this week's agenda that would amend our financial policy. It seems to me that it could be worded more, I don't know, maybe more *adroitly* is the right term." Dub nodded, offering no other response on his lined face, framed by the full head of gray hair. Nor did he comment about the fact that the *Tribune* article he had been reading explicitly recited some of the campaign promises spread about by Alece Jackson and Estella Jiminez, which was headlined: "Council to Consider Policy Guidelines."

If one thing was constant during his term as mayor, it was that everything changed, sooner or later. If Lamar had not grown so rapidly in the past ten years, maybe most of the older ways would have remained. Maybe households would all consist of children reared and loved in a two-parent family and all the townspeople would know one another and wear the same pride on their sleeves as neighbor helped neighbor. But things had changed from the day I-35 bypassed the square and cleaved Lamar into two separate communities linked only by one overpass and two underpasses. The old black community, the Camp, established in the late nineteenth century and once a place of pride and grit, now huddled just off the east side of I-35 no longer accessible by Third Street and abandoned by most of the younger generation. For the most part, the young ones had moved away to Fort Worth or Dallas. Even Leon Harris, Lamar's star wide receiver, had settled in Fort Worth and rarely returned to his hometown.

25

A few of them had earned college degrees and made enough money to move to the newer neighborhoods which had sprung up on the west and south sides of the square. Alece Jackson was clearly referring to the Camp when he called for more government assistance to the underserved, implying his constituents were entitled to the same economic development which had graced other parts of the city.

As he read the *Tribune* article, Dub had muttered to himself, "I wish it were that simple." The city development department each year directed large sums of Federal HUD money to deserving projects on the east side. However, few had primed the pump as everyone had envisioned since private developers, ever mindful of the bottom line, found other more promising places to spend their money. The mayor was acutely aware that entrepreneurial investments, controlled by the laws of economics, seldom followed the path of good intentions in the feel-good social projects dreamed up by politicians.

"Bobby, I think you have a point. This issue could become problematical or worse. I hope you and the other council members will agree to postpone any action on the resolution tonight. I would like to appoint an ad hoc citizens committee to review the whole question and return a recommendation to the council. What do you think?"

The mayor looked carefully at Bobby, perhaps the most level-headed one on the council, without revealing any of the thoughts which had crossed his mind while reading the news article.

Letting his lungs exhale, Bobby responded, "You sure have my support, Mayor. Ramsey and Leech need time to settle in before we launch into anything that might stir the pot."

Leaving the mayor's office, he wondered how Paula Ramsey, one of the new members, might view an effort to postpone action on the financial policy change. She had little opposition during the election campaign, and her views on most of the city issues were still a mystery. In her mid-forties, divorced with two children, she had come to Lamar ten years ago after the divorce and began work with a local real estate firm, where she had proven very adept at selling high-end homes to new residents. At five foot five, with short bang-cut hair, resembling a blond helmet, she was considered very attractive by the local bachelors and divorced men, yet she had spurned any serious romance, telling all that her task was to get her two kids through college. A graduate of the University of Texas, she had put to good use her degree in accounting and had an active CPA practice in addition to the real estate work.

Terry Leech, the other newcomer, was not such an unknown. An active member of the Johnson County Caucus, he made no secret in his campaign that he would favor any and all initiatives which echoed the Democratic platform, nation or state. His flashy ties and shoes perhaps revealed even more about his underlying character. He undoubtedly would find a challenge in sparring with the likes of Carl Jeffers.

SEVEN

A bright, warm May day dawned, rousing Ayazi from a restless night. He was soon up and in the small bathroom, which included a well-used shower in one corner, a sink, and a commode, luxuries he seldom enjoyed in Afghanistan.

The warm shower was a delight as it caressed his slim, muscular frame for twenty minutes. Drying in front of the mirror over the sink, he saw that his heavy beard was in need of a shave, a chore that had not plagued him before. To maintain his appearance as a native Mexican, he was instructed to abandon his proud beard and retain only the heavy dark mustache that hid his upper lip which supported his hooked Afghan nose. How many of his comrades on the other side of the world would recognize him today? He frowned, realizing he was thinking in Pashto, not in English, which must serve as his waking language in this new land. Maybe he could find a bookstore where he could purchase a small English dictionary to extend his limited English vocabulary. Dressing in jeans, shirt, and a sweat-stained cap, he noted the apparel's contrast with the long shirts, colored vests, and flowing turbans that had covered him since childhood.

Sleep eluded his tired body during the night as his brain repeatedly reviewed the events that had controlled his destiny since an al-Qaeda agent approached him several years ago in Khost Province. The Taliban was on friendly terms with Osama bin Laden and his followers but had no desire to act in concert with them because their actions on 9/11 had unleashed the American invasion, an invasion that took the life of Ayazi's father.

"Your exploits in harassing the devils from America have not gone unnoticed, my brother," the agent offered in Arabic, colored by his Palestinian accent.

"Our holy jihad would be well served by your assistance in dealing a death blow to the Western infidels," he continued when Ayazi merely stared in return.

Though he had feigned little interest in the flattering words, Ayazi was intrigued with the prospect of avenging his father's death, perhaps an act that might reach beyond the rugged mountains of Afghanistan, for it would only be a matter of time before the Americans again tired of their venture and retreated behind the barriers of their two oceans.

His Taliban commander was not pleased with the plea that one of his prized fighters be released to serve the Arab bin Laden, but Ayazi's contention that service in Allah's cause could be fulfilled in the worldwide jihad through many means proved successful. In August 2013, Ayazi began the long trek through the high mountains, as directed, to the al-Qaeda training camp in North Waziristan, an old tribal territory in Pakistan.

The training camp was well hidden in a series of caves which were not readily visible from the air. Recruits came and went during his eighteen-month stay. Already well versed in military and raiding tactics, Ayazi devoted most of his time to learning Spanish and English, two languages far removed from his native Pashto and the ubiquitous Arabic which dominated the camp. His other subject of study was the numerous methods of assembling, transporting, and detonating bombs and other explosives.

He still treasured the day when his training came to an end, and he was escorted by two fierce instructors to meet Osama bin Laden. Bin Laden's rhetoric was soft but mesmerizing, and before leaving the darkened cave, Ayazi vowed before the three men that he would become a martyr in the service of Allah and his prophet Muhammad. With laudatory remarks, bin Laden ordered further schooling be given so that Ayazi would be fully prepared to journey to America to confront the Western devil in his home ground. Thus began the long journey through India and tramp steamer across the Atlantic to San Fernando, Mexico, a few miles from Matamoros, one of the southern gateways into the United States.

Surveying each drawer and cabinet in the small kitchen, Ayazi thought back on the drive with Ali. Ali's dour silence and clipped instructions were puzzling. Not once had he smiled, glanced at Ayazi, or addressed him by name even though surely he must have been told that Juan Carlos Sanchez was, in fact, HajI-Ahmed Ayazi, an Afghan recruited by al-Qaeda. Ali's first and only instruction in Arabic revealed an accent common to Yemen, often heard during his days in the al-Qaeda camp. Was Ali envious of Ayazi's mission, or did he believe only Arabs were worthy to carry on the jihad and that Afghans were not true believers? Whatever the reason, Ayazi was left with a lingering feeling of destitution.

Before dawn, he had silently renewed the vow pledged in the presence of bin Laden, a vow now doubly ingrained by the slaughter of the great warrior in Pakistan by the American Navy SEALs several years ago. Bin Laden's personal martyrdom strengthened the resolve to visit vengeance upon the ungodly bastion of the West. The holy jihad would succeed totally and eventually to the rejoicing of all the martyrs now and forever residing in Allah's glorious heaven.

"By all that is holy, I will not rest until Allah's vengeance against the infidels is fulfilled by me," he muttered in Pashto as he prepared for his first day in America.

He spread his small prayer rug on the floor, knelt, facing east, and intoned, "God is great. God is great. I am witness that there is no God but the one God and I am his servant. For God is great, God is great. God is great. God is good. We are the servants of God. God is great, and I am witness that Muhammad is his prophet."

EIGHT

T he journey on I-35 with the newly arrived Afghan, *Sanchez*, had done little to quell Ibrahim a Salih's anxiety about the prospect of his carefully constructed plan. Three years of preparation were nearing conclusion and would bring home to America the true reach and determination of Islam. It all depended upon the dedication and courage of the Afghan and the three others that al-Qaeda was sneaking into the country.

During the drive to Lamar, Salih had observed the Afghan. He was wide-eyed, glimpsing for the first time the land of the infidels, and had done little to hide his disappointment when Salih sternly discouraged any discourse. At least the cell in San Fernando correctly instructed the Afghan to call him Ali and to recognize the red shirt he was wearing.

They should have sent a fellow Yemen, a Saudi, or some other Arab, like the other three who would soon be in place. How useful would an Afghan be without a truck-mounted machine gun and a turban? A pledge to immolate oneself with a bomb did not always assure final confirmation at the moment of sacrifice.

Pulling away from the apartment in Lamar, Salih admitted to himself that Sanchez at least looked like a real Mexican, except for his piercing green-tinted eyes. Tall, lean faced, and with a large mustache, Sanchez would fit in well with the Maladondo company. All but one of the four bombers, committed to martyrdom, were now in place. The last one should arrive in June, inshallah, and he would see that he was embedded, as the media termed it, well before the fatal day in late August.

* * *

Ibrahim a Salih, the first son of a Yemeni herdsman, had come to America in 1985 on a US State Department scholarship with the intent of returning to his homeland after gaining a college degree. In four years, he received a degree in electrical engineering from Virginia Tech but postponed his departure after he was hired by a small engineering firm in Baltimore. Encouraged by his employer, he studied the US Constitution and sufficient American history necessary to become a naturalized US citizen in 1992. With a US passport in hand, he no longer was concerned about his student visa and immigrant status, and he was assured that his employment could continue.

Success in America had come with such ease that he often felt guilty that his parents and two younger brothers struggled daily in the desert wasteland of Yemen. The charitable pillar of the Koran reminded him to periodically send money to them. His infrequent return visits to Yemen served only to confirm his desire to remain in America.

A professional convention in Dallas recognized his engineering work with a small plaque in 1998. Two months later, a Dallas engineering firm offered a new position he could not resist, and he left Baltimore for the Wild West, as his colleagues in Maryland called it. Terrorist attacks in East Africa and in the World Trade Center parking garage had only been passing headlines initially, but Ibrahim began attending a mosque in Dallas, guided by an Imam who held a militant view of the strictures of the Koran. Correspondence from his younger brothers echoed the same message, urging him to devote his Allah-granted wealth to the cause they had joined in Yemen, a cause underwritten by the son of an old Yemeni immigrant to Saudi Arabia, a man called Osama bin Laden. The brothers insisted that bin Laden's quest had indeed been glorified by the bombings in East Africa, the World Trade Center, and elsewhere.

Driven partly by loyalty to his brothers and partly by the Imam's teachings, Salih founded in 1999 the Palestinian Relief Organization and leased a four-hundred-square-foot office in a South Oak Cliff shopping center, not far from I-20. Appeals to the mosques throughout North Texas and beyond supplied thousands of dollars which Khalia, Salih's wife, carefully recorded in the PRO bank account before the money was forwarded to a Muslim organization in Palestine. Khalia was not permitted to know that much of the money was diverted on reaching Palestine, with only a small portion finding its way to the many camps housing Palestinian refugees. By September 11, 2001, the name Ibrahim a Salih was well-known by the leaders of al-Qaeda and Al-Shabaab in Yemen. Salih began to seek a more direct way in which he could further the common cause. The strident voice of Anwar al-Awlaki, the American-born al-Qaeda member, confirmed Salih's ardent determination to restore the Islamic caliphate, a determination undiluted by Awlaki's death in 2011 by a CIA drone.

His pledge in 1992 to the American flag, along with ten others being sworn as American citizens, was never with the intent to adopt allegiance to the United States. It served only as a means of securing the US passport and the other benefits of US citizenship. Any suggestion that his actions were in conflict with a loyalty to America would have only amused him. Loyalties in Yemen were far and few between, a luxury that his family could not afford amid the numerous tribes and other factions which abounded there. Survival was first and foremost in reaching one's goals.

NINE

The shock of 9/11 reverberated through the Salih household as it did throughout America. Not once in his communications with al-Qaeda operatives had Salih been afforded even a hint of that horrendous plan, and he was faced with anxious questions from Khalia and their two sons, who suddenly feared that their quiet Muslim-American world would morph into a despised group persecuted by the Christian land in which they lived. The two sons refused to return to school for two weeks. Salih had no choice but to lock the doors of the PRO, wondering if the FBI would soon appear to investigate its operations.

The Imam's exultation over the collapse of the Twin Towers was unrestrained when he and Salih met three days later on September 14. They joyously speculated about when and where the next great jihad would occur on American soil. Surely Allah had spoken through the martyrs who had commandeered the four airliners, and the Nation of Islam would soon be restored in all its glory to mark their sacrifices.

But months and then years passed and the war was taken to Afghanistan and Iraq while America continued its heathen ways. The fear of terrorism over the next ten years became manifested only by long-lined security checks at the airports, by flying US marshals, and by contentious pat downs, x-rays, and bomb-sniffing dogs the Americans came to tolerate while the shock of 9/11 was forgotten. Suicide bombers in Spain and elsewhere raised no panic in America.

Salih's PRO went back into operation and was given scant attention by the FBI even though the principals in a similar Dallas organization were convicted of abetting terrorism.

Fully committed to the holy cause and at risk of federal prison should the true activity of PRO come to light, Salih chaffed with the realization that bin Laden and his associates appeared content with such exploits as the bombing of the USS *Cole*. Were they intimidated by the annoying security measures following 9/11 and the multimillion-dollar security apparatus established by the NYC police? Shoe bombs and hijacked airliners were not the only means of spreading terror, nor was New York City the sum total of America. Yet bin Laden languished somewhere in the mountains of Pakistan.

Salih's engineering experience taught him that America, more than any other country, was sustained by, and prospered, because of its two hundred years of developing a system of energy consumption, a panacea that eluded feudal domains such as Yemen. How long would the economic giant survive if its energy supply was disrupted and people were compelled to live in the dark—without communications, without television, without heat, without commerce to deliver life-sustaining food? A true blow to America must do more than kill a small number of the millions who live in such splendor. In 2011, when the tenth anniversary of 9/11 passed without any display by al-Qaeda, he began to put his American education to work.

The research came easily. Already familiar with the electrical grid in Texas, he accessed the website of the Electrical Reliability Council of Texas and traced every generating plant, every high-voltage transmission line, and every transmission station in the Metroplex. Each day and each hour, the scheduling of electrical power was carefully coordinated throughout the state and with interconnections into neighboring states. Any loss of power on the widespread grid would automatically initiate connections and disconnections necessary to reroute power and, if necessary, cause rolling blackouts to maintain the grid's overall integrity. What the system could not do was overcome a sudden and simultaneous destructions of a number of key switching stations. The most vulnerable time was late August when Texas heat dictated the highest consumption of electrical power almost every day. If the correct stations were simultaneously put out of operation, a massive portion of the state would be plunged into chaos for days, maybe for weeks. The terror engendered by such a catastrophe would be compounded by the fear that such an economic and safety relapse could occur anywhere in the country. If removal of shoes at airport security was America's answer to one hapless shoe bomber, what massive and costly recourses would be needed to secure the millions of miles of electric transmission lines and switching stations throughout the country?

Six months rolled by before Salih had tested and retested the plan on a grid pattern he traced on a carefully devised scheme. Finally, he submitted the plan to Ayman al Zawahiri, the heir apparent who claimed al-Qaeda leadership after bin Laden's demise. Because US security after 9/11 had advanced SIGINT (signal intelligence) to an art, Salih was forced to personally deliver the plan on a visit with Khalia and the boys to see her family in Damascus. Internet transmissions, even with codes, were not sufficiently safe to convey Salih's enthusiasm for the grand plan. It included details he specified for insertion of bombers into the US, through a liaison he established with one of the drug cartels in Mexico.

Contributions from PRO and money directed from al-Qaeda carefully placed in Mexico had bought fake driver's licenses, untraceable vehicles, and a base camp in San Fernando where the bombers received training before being smuggled across the Rio Grande. The cartel, being impressed with the cash available from the Middle East, had even arranged for Maladondo's cousin to steer Sanchez to his new job in Lamar.

* * *

The good life in America over the years found its way to Salih's waist, and he no longer carried his six-foot frame with the lithe step that once kept pace with the goat herds on his father's barren farm. His beard now revealed more gray than black, and his hair had receded midway back on his mahogany skull. His rimless reading glasses, under a furrowed brow, gave his face the appearance of a kindly professor. But he was not frowning about class examinations. With only two months before the jihad, he could not avoid the nagging doubts and concerns as he drove the black pickup to the DFW airport.

Exact timing and coordination was needed among the four bombers to assure the downfall of the grid and its maximum impact on the power supply. The logistics of acquiring, training, smuggling, and embedding the bombers entailed far more people than he liked, and he constantly feared that detection or misstep of any one of them could sabotage three years of work. The fourth bomber still had not crossed the Mexican border, a fact that threatened the entire plan, which would not succeed without destruction of the four carefully selected stations. None of the four martyrs-to-be were aware of the others, nor did they know him, *Ali*, except by sight, and only when he chose to contact them in person or via the time-limited cell phones he had provided. Even the agents who had constructed the vest bombs had no knowledge of their intended use, or when. He alone was responsible for delivering the bombs, together with city maps and oral instructions of street locations where the stations would be found. Most importantly, each bomber would be instructed to carry out his jihad at a precise time, on a day which he had yet to reveal.

His mind turned to the Afghan when he stopped to take the parking ticket at the airport entrance. His initial impression of the tribesman had improved as he observed the ease with which the Afghan took his place among the Maladondo workmen. That concern was now replaced by the delay in the arrival of the last bomber. Did Zawahiri not understand that all four must be in place? The old Egyptian scholar, at times, seemed more concerned with solidifying his reign over al-Qaeda than assuring the success of the strongest blow he could deliver to American conceit and power.

He guided the pickup to the curb at the departure level of Terminal D and immediately spotted the courier who was to begin the long trek to Pakistan.

Abdullah, known only by his single name to Salih, waved as he strolled toward the pickup.

"Greetings, brother. I feared you would not arrive before my flight left."

"Yes, I know. Only in America do people work so hard to be on time. May you go with God, and here is the letter you must guide to the hand of Zawahiri," Salih replied, handing over his written plea to speed the arrival of the fourth and last bomber.

Abdullah, the past two years, had proven to be a reliable courier, unremarkable in any way, and totally unknown to the US watchdogs as far as Salih knew. The long ability of bin Laden to escape the vengeance of America was largely due to the fact that trusted couriers like Abdullah had eliminated the risks imposed by internet communications. The Americans had satellites and drones in every sky.

Salih left DFW, turning toward Dallas and home. All was ready, if only Zawahiri would take steps to assure the final, crucial arrival.

TEN

T he gavel banged loudly on the wooden base, and Mayor Fanning announced, as always, "The council will come to order. All rise for our invocation and remain for the Pledge of Allegiance."

The fifty or so people in the chamber rose, watching Reverend Clete Jones, a black minister, approaching the microphone at the speaker's podium, next to the secretary's desk. Bowing his head, he proceeded to call down God's blessing on the assembly, asking for guidance and wisdom of the elected officials who looked down from the dais.

Protestant ministers, Jewish rabbis, and Catholic priests performed the opening ritual at each council meeting without protest from Atheists or others who might claim to be offended by a public religious display in a government house. Bobby had once remarked to himself that no Muslim Imam ever offered an opening prayer, presumably because there was no mosque in Lamar.

The council chamber was dominated by the curved, raised dais situated near the south wall, behind which were nine large high-backed swivel chairs clad in black leather. Before the recent redistricting, based on the 2010 census, the mayor and four council members sat with the city attorney and the city manager, gazing at the public in attendance. Now there were no vacant chairs as Terry Leech and

Paula Ramsey were to be sworn in with the incumbent, reelected council members.

Hands over hearts, the council, staff members, and the audience recited the pledge to the American flag, resting behind the dais, swearing their fealty to the nation for which it stands. In schools, at the Rotary Club, Boy Scout meetings, and a multitude of public gatherings, the pledge was spoken so often it would not have surprised Bobby if he had turned to observe many in the audience with eyes gazing anywhere but the flag or with hands texting on ubiquitous iPhones. But the council, turned toward the flag, never observed the loyalty of the audience.

Bobby opened the heavy docket notebook and followed the usual agenda as the city secretary intoned the items set out. First, recognition of special citizens, proclamations exclaiming Lamar Cleanup Week and other notable events, and awards to worthy recipients. Next, under zoning matters came a review of changes in the zoning classification of various plats and plots of land in the city that had first been approved or denied by the council-appointed members of the zoning commission.

Next, a perfunctory approval of the consent agenda before addressing individually a few of the consent items which had elicited inquiries from a council member for a staff explanation or perhaps debate among the council members. Finally, before adjourning, the council would hear comments, inquiries, requests, or complaints from citizens sufficient to justify their attendance and delivery of a speaker's card to the city secretary.

Bobby had been through the routine so many times he had lost count. The council met at 7:00 PM on the first and third Wednesday of each month, with few exceptions, in order to comply with a provision in the city charter, the city's constitution, which proscribed the operation of city government. Many other meetings occurred periodically as called by the mayor to address special issues or agendas.

The next item called by Madam Secretary in response to the mayor's signal was the application of Payton Energy Company for a gas well pad site drilling permit in the southern part of District 3, the item Bobby had reviewed and fretted about over the weekend. It was no surprise that the audience included about twenty people wearing T-shirts and printed shirt buttons proclaiming their solidarity in opposing the application, evidencing their general enmity to any and all drilling in the city. Payton was only one of five drilling companies in the city, and a request by any of them for city approval of gas-related activity signaled a call to arms for the anti-drilling crowd.

Bobby counted at least a dozen faces which graced the chamber almost every time the agenda included an item related to the exploration, production, and transportation of natural gas. He could recall no other activity in Lamar which had stirred up more interest among the citizens, an activity on which many people seemed not to agree. Modern technology and *horizontal* drilling had opened up the Barnett Shale formation to gas production for the first time around 1998, and the play, as the petroleum engineers called it, had slowly moved through Tarrant County and into Johnson County. The Texas Railroad Commission, for almost a hundred years, had been tasked with the review and approval of oil and gas well drilling applications throughout the state, but inside incorporated city limits, municipalities were authorized to adopt restrictive ordinances and prohibit drilling unless the municipality likewise issued a drilling permit. While a few oil wells and gas wells were drilled over the years outside of Lamar, the Barnett Shale boom was now a hot topic in Lamar.

Payton Energy, wanting to drill closer than the regulated six hundred feet to a number of residences, had failed to get one of the affected property owners to sign a waiver to the set-back requirement, and Payton's spokesman was present to persuade the council to grant the waiver in spite of the protest from the holdout property owner. First came Lamar's gas inspector to the podium and outlined the basic facts of the application, the ordinance requirements for a waivers, and a map showing the plat location and the nearby residences.

"Mr. Sanford, do you have any questions?" the mayor asked, knowing as usual that the member from the impacted district would be the first to weigh in on the application.

"No, Mr. Mayor. I'm ready to hear from anyone who signed up to speak," Bobby replied, knowing that the Payton representative was first, followed by many of the T-shirt-clad members in the audience.

Payton Energy presented little in addition to the facts outlined by the gas inspector. The representative was making his first appearance before the council. Their usual presenter, a young woman, blond, and sporting a svelte figure wrapped in tight clothing, was absent, causing Bobby to wonder if she were on vacation or had found other employment. Pulling his mind back to the matter at hand, he asked the Payton agent if his company had made an attempt to obtain a waiver from the owner who had not signed.

"Yes, sir, we met with all the affected property owners and offered a sizable payment if they would approve our application because the well proximity and noise would affect them somewhat. Mr. Markham said from the get-go that he would not agree, and he has continued to refuse."

"Did you ever pay Mr. Markham a bonus to sign a lease, giving Payton the right to drill for gas under his land?" Bobby had pursued that line of inquiry on previous cases, spurred on by his years of law practice dealing with oil and gas leases. Texas treated such leases as a grant of property rights, and many argued that a lessor could not lawfully take money for a lease and then block the lessee's right to recover the minerals the lessee had already paid for. Certainly, if Mr. Markham's lease had contemplated that Payton could and would locate a well directly on the surface of Markham's property, the Texas courts would probably grant an order enjoining Markham from keeping Payton off his property. But development of gas reserves from remote locations through horizontal drilling was raising many legal issues not yet resolved in the courtroom. Bobby had yet to learn of any attempt by Payton or any other gas exploration company to press the matter.

Glancing to his left, Bobby recognized a frown crossing the mayor's brow, a sure sign that the mayor was not interested in esoteric legal questions and was anxious to move on.

"Thank you. I have no further questions," Bobby hastily stated, not waiting for an answer. The next speaker was no surprise. Charles Unsel, president of Sane Citizens Against Drilling (SCAD), was probably in his late sixties, retired from federal government service, and a frequent spokesman for those who believed that the city was but moments away from an apocalyptic disaster if another gas well was drilled.

"Charles Unsel, 4328 Bluebonnet Avenue. I am the president of Sane Citizens Against Drilling, and I am representing the many, many citizens in this city who have genuine concerns for our safety and health and the health of our children and grandchildren. Mr. Mayor, I am speaking for the fifteen or so citizens behind me, and I understand that I will have ten minutes to speak."

"Yes, sir, Mr. Unsel, you may speak," the mayor responded, resigned to hearing what had been presented many times during the past ten years.

Bobby smiled, his mind recalling Carl Jeffers's description of Charles Unsel six months ago as they had a late-afternoon beer at Mac's BBQ.

"He is a true SAP, in fact an archetype."

"What do you mean?" was Bobby's baffled reply.

"He is a creature known as a self-appointed pontificator. Self-appointed because he pretends to represent a vast array of citizens. Not elected by anyone but appointed by himself to represent these unidentified minions, all of whom are advertised as sharing his views and rantings. An SAP must meet certain requirements to merit the designation."

"Really," said Bobby, reacting to Carl's obvious research into this new and wonderous category of humans.

"First, a true SAP must create a cause, one presumably shared by many others. Next, he must develop a resounding mantra, a phrase, or a goal to be repeated at every occasion." Carl was warming to the diatribe.

"But that alone will not suffice. He must then establish an organization and appoint himself as its head. The organization must be labeled with a name which connotes a widespread following, such as Concerned Citizens for...whatever or Concerned Citizens Against...Alliance is also powerful, and the addition of a far-reaching geographical scope is desirable. When all this is in place, the SAP must court the media to promote his cause, but more importantly, to promote himself as the exalted leader possessing the true insight to present the mantra. Finally, once he is established, it is essential that the SAP maintain his credentials with frequent appearances before public bodies, such as city councils, commissions, legislatures, or other tribunals. Repeated appearances provide pleasing fulfillment and vindication for his very existence."

Bobby had laughed so, he could hardly sit up in his chair. When he subsided, he toasted Carl with his beer bottle and proclaimed, "For an old gunny sergeant, you are pure genius. Unsel meets every qualification."

"Maybe we should present him with a plaque the next time he comes to the hall. I'll think about something that won't offend him too much!" Carl laughed.

Working hard to suppress the wide grin on his face, Bobby returned to the matter at hand as Unsel droned on. "Every day in the news we learn of oil wells, gas wells, and pipelines which blow up, blow out, and erupt, damaging untold property, injuring innocent victims, and polluting the air we breathe. Is this city so desperate for money that it must sell the public's safety to the barons of the gas industry who are concerned only with the almighty bottom line? Do you believe the citizens of this city take comfort in the paltry royalty checks they receive while they await the next catastrophe? And it will happen! The only question is when. Time is running out as more and more wells are drilled, and this dangerous explosive gas is piped through our streets, backyards, and next to school grounds with play-ing children. You must stop the drilling!"

Unsel's clipped white goatee bobbed with each word, lending the appearance of an ancient prophet, indeed a pontificator of gloom and doom.

Bobby could almost hear him proclaim his wish for a gas well explosion that very instant, a vindication of his prediction and dili-gent effort to bring the council to its senses.

The bell rang, signaling the elapse of Unsel's allotted time.

Knowing the drill quite well and knowing the media would be back when the next gas matter came before the council, he stopped and whirled to return to his seat.

Perhaps frustrated by the repeated parade and display from SCAD, Bobby called out, "Mr. Unsel, before you sit down, let me ask you. Do you understand that the only issue before us tonight is whether we should grant a waiver to Payton Energy as permitted by our ordinance? We are not addressing the design of the ordinance or the elimination of the ordinance. Those issues were decided some time ago after hearing input from all those who wished to be heard."

"What?" Unsel replied, seemingly shocked that anyone on the council had responded to his presentation. "That is the issue, Mr. Sanford. Drilling is wrong and the council should enact a moratorium before it is too late!"

Cheers and applause rose from the SCAD supporters, which lingered until the mayor rapped his gavel.

Pleased with himself, Unsel returned to his seat, accepting the smiles and nods from his gallery.

A handful of additional speakers came forth, repeating Unsel's theme, except for one man who stated he had leased his minerals to Payton, urging the council to let drilling go forth.

Bobby and the other members knew, as from the beginning, that it was a question of weighing the desires and rights of the mineral owners who wanted their gas produced against the rights and concerns of the surface owners near enough to the drilling operations to be inconvenienced or endangered. The six-hundred-foot limit itself had been a compromise but was not intended as a binding rule, which could not give way to those individual facts affecting a particular well site. King Solomon's quandary had nothing on the council, which sat both as a legislative body and a judicial body.

Convinced that far more people would benefit than would suffer, Bobby moved to approve the Payton application, and it was passed by a unanimous vote. The SCAD delegation filed out, pausing outside the chamber while Unsel spoke heatedly to the *Tribune* reporter assigned to the city beat.

The next agenda items were dealt with in short order and finally reached the citizens' presentations for those who wished to complain, ask questions, or otherwise address the council. One of those speakers was the Reverend Jeremiah Benjamin, a rather large African American with a deep and resounding voice.

ELEVEN

A s always, Anna peered around the open door rather than simply walking in. Carl had the impression that she was afraid something secretive might be occurring in his office whenever she came to deliver a message.

"The mayor would like for you to drop by his office if you're free, Mr. Jeffers."

"Sure, tell him I'll be there in a minute," Carl responded, surprised he had not been summoned earlier. It was pushing ten o'clock. Last night's council session ran until ten thirty. Maybe the mayor had slept an extra hour this morning.

Heading down the hall, toward the mayor's office, wishing he had skipped coming to the hall until tomorrow, Carl noticed a tall man visiting in Bobby's office. Bobby glanced up at Carl and waved, and his brow frowned and rose to transmit some unspoken message, a message of sympathy, perhaps.

With the phone pressed to his ear, the mayor pointed Carl to a seat with his free hand and continued to listen to the resounding voice echoing from the telephone.

"I understand completely," the mayor spoke rapidly as the caller's obvious tirade wound down.

"You're welcome anytime. We're glad to hear from anyone who's extending a helping hand." A pause. "I know, I know. We'll see what we can do. Yeah, well, call anytime."

Carl admired again the gifts, trophies, and tributes adorning the walls of the mayor's office. A collection of many years.

As the phone was placed in its cradle, Carl anxiously opined with "Good morning, Mayor." Carl had never addressed him as Dub if the two of them were in the city hall.

The mayor did not appear pleased.

"Carl, do you know who I was talking to?" a rhetorical question, hanging in the air as he went on.

"That was the Reverend Jeremiah Benjamin, the man you called on the carpet last night. He was not happy with you, and he is not happy with our city. In fact, he has expressed, as he puts it, his outrage to a reporter from the Fort Worth *Star Telegram* who happened to monitor our meeting."

"Mayor, all I tried to do was—"

"I don't give a damn about what you were trying to do!" The interjection almost exploded from the mayor's mouth. "Here we are just finished with the election, and you decide to conduct a debate on race relations with one of the biggest leaders in the Dallas black community. Am I right or am I wrong?"

Carl waited for the storm to subside and then responded as he remembered the points he had rehearsed lying in bed at dawn.

"Mayor, we don't need anyone coming down here from Dallas, all dressed in an expensive suit and diamond rings, telling us how we should spend our taxpayers' money. He was arrogant and patronizing. What does he know about our town and what is right or wrong here? He doesn't know who is underserved, as he puts it, or who has been neglected. Jim Grant says the reverend has been out in the Camp for a week, telling everyone how he is going to city hall and get them what they deserve."

The mayor was listening, but was he buying?

Carl continued, "Did you notice? The brochure he handed out suggesting how our funds should be spent included a $1,500 honorarium for the reverend himself. I suppose that was his fee to compensate for his work on behalf of our citizens. The reverend is not interested in helping anyone but himself. Jim knows everyone in the Camp, and he says no more than ten people have spent any time listening to the reverend, and Jim knows better than anyone." Carl paused and went on as the mayor stared impassively at him, "No one wants to see the black people in this town do well more than I do. And most of them have. I don't have Jim Grant managing my store because his skin is black. He does that and is my partner because he is the best. I would never insult him by calling him underserved or disadvantaged. He doesn't want to be dependent upon a handout of public money, and he was so mad to see the Reverend Benjamin nosing around the Camp he threatened to run him out!

"So I don't think we do Jim or his folks any good by listening to the likes of the reverend and nodding our heads as if we agree with his propaganda. Benjamin knows what he is up to. He has no reason to act insulted or disrespected because we chose to expose him for what he is."

"And what is he, Carl?"

"He is no more and no less than a hyena, preying on his own people as long as he can make a nickel by sucking money off the public teat!" Carl was becoming heated.

The mayor was now pacing around his desk. "Well, I guess we're all lucky you didn't say that last night. We could have made the ten o'clock news on TV."

"Dammit, Mayor, you know what I mean. How well-off is any-one that has to depend on government money instead of standing on their own two feet? Does anyone think Condoleezza Rice, Barack Obama, or Colin Powell got to where they did by crying about how underserved they were? I'll tell you who is underserved in this town. It is the sixty-five-year-old retiree who has worked hard all his life and now pays more and more taxes from his retirement income while the city prospers and his house assessment goes up and up. He pays more taxes each year than the underserved folks but gets no more police protection, no more fire protection, and no more public streets. For each dollar he pays in taxes, he is the one who is underserved."

The mayor halted his pacing and simply looked at Carl with a blank stare. The diatribe was nothing new to the mayor. He had heard it in the coffee shops and at the neighborhood meetings. But what did it solve?

"Carl, everything you say may be true, but it won't sell. You know, after twenty years in this office, I have to agree with something I once read. 'Politics is the art of avoiding substantive dialogue about public issues.' And you know, that is closer to the truth than you and I might care to admit. Don't ever forget that the goal of politics is to get elected and reelected. If you're not sitting here, you can't do much about guiding the ship of state. If you don't believe that, the media damn well understands it. So when that newspaper reporter calls you about last night, I hope you will tone it down just a little. Getting our city written up as a community that doesn't care about helping its poorer citizens will not help anyone who lives here"

With that, the mayor stuck out his hand, tacitly directing Carl to the door.

TWELVE

R eturning to his office, Carl pondered the meeting. What did the mayor truly think about the effrontery of the Reverend Benjamin? Had he agreed or disagreed with anything Carl had said?

But one message was very clear: don't rock the boat. Was that leadership or just political expediency?

From boot camp to his final days in the Marine Corps, Carl had learned that discipline and defined goals were the keys to one's success. Eighteen months in the Middle East during Desert Storm confirmed his belief that divisive and irrelevant sidetracks were not only counterproductive but could quickly lead to death when your opponent held a gun. He fought side by side with Jim Grant, and when they both mustered out in 1995, Jim had persuaded Carl to move to Lamar, the *best town* in Texas, according to Jim. Their mutual respect was forged under fire, and Jim eagerly accepted Carl's invitation to manage Carl's first election campaign for a seat on the council, exclaiming, "Gunny, you are the man! Anyone who can move a company of badass Marines like you did in Iraq should have no trouble."

Carl had laughed and expressed his lingering doubts about an elective office. "I'm not sure the Marine Corps and politics have much in common."

"Yeah, it's damn sure different, but we'll get you there and then you can teach the town a thing or two. I'll get you the votes from the Camp for sure!"

Jim delivered as promised, helped by the fact that Carl's Auto Zone store, managed by Jim, enjoyed a large trade from the Camp.

It had not taken long for Carl to champion the expenditure of certain Federal CDBG funds for home improvements in the Camp when the council programmed those funds shortly after his first election. The Camp voters stood behind him ever since.

He challenged the Reverend Benjamin, confident that the black people in Lamar did not need and did not want some self-proclaimed crusader from Dallas. They were not interested in someone painting them as downtrodden and still enslaved by the angst and anger of a people forcibly transported years ago. His days in the corps had irrevocably convinced him that skin color was not a criterion of personal worth or entitlement. Jim Grant had proven it when he rescued Carl in a firefight on the Iraq-Kuwait border.

How long would it take before characters like Benjamin were escorted from the political stage, he wondered, and looked up to find Anna standing at his door again.

"Mr. Jeffers, Mr. Sanford says he would like to visit with you, if convenient," Anna timidly reported.

"Sure, I'll be right there," he replied. Anna must have been born a schoolmarm, he thought, noticing her quiet and submissive demeanor, which she projected to everyone in the council office.

"I hope I didn't interrupt anything," Bobby said as Carl lowered his large and trim frame into the armchair by Bobby's desk.

"No, no. I was just licking my wounds. The mayor chewed my rear pretty good about my discussion last night with that Benjamin carpetbagger."

Bobby laughed. "Carpetbagger may be the right description. But the newspapers prefer the term *activist*, a more neutral word since those folks provide the paper with contrary views on every issue. You know controversy is the lifeblood of the media. No controversy, no paycheck."

Carl smiled, "I've damn well learned that since I've been here," brushing his hand through his thick salt-and-pepper hair that afforded him a certain statesman's stature, far different from the shave-headed warrior he presented in the corps.

A slow smile crossed Bobby's face, provoked by his memory of Carl's early days on the council when his Marine mantra frequently landed him in the *Lamar Tribune* and once or twice in the *Dallas Morning News*. Comments from a public servant which transgressed politically correct guidelines were more cherished by the media than the trite "man bites dog" story.

"Carl, if your behind is really sore, you don't need to sit in that chair," Bobby joked, noting the glum look still resting on Carl's groggy face.

"Hell, I guess I'll survive. I've been chewed out before by a two-star general. That's one you never forget." Carl's face rumbled into a smile. "But I got to tell you, Bobby, sometimes I don't understand the mayor. He said he didn't disagree with most of my concern about the likes of Benjamin, but he was hot under the collar because I expressed it. Go figure!"

"Yeah, I agree. Sometimes I think he's too cautious. I've had the same reaction from him when I talk about the employees' pension. But what the hell, you've survived to fight another day."

Carl laughed. "Well, I got to get over to the store. A new shipment is coming in today."

Bobby saluted a farewell to Carl, sat back in his chair, and ticked off the other council members in his head. The mayor, Alece Jackson, and Estella Jiminez never seemed bothered by the question of how the city was ever going to pay the future pensions. But the new members, Terry Leech and Paula Ramsey, were not yet introduced to that problem. It would be interesting to see how eager they might be to dip their toes into that swirling pond.

THIRTEEN

The Reverend Benjamin was stuffing his Blackberry into his jacket pocket, fire in his eyes, as he left his shining black car by the curb and stomped toward the front door of Alece Jackson's office on the south side of the square. He let go when he entered.

"Alece, you nigger mothafucker, you done told me you and Jiminez would see that I got treated with respect. That honky Jeffers laid into me with both feet!" Jerimiah Benjamin was not happy on the sunny Thursday morning.

"Hold on, Jerimiah. How was I supposed to know what Jeffers would say?" Alece was reeling, on the defensive, an unfamiliar position for the first and only black on the Lamar council.

"What? You's supposed to know! When the coalition agreed to support your sorry-ass campaign, you swore you'd get Jiminez, and now Leech and Ramsey, to vote for the finance policy. All's I had to do was show how our folks have been crapped on, especially here in the Camp. I don't like bein' kicked in the ass!"

Benjamin rocked his large three-hundred-pound frame forward in the chair, an aroused hulk ready to leap atop Jackson's desk. Sweat beaded on his dark brow above his flashing black eyes.

Jackson scrambled to get the storm calmed. "I know, I know. But it ain't my fault. I talked to Leech and Ramsey before the election. They listened, but they've only been here a few days. They can't vote that quick on the policy, not with Fanning looking down their throat and telling everyone it has to be postponed."

"So you just let me walk in and get my ass chewed?" Benjamin was not going to be mollified.

"Listen, Jeremiah, we can get this done. Just might take a little longer, but when we do, we can get other cities to stop burying the needs of our folks. I'm in the Black, Brown, and Tan Coalition for the long haul. If Obama ain't goin' to get it done from Washington, we got to start at the bottom."

"Nice speech, Alece. But the next time you ask me to come, you better make sure I get the respect I deserve. I damn sure let that mayor of yours know about that this morning. I'm goin' be the new president of the coalition come October, and if you don't stand with us, we'll find a new candidate next time."

Benjamin pushed to his feet and glared for several seconds before walking out, on his way back to Dallas.

Jackson watched him go through the door, almost brushing the jambs on both sides.

The coalition's support, mostly money, had propelled Jackson past his two opponents in 2013, and he had been eager to sign on with their plan to establish more liberal local governments in the Metroplex. The effort had made little progress, however, even before the election, and he was angry that it was his loyalty being accused, as if everything hinged on a small policy change in Lamar. Hadn't he been the one to get the *Tribune* to print an editorial favoring the change?

Watching Benjamin's car speed around the square, he recalled he had not been opposed in the latest election. Maybe he could just do without the coalition. If others on the council were aware of his alliance with the coalition, his influence at the dais might go south and not just with Carl Jeffers.

He suddenly remembered he was going to have lunch with his nephew, Elisha, at Maudie's. "I'll be back after lunch," he called over his shoulder to his part-time secretary before throwing his suit coat over his back.

* * *

After graduating from Trimble Tech High in Fort Worth, Jackson served four years in the Army before moving to Lamar. Bright and articulate, he worked at a number of jobs, finally opening his own business as the local contact for a national firm marketing home products. He never forgot the loan received from Elisha's father which got him started. When his sister called, he was happy to set the lunch date with Elisha, a junior at UTA.

"He is very interested in politics, Alece, and wants to talk to you about taking a political science course this fall."

His years on the council comprised his only political course, but he had learned a great deal in a short while. He often wondered how his election might have gone if he had run as a Democrat. Not a formal member of that party, neither he nor any on the council doubted where his political sympathies lie, but municipal elections in Lamar, and generally in the other Texas cities, were nonpartisan. It had been much simpler during the campaigns not having to recognize, and support, some platform put together by people he didn't know and who, for the most part, were still a product of the ever-present White Establishment. It was to counter that establishment that prompted him to accept the push from the brothers. But having avoided the pressure of running as a political party member, was he now forever bound to remain loyal to the precepts of the coalition?

His thoughts were interrupted as he walked through the door of the restaurant.

"Hey, Alece, your nephew's over there, waiting for you," Maudie greeted from her stool.

"Thanks, Maudie," he responded, stepping around a table loaded with six workers wearing Maladondo work shirts.

FOURTEEN

As his uncle neared the table, Elisha rose, towering over him. "Elisha, how's it goin'? I ain't seen you in almost two years. What you been eatin' to make you so tall?"

"Just what the coach tells me to, Uncle Alece. He says I can make the varsity." His chest swelled at the prospect.

"That sounds good. You sure showed when you played at Lamar High." Pulling out a chair and sitting, he went on, "Maybe the NBA might look at you soon."

"I don't know, Uncle. The coach says I got to understand that six feet, five is not very big anymore. But that's why I wanted to talk to you. I saw you at a council meeting back in March, and I got to thinking about maybe politics is what I should do when I graduate."

They paused as the waitress wrote down their orders and then returned to the discussion. Jackson was proud of his sister and her kids, Elisha and Kinasha, and pleased that Elisha had ambitions. His own education was limited to the school of hard knocks.

"You looked like you belong on that council, Uncle. I noticed you had plenty to say."

"Well, that's the truth, Elisha. That's why I'm there to give a different viewpoint. Not too many people in this town ever thought they'd see a black sitting up there."

"Well, what do you all do? What do I need to do?"

Laying aside his fork, Jackson responded, "You know I never went to college. Couldn't afford to. I don't know what they can teach you about politics, but it took me almost a year to figure out what was goin' on. Still not too sure sometimes. One thing is, I had to listen and figure out where the others are comin' from. I mean what's pushin' their buttons. You can't get them to vote with you if you don't know that.

"Jiminez and I speak for a lot of folks who are due more attention. We got an old swimmin' pool in the Camp that needs fixin'. We don't have a park that anyone can use without gitin' mugged. So we talk about more help for folks that still haven't been served by the city. And now the government in Washington is cuttin' back subsidies for people who can't pay their rent or who need help fixin' up their homes. Some of that money called CDBG has got to be replaced with city money. Even Fort Worth set up a trust fund years ago to take care of those problems."

Elisha was eagerly leaning forward. "That's what I want to do. If I can do it too, maybe I will run for president someday. If Obama did it, I can too!" Elisha gushed.

"Yeah, Elisha, we all thought that was okay until he sold out and forgot all the changes he promised, another Uncle Tom." Jackson almost spit out the words.

"An Uncle Tom? What's that?" Elisha looked puzzled.

"Where you been, boy? Don't you know there are some who make it and then forget about their brothers? Don't your momma and daddy teach you nothin'?"

Elisha cast his eyes down, not following the turn in the conversation as Jackson went on, "When I was a little boy, my granddaddy, your great-granddaddy, would tell me about the things that happened to some of his pals when they lived outside of Waxahachee. Black folks would get beat up by white folks and the police would just ignore it. We're still goin' have to fight for everything we get. We got to hold together. People of color are a long way from bein' equal. Every time we say the Pledge of Allegiance before our meetings, I have to laugh when it says 'liberty and justice for all.' The *all* they're talkin' about is only those people who were not owned as slaves."

Elisha sat silently, surprised by the outburst. This was not something he had seen or heard at UTA. He skipped back to his uncle's comment about the grandfather.

"Yeah, I heard about your granddad from Mom, but I don't know much about your side of the family. I don't even know if you ever had any kids."

"Well, no. At least none I ever owned up to," Jackson said with a grin. "But don't tell your momma I said that." Returning to his lecture, Jackson resumed, "We're not gonna get the respect we got comin' unless we fight together, Elisha. That's why I'm tryin' to help the coalition, the Black, Brown, and Tan."

"Black, Brown, and Tan. What does that mean?"

"'It means if your skin ain't white, you got to stand up and be counted together!" Jackson stopped, looking around to see if anyone was listening to his lecture to his nephew. Were Elisha's folks goin' to send him out in the world unprepared?

They finished up the meal in silence, Elisha unsure about pressing the political agenda any further.

Out on the sidewalk, Jackson parted with his nephew, saying, "Elisha, I hope you get into a class to learn about politics. But don't be afraid to ask some questions about what I told you. If you're gonna be in politics, you gotta know about all of it. If you're gonna help the folks who elect you, you gotta stand up for 'em."

FIFTEEN

The vote at Wednesday night's council meeting was unanimous in favor of the Payton pad site application, a vote which relieved Bobby's usual anxiety, which arose each time a drilling matter appeared on the agenda. In his mind, SCAD and several other SAP groups were not going to cease their monotonous drumbeat. They, and the op-ed writers for the *Tribune*, studiously avoided any recognition of the hundreds of jobs and rising sales tax collections which had been brought to Lamar by the Barnett Shale activity.

He turned into the square, narrowly missing a car that was determined to ignore the one-way sign and searched for an open parking space near Maudie's Café. It was about fifteen minutes before he was due at a meeting at his council office. He tried to keep council meetings at a minimum on Fridays to provide more time in the law office. Public service commanded more of his attention than he had imagined when he first decided to seek a place in city government. But it was intriguing, albeit frustrating at times.

"Bobby, what brings you into my modest establishment so early in in the morning?" Maudie greeted as he stepped through the door. As usual, Maudie was seated on her high three-legged stool near the cash register.

"I'm in need of some coffee, Maudie, and maybe a little advice," Bobby replied.

"Well, you know where the coffee urn is, so get yourself a cup and come back and tell me what words of wisdom I can impart this morning," she said, directing with a wave of her hand over the head of a tall, rawboned man holding out his check and a well-worn credit card.

Bobby nodded and headed toward the kitchen door. Maudie Sue Walton was seldom seen off her stool, but her antennae captured almost every movement, gripe, event, and future scheme in Lamar. Her observations and predictions were never far off the mark. She had dropped a number of hints during Bobby's campaign which were not only astounding but also accurate.

The coffee mug was large and the coffee was hot, black, and brewed to kick-start anyone's day. Bobby carefully cradled the mug and set it on the counter near Maudie.

"Bobby Sanford, I congratulate you again. Your election proves that there are a few people in this town who have some common sense."

Maudie's head waggled and appeared to duck and dodge behind the register. Even on the stool, she still had to look up to see her customers. Bobby was not sure he had ever seen her standing. She was a small but obviously tough lady.

"Thanks, Maudie. There have been maybe a one hundred or more gas wells drilled in Lamar in the past ten years, and a lot of people are concerned that the drilling is, or is going to be, dangerous and unhealthy for our folks. Everyone talks to you sooner or later. What are you hearing about it in the city?"

Maudie gazed at him, frowned as though she was calculating some difficult puzzle, and delivered her words of wisdom. "Bobby, I guess folks talk differently in this place than they do over at your council meetings, but I can't remember more than one or two people that have complained about the drilling, and some of those were bitching about how long they had to wait for their royalty checks after a well was drilled. You know most people don't have a well near them, and they just go on without any thought about it as far as I can tell."

Bobby listened intently before asking another question, "Well, what do you personally think about it?"

Maudie straightened her shoulders and leaned over the top of the register. "Let me tell you about that. When Clyde decided to move on to the Pearly Gates in 2001, I was left with this café, a small house, and a lot of unpaid estate taxes and sales taxes. I sold the house to pay the taxes, rented another house, and kept this place going. By then, most of the folks were taking their business out to franchise row on the interstate, and soon after the funeral, the cook left and went to Fort Worth. I would have closed up if the good people at city hall had not come by on a regular basis.

"But then, when the gas companies and their subcontractors came to town, the business doubled in about six months, and sometimes I don't have enough tables at noon when the drillers, roustabouts, and other hands come in for lunch. They order everything on the menu and leave big tips for the girls. Mister, I love the gas business!" Maudie rocked on the stool and threw both arms in the air.

Bobby smiled, "Are you getting any royalties?"

"Are you kidding? I sold the house and the minerals before all this happened. I guess the guy that owns the house I rent may get royalties. I've never asked him."

SIXTEEN

"Bobby! Are you listening to me?" Becky barked, standing in front of his chair. "You have been off on a cloud ever since you got home," she went on, waving her hand in exasperation.

"Okay, okay. I'm sorry, I was just thinking about some stuff at the office," he replied, pulling himself back to the present.

"Libby called this afternoon. She'll be home this weekend since her Friday class is cancelled for some reason. She wants to know if she can invite Josh over for a cookout on the patio on Saturday." Becky tossed her blond hair and bobbed her eyebrows in that well-known fashion designed to signal that his agreement was expected. It was a gesture that had captured him over twenty-one years ago when they had meet at a law school cocktail party, and he had learned many times not to ignore it.

"Sure, that would be fine," Bobby properly replied. "I think it's time for us to get to know him a little better. He seems like a nice kid, but he is several years older than Libby and we need to do a bit of due diligence."

"Due diligence?" Becky exclaimed with a laugh. "Bobby, this is not a real estate transaction. But I would like to know him better too. Libby sometimes gets ahead of herself."

Bobby smiled at that remark, recalling how forward Becky had been on their first date. Like mother like daughter?

* * *

The shopping list sat, undisturbed, on the Saturday morning breakfast table. Hamburger buns, charcoal, pickles, coleslaw, and key lime pie, all dictated by Libby, who was determined that her parents would field an impressive domestic scene when Josh arrived that evening. The beer was ready to be iced down in the cooler and much of the repast was waiting in the refrigerator.

"Dad, don't forget to go to Maudie's for the coleslaw," Libby admonished as she reminded him for the third time, hoping to rouse him from the council agenda book in his lap, which carried the issues for the coming Wednesday session.

"Libby, sweetheart, Josh is not coming for hours yet. Just relax. It's just a cookout on the patio." He turned to the next agenda item and groaned aloud. "Why is that damned financial policy thing coming up again? I thought we had postponed it for at least six months."

Becky turned from the sink and asked, "What is the problem now?"

"Well, the mayor and I talked about this already. Estella Jiminez, Alece Jackson, and now Terry Leech, I hear, want to change our financial policy so it will require the city to spend more money in any part of the city that is deemed underserved. It's an attempt to permanently earmark a part or the budget to spend taxpayer money in their districts. In other words, spend city dollars to reassure their reelection!"

"Well, that's only three votes," Becky replied, rinsing out the sink. "That won't pass, will it?"

"It's not a question of whether it will pass or not. They know that. But it will stir up that old battle of the have-nots versus the haves. They will look like heroes in their district while they make the city look like a scrooge. It's the worst kind of demagoguery, and they damned well know it! If I and Carl and the others oppose it, the press will paint us as elitists who want all the gravy for ourselves." Bobby was angrily pacing the kitchen now.

"Dub Fanning has worked for years to keep the council away from that kind of dispute. Look what that infighting has done in Dallas and other places."

Still mumbling, he put away the agenda book and picked up the shopping list. Halfway out the door, he heard, "Bobby, forget about the council meeting. We're going to have a good time with Josh this evening." Becky always had her eye on the ball.

He arrived precisely at five thirty, looking like an all-American athlete in the latest cut of summer shorts, a light blue golf shirt, and brown Top-Siders. Libby was beaming as they walked out onto the patio, holding his arm as if to display him to the world. Bobby shook his hand, admiring the young man's strong grip and sincere face.

"How are you, Josh? Haven't seen you since the election. How are things at the engineering company?"

"I'm fine, Mr. Sanford. Been busy lately. You know, I guess, we're putting in the gas pipeline on the Payton pad site on South Adams. At least we're doing the engineering work I mean."

"Good. I suppose Payton is still a month or two away from finishing their site work there?" Bobby queried.

The conversation soon turned to subjects more interesting to the ladies as the beer and other drinks were passed around. Josh Powers's stint at Texas A&M and his high school days in Austin were already known through reports from Libby, who had made the usual inquiries during the several months she and Josh had dated. Josh was living in a bachelor pad in Fort Worth, and Bobby and Becky were not sure how many times he had visited the TCU campus to see Libby. But it was clear that Libby found him very charming. She proudly showed him about the house and yard, exercising the Texas ritual for all houseguests.

After Josh pulled out of the front drive late in the evening, Becky remarked to Bobby, "You know, I like that boy. I can tell that he was well raised by his parents. And he is so cute!"

"Whoa, lady," Bobby retorted. "Libby is just a junior. I don't want to hear any talk about serious beaus until she gets out of school.

She is interested in going to law school, and I don't want to lose a law partner someday. Wouldn't Sanford and Sanford sound good?"

"Well, don't worry, dear. I'll talk to Libby and tell her to cool down. He is at least four years older than our little girl, and we can't let her get into something that might not work in the long run," Becky intoned solemnly.

"Yes, Mother Superior." Bobby cracked with a smile while agreeing wholeheartedly.

SEVENTEEN

"Okay, it's three o'clock and we'll call to order the pre-council meeting," Mayor Fanning announced in his low-key voice, revealing the gravel-laced tone common to ex-smokers of his age.

The pre-council sessions occupied a comfortable room immediately adjacent to the main council chamber. It accommodated around the walls about twenty or so staff members and interested citizens who cared to attend the presentation/discussion sessions that always preceded the formal council meetings where the council business was formally transacted.

"Well, I welcome, first off, Terry Leech and Paula Ramsey, our two newest members. You haven't been officially sworn in yet, but we've made places for you at the table, so please have a seat," Fanning stated, pointing to the two new chairs abutting the large oaken conference table filling the center of the room.

The returning incumbents smiled and muttered congratulations and welcome as Leech and Ramsey followed the mayor's directions.

Art Isham the longtime city manager, seated next to the mayor, quickly ran through some of the routine matters on the pre-council agenda which drew little discussion around the table before coming to the budget update.

"As we all know, this year's budget will not be easy. The economic downturn is continuing while demands for more roads and other infrastructure are running far behind. Tax revenues have declined the past six months." Isham's face, while always reminding Bobby of an aged basset hound, looked even more dire when addressing the budget and left no doubt that the upcoming budget sessions would be a game of trade-offs.

"Our budget director, David Watson, is going to bring us up-to-date on where the budget stands as of today. David?"

"Good afternoon, Mayor, council members." Watson nodded to those sitting around the table before continuing. "Art has correctly pointed out that this will be a trying year to balance the budget. A big part of the challenge comes from the unfunded liability of our employee pension fund. This liability has continued to grow at an increasing rate over the last few years, really ever since the economy went downhill in 2008 to 2009. This was discussed when we put together our current budget. At that time last fall, there was a consensus of the council to look for possible solutions to the problem.

"My staff and I have done a lot of searching. What we find is that the unfunded accrued actuarial liability, which was about $62 million last year, has now grown to over $70 million. That's about equal to our total budget for last year. If you will look at the hand-outs in front of you, you will see on page 4 a graph which shows that the liability is going to keep increasing and could reach over $100 million by 2025. In other words, if the council doesn't make some fundamental changes in the retirement plan, the city will have to substantially increase its annual contributions to the pension fund, and I mean more than double what it's contributing today."

By now, the council members were staring at Watson, wondering if the latest news was real or just more hype engendered by the stories of municipal bankruptcies around the country.

Carl Jeffers broke in, "David, we just increased our contribution in the last budget. Didn't that fix the problem? We just don't have the money to up the ante again."

"Yes, sir, the contribution was increased. The problem is, 75 percent of the fund's annual needs come from the fund's security investments, but those returns have remained very modest since

2008. Under Texas law, the city must make up the difference, and the hole just keeps getting bigger."

Carl again spoke out, "But how can that be? The fund was in great shape just a few years ago. We even changed the plan formula so our employees' pensions would be better."

"That's right, Mr. Jeffers. But that occurred when the fund's investments were earning at a very high rate in the late '90s, and no one thought that the market would ever turn down."

The discussion had not only riveted the attention of the council. With few exceptions, all the other persons in the room were city employees, and as potential pensioners, they were paying close attention. Sitting back against the far wall, Ron Blake, the Lamar Police Officers Association president, and Jack Culberson, president of the firefighters' association, were side by side, acutely attuned to Watson's presentation.

"Well," Jeffers continued, "we'll have a helluva time coming up with more pension contributions in our next budget. Maybe we need to change the plan if we can't afford to pay the tab. I don't think any of our taxpayers are in the mood to see their taxes go up. I get complaints every week that taxes are already too high."

The ball was now back in Watson's court, and he replied, "I think the city has two choices. One is to pay the liability as it grows but spend a great deal less money on other city services. The other is to seek relief in the bankruptcy court. San Jose and Vallejo in California are two cities that have gone to court and laid off a large number of employees in order to divert money to cover their pension liabilities. That's not a happy solution for the citizens and certainly not a happy result for the employees who lose their jobs. The only other choice is to find some way to change the plan so that the future pension payments are reduced."

Jeffers jumped in again, "Good! Have you found any changes we can make?"

"I'm not sure. I've talked to the city attorney, and he says there is a provision in the state constitution which says, and I'm quoting, 'A change in retirement benefits of a public retirement system may not reduce or otherwise impair benefits accrued by a person.' A recent case in Fort Worth caused the attorney general to issue an opinion saying the constitutional provision means our retirement plan cannot be changed for any of our employees if it means that employee can no longer earn the same benefits he can earn today. So we may be prohibited from making any changes, except changes that will increase an employee's pension."

Bobby was stunned and launched into the discussion. "You mean to say Texas law requires us to keep paying until we go broke? We can never alter the pension plan to meet changing economic conditions from time to time?"

Watson held up both hands and replied defensively, "I'm only telling you the law as it was reported to me, Mr. Sanford."

The mayor leaned into the table and said, "Now, David, as I understand it, the constitution affects only the plan as it may apply to present employees. What I suggest is that we look at changing the plan only with respect to new employees we hire in the future. In time, all the employees would fall under the new or changed plan, right?"

"Yes, Mr. Mayor, that's true. But it will take several decades before all our present employees are gone. In the meantime, the city's unfunded liability is going to continue to increase. We talked about this last year, and so I put together some figures to show what would happen if we went from a defined benefit plan, which we have today, to a defined contribution plan, which is more like the pension plans found in private industry. It pays an employee an accumulated fund at retirement rather than promising a fixed monthly pension for as long as the employee lives. It's the only way, I think, that the pension payments can be made truly responsive to changing economic conditions and investment earnings. Under our current plan, the taxpayers are, in effect, guaranteeing that an employee will receive a certain sum for his whole life even if the economy goes into the tank. If you will look at pages 4 and 5, I show how a defined contribution plan would work."

"Well, thanks, David. I think all your work gives us food for thought," the mayor rejoined. "It is so important that we get this right. We depend on our employees for their dedicated and loyal service. We must remember that a promise made is a promise kept."

The mayor turned to the city manager, sitting on his right, and asked, "What's the next thing we need to address today?"

David Watson folded his papers and sat down, surprised that the mayor was dismissing any further discussion about the pension question.

Bobby and Carl exchanged glances, as if to inquire as to the reason the issue was not being pursued to some conclusion, a conclusion which could solve the problem. Neither of them noticed as Ron Blake and Jack Culberson quietly rose and left the room, whispering behind their hands.

EIGHTEEN

Sergeant Ron Blake, a ten-year veteran of the Lamar Police Department, proudly wore his silver badge as one of the 130 police officers under the command of Chief Harold Knebler. His days on the beat were rare, however, since his election as the president of the Police Officers Association, a responsibility which he exercised diligently and, by some accounts, too zealously. His campaign for president of the POA had been noted for his repeated vows to bring about the hiring of more officers and the raising of both pay and retirement benefits for the union members. The POA's quarterly publication, the *Badge*, always carried the "President's Page," bearing Blake's photograph along with exhortations concerning his latest efforts and progress on behalf of the membership. He enjoyed his role as POA spokesman and relished his political chores which largely removed him from the day-to-day duties of a police officer although his salary was still paid by the city. Such was the arrangement memorialized in the written contract executed by the city and the POA two years ago and soon to be renegotiated upon the contract's expiration.

One of Blake's presidential duties included periodic luncheons with individual members of the council to visit with and inform those members of the latest concerns being addressed by the POA.

Sitting in one of the booths at the Western Steak House, Blake reviewed his notes while waiting for Bobby Sanford. At six foot five, he easily filled one side of the booth. His broad shoulders and narrow waist were imposing even though he was not wearing his police officer's uniform. With his badge and sidearm strapped to his belt, above his jeans and cowboy boots, and with his cowboy Stetson perched on the table, Ron Blake could have been easily mistaken for a Hollywood Western sheriff, a stalwart bastion of the law. His appearance had always been one of his greatest attributes when confronting citizens that were failing to exhibit proper respect for law and order in Lamar, an appearance which he readily displayed in promoting his views on the fair needs of the POA members.

The meeting with Sanford would be an important one. Renewal of the police contract next year could hinge in large part on the POA's success in blocking the ever-growing complaints directed at the employees retirement plan. The plan itself was a product of the POA's efforts, along with the firefighters' association, to continually upgrade the plan formula to produce adequate pensions for those who retired from city service. Sanford had not always been supportive of the plan amendments the past few years and had lost the POA's endorsement in the last two elections. Many in the POA believed their endorsement in his first election was a large mistake, a mistake which Blake had faulted when he ousted the prior POA president. Nonetheless, his relationship with Sanford remained cordial, but not as warm as Blake wished since support of every council member would be crucial in the coming contract negotiations.

Ron rose as Sanford approached the booth. "Hey, Bobby, how's it goin'?"

"Hey yourself, Ron," Bobby replied, shaking Ron's hand as he slid into the opposite side of the booth.

"I'm glad you could make it, Bobby. It's been awhile since we talked. Bert, our VP, was going to join us, but he got called to fill a spot down at headquarters. He said you could have his dessert." Ron smiled at his small attempt at humor.

Bobby grinned. "Dessert and I don't seem to get along too well these days. My clothes don't fit well anymore."

Bobby cast his eyes on Ron's face, hoping to fathom what might have prompted the luncheon invitation. But before either could speak, the waitress arrived, pen in hand, leaving no doubt she was busy and wishing to waste no time for them to dawdle over the menu.

After both ordered and Ron signaled the waitress that the check would be his, he began his standard gambit.

"Bobby, as usual, it's budget time again in a couple of months, and I know there is talk about reviewing the pension plan. You know the council wrestled with it back in 2011 when the economy didn't look so good. But I want to show you some figures on what the retirement fund's investments have done the last year. It's up about 7 percent and the fund's trustees say it has regained its full strength again. The fund's actuary is feeling comfortable about it. I know our membership is very concerned that we don't hear more talk about changing the plan. That plan has let the city hire qualified recruits and, better yet, has kept our force intact. Other cities around here are always trying to hire away the officers Lamar taxpayers have paid to train." Ron paused to see what reaction he was getting.

"I understand, Ron. I agree that police and fire safety are a large part of the city's responsibility. But I think the council has a duty to maintain a lot of other services too. I'm sure you know that personnel costs across the board, including retirement pay, consume 70 percent of our budget. So I can't promise you that some civil service costs are not going to be reviewed in our budget. You know my position. I think retirement pay is a very important subject not only for city employees but also for the taxpayers who have to stand behind every retirement commitment the council makes. The economy's down-turn the past few years has put a real spotlight on what happens when earnings don't match the funds needed for future retirement obligations. What are we going to do if those earnings don't continue to grow next year or the year after?"

Bobby had learned in times past not to debate about what the fund's trustees or actuary cited as to the fund's earnings since the figures were often skewed or presented for selected time periods that gave a distorted picture of what lay ahead. In fact, the plan had been "sweetened" over the years because the council too often failed to review the impact of plan changes over the long run.

Ron sat with his eyes open and unblinking. He had heard this speech before, and it was not pleasing. Sanford was beginning to find sympathetic ears on the council, and even a few nodding heads were seen during David Watson's recent presentation at the pre-council meeting. Some of the council members were beginning to view the upcoming budget with alarm. He tried another tact.

"Well, Bobby, I see your point. But not all our members are able to understand why they and their wives and their children cannot rely on the city to see them through when they have to retire, especially after putting their life on the line for the taxpayers. You know they could be doing something else in a lot of other jobs. It's not easy for me to explain to them how other city costs may be more important. And I don't think that issue will get any easier when the collective bargaining agreement comes up for discussion next year."

Bobby felt a flush rising under his collar. This song and dance had never changed and was taking on the sound of a threat. Did Ron really believe he was naive enough to think the rank and file fretted every day about their retirement some years down the road? And was Ron actually due some sympathy for the feigned hardship he claimed to endure as the union president?

"Well, these are not simple subjects, Ron, but I know you are wise enough to explain it to our police officers," Bobby muttered, hoping the sarcasm was not too obvious.

With their respective positions clearly reconfirmed, the meal was concluded as the retirement talk ran its course and turned to less obtrusive subjects. Before they left the table, Bobby insisted that Blake take a $20 bill to cover part of the check. Neither his constituents nor the media needed to think he was satisfied to take anything of value from anyone lobbying him for a vote.

Driving back to his law office, Bobby was anything but sanguine about the upcoming discussion on the pension plan nor next year's police contract negotiations. The POA was making it clear that the new contract must lock in the current plan provisions if the city hoped to reach an agreement. Candid conversation was essential, but the lunch session did not lessen his fear that intransigence would again get in the way of reaching a common ground. Government pension plans had long existed on the supposition that public employees were underpaid and, therefore, were entitled to higher retirement pensions, but today their pay, in fact, often exceeded that enjoyed by workers in the private sector and exceeding the city's ability to pay. Alarm bells were still sounding across the nation as states and cities struggled to fund such plans, yet civil service employees continued to beat the same old drum. Even the bankruptcy of numerous cities had failed to bring needed reason and logic to the bargaining table. Police and fire association leaders were behaving no differently than private sector unions that he often faced in his law practice. They insisted they were entitled to more and more, and it was the sole responsibility of the city to worry about how to pay for it all. One of Blake's reports in the recent *Badge* had gone so far as to rant about the enemy, which the POA was facing in light of concern that some citizens were expressing over the pension liability. He had called it a class war. Warfare between taxpayers and their civil servants was the last thing the city needed. How secure would citizens feel if they were labeled the enemy by a force which wore sidearms on the street every day, a force sworn to protect those same citizens? Pulling into the parking lot, he vowed to seek a session with the mayor, who had been down that road many times.

By three o'clock, he finished his online research for cases that might support a longtime client's position he was advocating. The written brief was due at the district court next week. Still rolling over in his mind the most salient manner in which to fashion the brief, he dialed the mayor's office.

"Hi, Nancy. This is Bobby Sanford. Do you think the mayor might have time tomorrow morning to visit with me?"

He waited patiently as Nancy checked the mayor's calendar and finally answered in the affirmative. "Nine o'clock looks good."

"Great, nine would be fine. Tell the mayor I appreciate it, and I'll be at his office then."

He next called the Auto Zone store, where Jim Grant answered on the third ring. "Mornin', Jim. This is Bobby. Is Carl there?"

"Yeah, Bobby. He's out back checkin' some inventory. Hold on." The sound of laughter came over the line as Jim and a customer resumed a conversation which had been interrupted by the call.

"This is Carl Jeffers. What can I do for you?"

"Hey, Carl. This is Bobby. I had lunch with Ron Blake today, and I'm concerned about how we're goin' to get him and his folks to come to the table on this retirement fund problem. I've got a meeting with the mayor tomorrow morning at nine o'clock. He has had a lot more experience with this than I have. I was wondering if you could join us at his office."

"Sure, I'll be there. Ron and I have shared lunch too on several occasions. Maybe the mayor can make some sense out of it. It's a real problem."

NINETEEN

"Gentlemen, have a seat." The mayor was in a cordial mood and smiled broadly, waving at the seats opposite the small table in the center of his office.

"Dub, I hope you don't mind my asking Carl to join us. He and I have a concern about the same problem."

"No, glad to see both of you." The mayor relaxed in the chair he always used at the table.

Bobby proceeded, "Well, it's the same old question about the employee retirement fund. I know we have looked at it over the past several years, but the unfunded liability keeps growing. But what really concerns me is I had lunch yesterday with Ron Blake and he made it very clear that the POA is not going to stand for any changes in the plan, and that issue is going to be on the table during the contract renegotiations. As he stated in the *Badge*, the liability must be met with contributions from the taxpayers. But that can't be the solution. The market downturn has proved that." Bobby halted, shifting in his chair, which never seemed comfortable in the mayor's office.

"Well, I agree we do have a problem, just like a lot of other governments around the country. What do you fellas think we can do?" Fanning had been in the game long enough to know how to return any ball that they hit over the net.

"Mayor," Carl chimed in, "I reviewed the history of the plan, and it seems this council and prior councils have often modified the plan to satisfy the employees' claims that we were not providing benefits as good as other cities, what they call benchmarking. I think it should be called bootstrapping. It looks like keeping up with the Joneses is now going to have us go over the cliff with those other cities that face the same problem. The police and fire reps have lobbied me, and I guess the rest of the council, to keep our hands off the plan. Their suggestion that council members should be voted out of office if we take action is a little heavy-handed. They are not even subtle about it any more." Carl was beginning to turn red in the face.

"I know, Carl. Everyone who wants something from the council sooner or later lets you know their vote is hanging in the balance. They even told me last week that they think our budget director is using false accounting tactics to overstate the unfunded liability, and we would be smart to think about getting a new director. I guess their theory is, if you don't like the message, kill the messenger and get a new one."

Bobby's eyebrows rose as this new tidbit hit his ears. He leaned forward to reply, but Carl spoke first, "Mayor, it sounds like it's a question of who is running this city—the elected council or the city employees. If the employee unions get their way, our taxpayers will have to pay forever."

The mayor said nothing, waiting for Bobby's input, as he looked Bobby in the eye.

Bobby leaned over the edge of the table. "Dub, I share Carl's feelings. As I told Ron Baker, police and fire protection are very important, but there has to be some limit to what we can afford. We can't run those departments solely based on what their unions want. There are cities in California that have been financially wrecked by unaffordable police and fire payments. They have been forced to abandon a lot of city services and lay off hundreds of employees, including police and fire. And worst of all, how will those cities keep a sustainable population? Who wants to pay any city taxes in a city that has no public services?"

Bobby's voice was rising as he contemplated Lamar suffering the same fate.

"I don't think we're as bad off as California," the mayor replied. "But our hands are tied by Prop 16, that change in the Texas Constitution that David Watson spoke about the other day. Our employees claim that provision forbids any change to a public employee pension system that will lessen their future rights and pension accruals. And the AG has issued his opinion agreeing with that position."

Carl was now out of his seat. "Mayor, I can't believe the AG is the one who decides the law in this state. I thought that was a job for the courts!"

"I know, I know," said the mayor, waving his hand at Carl. "But as a part of the Texas government, this city is bound to follow the AG's opinion, at least until some court says otherwise."

"Dub, are you saying the only way out of this hole is to keep raising taxes? That the city is forever bound to a plan that may threaten our fiscal viability?" Bobby was sharing Carl's agitation.

"Well, I guess we can always pray that the stock market keeps going up, but we know that will not happen. People in this country were shocked in 2008 and 2009, and it will happen again."

Bobby again. "Why can't we get this problem in front of our citizens? They are the ones who have to pay in the long run."

"I believe you have reached the crux of the matter, Bobby. But how many of the council members are willing to define this issue and put it in front of the voters? Are you, Bobby? Are you, Carl? How many of the council members rely every two years on the POA and the firefighters' association to assure their reelection?" Dub Fanning knew that fear or defeat at the polls was a major contributor in the past council deliberations affecting retirement pay. He had little hope that it would change because Sanford and Jeffers recognized the dilemma and were willing to confront it.

The meeting concluded with the mayor's return to his recent suggestion that efforts be made to persuade other council members to consider changes in the plan only with respect to new employees hired after a certain date.

"That step may not cure the whole problem, but it won't run afoul of the AG, and it will show that we're trying to address the issue." The mayor's voice did not sound very convincing as Bobby and Carl bid farewell, still troubled that any council action would only succeed in lulling the citizenry to sleep, much like the actions of prior councils.

TWENTY

The Lamar Police Officers Association's headquarters sat in a nondescript one-story building five blocks south of the city hall. Once used as a dentist's office, the association had turned it into four small offices surrounding a fifty-person meeting hall. The hallway walls were almost totally covered by carefully framed pictures of the association's elected officers, past and present, as well as police officers who had received distinguished awards over the years. Prominent near the door to the meeting hall, the smiling-face portrait of Ron Blake greeted all who entered.

Across the hall, in his office, Sergeant Blake sat with his feet propped on his desk as he spoke with Alberto "Bert" Esparza, the association's vice president.

"We better have more people at tonight's meeting than we did last month. What the hell do they think the association is anyway, a club just for you and me?" Blake was anxious to alert the members of the city's apparent effort to attack the employees' retirement plan.

"I don't know, Ron," Bert replied. "It seems everyone is getting too complacent."

"Yeah, I agree. I'll see if I can light a fire under them tonight. Did you get those changes over to the printers in the article we're putting in the *Blade*?"

"It's ready to go, Ron, but I still think some of the remarks in there are going to stir up a lot of trouble. Some people won't be happy when they're called the enemy again. We need every vote we can get on the council."

"Let me tell you, Bert. Some people are the enemy, and the worst is that budget director, David Watson. That idiot has brought to the council a proposal to change our retirement to a defined contribution plan. I guess he doesn't know his own pension will be slashed just like ours. I don't believe the mayor is going to jump ship on us, but some of the council members talk like Watson has a good idea. We've got to find a way to get Watson out of city hall before his propaganda poisons the whole place. I had a talk with Jack Culberson after the last pre-council, and he is just as concerned. He says the firefighters' association will stand with us. He even said he has a cousin who works in the budget department that believes Watson has upset everyone. We are going to meet with his cousin tomorrow to see if he has some ideas about how we can force Watson out."

Blake took his boot-clad feet off the desk and stood to his full six feet, five inches.

"Let's move. It's time to get the meeting started."

The turnout was better than expected, and Blake led the forty-plus officers in the Pledge of Allegiance while his thoughts reviewed the speech he had prepared. Following the budget report and other routine business matters, he stood and began.

"I want to thank all of you for coming out tonight. The new issue of the *Blade* will be printed tomorrow, and in it you will find on the 'President's Page' a discussion of a very important issue that can seriously affect you, your wives, and your kids. The newspapers have been full of articles the last few years about municipal and state pension funds. There are certain people in the city who are trying to make it look as if Lamar has got a pension problem.

"They are deliberately using false accounting tactics and exaggerated figures to claim that Lamar has a huge and dangerous pension liability. What they don't tell you is that any funding liability is directly due to the failure of the city to make contributions to the pension fund as required by law. Instead of living up to their obligations to their police officers, their firefighters, and their general employees, the city councils have decreased their contributions and have spent the money on other matters.

"We have fought for many years to get a fair and decent pension system, which we deserve after putting our life and limb on the line for the city's citizens. We don't have any Social Security like people in the private sector, and now there is a move to take away our pension plan and replace it with something not even as good as Social Security. Their first step is to change the plan for new employees. How would you like to patrol your beat with someone who is treated differently and who will resent you because of it?

"I will be watching this attack very closely, and so will the president of the firefighters' association. And you can help. Talk to your family, your friends, your neighbors. Let them know that safe protection from crime in this city is going to be forever jeopardized if those changes are put into effect. People need to talk to their council representatives and let them know that taking hard-earned benefits away from all of us will mean the best and brightest will no longer want to work on their police force. There is going to be warfare between the haves and the have-nots. We've fought too long and too hard to get our pension benefits, and we cannot let the city budget director and the city council take it away from us!"

A cheer rose from the audience as Blake pounded the podium with his large fist, threatening to crack and split the wood.

Sitting nearby, only Bert appeared less than enthusiastic. While at A&M, he had minored in economics. The daily news stories concerned him when reporting other cities, some large, some small being forced to the bankruptcy courts when their pension funds hit the skids. In too many of those cities, employees had not only lost large portions of their accrued pensions, but many had also simply been laid off. A deep knowledge of economics was not necessary to realize that a layoff rendered moot any discussion about what was or was not a reasonable pension. Bert was tapped to be the association's representative at the bargaining table when the new police contract came up for renegotiation soon. If Blake and Culberson were bent on extending their respective labor agreements with no pension plan changes, it was going to be a long and bitter fight.

Back in his office, Blake called Culberson at his home to launch the next step.

"Jack, I've got our people ready to fight this pension thing. We are going to make every council member know that our folks will remember at next election those who have attacked our pension rights. But we need more. When can you and I get together with your cousin?"

"That's great, Ron," Culberson replied. "I just got through talking to him. He says there are two or three people in the budget office who have had run-ins with Watson. We can meet with them next Friday and see if they can give us some help. If Watson is not doing his job right, it should be brought to the attention of Art Isham. The city manager is who he works for."

Blake was smiling as he assured Culberson that the POA would do whatever was needed to pursue Watson out the door. They both viewed it as their duty to protect every dollar their members were entitled to receive from the city. In fact, their leadership roles depended on it.

TWENTY-ONE

He was beginning to find his days becoming more comfortable after six weeks in Lamar, and he welcomed the hot July sun which reminded him of the heat of Afghanistan. Ali's instructions were true, and he had discovered the pickup waiting behind the apartment, a small blue truck with over one hundred thousand miles on the odometer. He had stared at the battered Texas license plate on the rear bumper, wondering if it was validly registered with the authorities, stolen, or recovered from a junkyard. Authenticity of governmental registration had never been a concern for the Taliban's fleet of pickups in Khost. The rear-mounted machine guns and other weapons negated any need for a license to travel any road, but Ayazi was now going to move about with only a fake Texas driver's license in his pocket to confirm his "citizenship."

Omar, his American-born instructor at the Warizaristan bin Laden camp, assured him that his handlers in America would be very careful and clever to confirm that his accommodations, job, and his transportation would arouse no notice or suspicions and, most importantly, would have no traceable connections to themselves. Omar led him through an endless supply of photographs, videos, and movies which Ayazi had studied for months. They depicted typical American street scenes, grocery stores, public buildings, automobile traffic, schools, sports events, and American idioms to prepare him for his mission.

He had spent most of his first few weekends in Lamar driving the streets, refilling the gas tank at the Valero station on I-35, purchasing small items at a 7-Eleven store and other random contacts with the local scenes. Speaking with clerks and an occasional customer, he learned that his limited English seemed to raise no curiosity.

At 7-Eleven, he found many boxes which announced that they contained wheat and oat products used by Americans as breakfast foods. He purchased several boxes, some boxes of raisins, and what was labeled as bread. None of the foods resembled the pilau on which Ayazi and his family had subsisted in Afghanistan. He vowed to find the barley, wheat, onions, raisins, orange peel, and lamb to make his own pilau.

Referring to the piece of paper given to him by Ali, he had found the offices of Xavier Maldonado and Company on a narrow street east of I-35, a street that hosted a number of commercial businesses.

Behind the office, a lot fenced with steel wire was filled with dump trucks, backhoes, and other machinery which were clearly used for the excavation business in which he was to be employed.

On the first Monday in Lamar, he had entered the small office at the Maladondo company and was greeted by a young girl that looked no different than many he had seen in San Fernando, Mexico.

"I am Carlos Sanchez. I have come to work," he stated, hoping she had not expected him to speak in Spanish.

"Yes, we are expecting you," she replied with a broad smile. "Please have a seat." She pointed to a worn red sofa by the far wall.

Another woman soon led him to an interior office with small table and two chairs. She asked him to sit and placed before him two forms. "Fill out these lines," she said, pointing rapidly. "I will return soon." His writing skills were minimal, but he recalled the drills he had completed with Omar, and the woman seemed satisfied when she returned and scanned the forms.

Eventually, a man came and silently gestured for Sanchez to follow him out to the lot behind the building. Walking up to a short, rotund man dressed in dirt-stained jeans, a short-sleeved shirt bearing a Maladondo logo, and broad-brimmed cowboy hat, the guide said, "Lobo, here is that new hand we talked about. He looks strong enough to fill out that crew you will need at the South Adams pad site."

Lobo grunted and ordered Ayazi to bring his pickup down the drive and park it in the lot. "Then come with me."

He had passed his first real test in becoming an embedded sleeper, a term which Omar used in describing how the jihad would prevail over the infidels.

* * *

Six weeks and the cell phone sat silently in his pocket by day and on the bedside table at night. But it never once rang. Had Ali and his colleagues, whoever they might be, forgotten him? Or had they been discovered and arrested? Without any telephone number or other means to contact Ali, Ayazi anxiously awaited the instructions that would lead him to his glorious martyrdom.

Finally, returning home in his dirt-stained clothes late in July, he was surprised and excited to find Ali's black pickup parked at the curb. As he entered his apartment, he saw Ali sitting on the sofa, a can of cold tea in his large hand, taken from Ayazi's refrigerator. Startled, Ayazi suddenly realized he was not the only one who carried a key to the apartment.

"Greetings in the name of Allah," Ali intoned in Arabic, which sounded strange after two months of hearing only English and Spanish twenty-four hours a day.

Ali wore a slight smile on his lined face as he gestured Ayazi to sit in the only chair in the room. As Ayazi sat, Ali reverted to English, saying, "I see you have become accustomed to your new home." He continued, "We have been watching and are pleased that your work has gone well."

This was the man that had barely uttered four sentences when he had transported Ayazi in May. What was his purpose arriving unannounced? Was the jihad ready to commence? Ayazi merely nodded and waited for some possible explanation.

"You will be pleased to know a glorious plan is unfolding. Soon you will be a part of a massive attack against the nonbelievers. You and other soldiers for Allah will attack the electrical grids in Dallas and Fort Worth. Without power, the Americans will not be able to operate their cities and towns, people will die, and commerce will come to a halt. But the greatest effect will be the spread of terror here and over the entire country as they understand the Nation of Islam has the power to destroy their very heartland!" Ali waved his hand in a grand flourish, as if he could envision the chaos and terror which Ayazi would help spread.

"I will inform you and the others when we are ready to proceed. In the meantime, I have placed in the closet the explosives you will carry. On the table is a Fort Worth city map to guide you to the electrical substation which will be your target. On the small piece of paper, I have written the address. Memorize the address, then destroy the paper. In the next two weeks, go to the substation and learn where you can gain access. Timing is very important, and you must be able to perform your task when the time comes."

At last! Ayazi smiled. The jihad is coming. His heart was pounding as he followed Ali to the black pickup and watched him drive away.

TWENTY-TWO

The work with Maladondo was going well. In fact, he had performed so well they had let him operate the backhoe at the pad site, and after six weeks, he was appointed foreman on the job. His English was improving daily, as was his Spanish, which he spoke with most of the Maladondo hands. The Texas driver's license enabled him to open a bank account near his apartment, and it now held over $3,000—earned in a capitalist country!

Ayazi understood that his handlers in Dallas were reluctant to maintain more than minimum contact. Any misstep by him could lead to them if the ties were too obvious or too frequent, but while he was willing to endure his emersion among the infidels, he yearned for contact with his Muslim brothers.

There was no mosque in Lamar. The mosque he found in West Forth Worth was only a thirty-minute drive, but Ali had warned him against making any contacts there. "Not all true believers understand the jihad which we must carry out, and they might question your origin and your recent arrival here," Ali had declared on his last visit.

Ayazi's visit to the substation revealed a rear entrance which could be easily breached by forcing it with his truck when the time came, and he replayed the scenario again and again in his mind. It had been several weeks since the exciting evening of Ali's announcement of the plan. But again, nothing except silence. Surely, Ali and the others in Dallas realized by now he was committed to the jihad.

A commitment to death for the glory of Islam was divine, but waiting was not easy, he thought, as he waited on the backhoe for the crew to clear a large tree limb which was blocking the pipeline trench. From where he sat, he could see the gate that blocked the entrance to the pad site and was surprised when three large vans pulled up to the gate and stopped. The security guard at the gate was still speaking to the driver of the first van when all the doors opened and twenty-five or thirty people stepped out, carrying banners and signs. Yelling in unison, they arranged themselves in front of the gate and began marching to and fro. By now, all the Maladondo crew had ceased work, a stoppage soon repeated by the crew on the well rig drilling floor.

Unsure of the meaning of the disruption, Ayazi climbed down from the backhoe, told his crew to stand aside, and began walking toward the gate. The ebb and flow of human bodies was not unlike some of the events he had witnessed in Afghanistan, and he knew that his role as foreman demanded more knowledge of the unfolding events before he directed the crew to return to work.

Nearing the gate, he could see that the parade or demonstration was being directed by a slight man with a white goatee. The signs on their shoulders bore the word *SCAD* and demanded, "Stop drilling!" or "Killers go home!" The security guard stood before the closed gate, his arms crossed over his chest. He repeated to the man with the goatee, "You can't block this drive. Go away or I'll call the police."

Ayazi stood and watched for maybe five minutes before two police cars arrived, along with two television vans. The vans stopped in the road and raised antennae into the afternoon air. Quickly, two camera crews began roaming among the marchers while a reporter began interviewing the goateed man.

Ayazi was growing nervous, observing the policemen as they were urging the demonstrators to return to the vans. One of the policemen approached the gate to speak to a man wearing a Payton hard hat. Ayazi turned and walked back to his work site. An interview with a policeman could be very dangerous, especially if he was asked to explain who he was. To the Maladondo employees, he was simply another Mexican recently settled in Lamar with an unusual accent, but official inquiry could lead to too many questions.

Time was growing short, he thought. The Dallas brothers must move rapidly. Martyrdom could not wait forever.

TWENTY-THREE

T he pilau was good. He ate it slowly, sipping the hot tea, watching the small television in front of the sofa. Somehow, though, the orange peel and the onions were not the same. The pieces of lamb, browned by him on the electric range, were bland, lacking the pungent flavor and texture of a rangy Afghan lamb roasted on an open fire. The American lamb seemed bloated, over-fed, and without character, like the American people.

He remembered every detail of his mother's weekly preparation of pilau for the family, details which he scrupulously followed. His pilau was close but would never match her magic.

The ten o'clock newscast was beginning when he picked up the empty bowl and took it to the small kitchen to wash it clean. But first he washed his hands, giving special attention to his right hand with which he had plumbed the bowl. He was now proficient with fork, knife, and spoon, but pilau was meant to be eaten with the right hand like most Middle Eastern dishes. He smiled as he rinsed his hands, remembering that he no longer had need for his left hand to clean himself since the infidels had stocked their stores with tons of toilet tissue.

Was his mother still concocting pilau every week, perfected with the raw wheat and barley from the local market? Was she even alive? The day he and his father had last left their home, his father had made his younger brother, Hamidi, swear he would remain home and care for his mother. Hamidi, only fourteen years old, had longed to join them and take up arms with the Taliban. Had he remained true to the pledge given to his father? Ayazi shook his head, clearing the memories from his thoughts. He would never again see his mother and brother and sisters. He must take comfort knowing that soon he would see his father in the glorious kingdom, knowing his father would proudly greet his son for accomplishing a holy jihad in the name of Allah.

He returned to the sofa and watched intently as the report of the afternoon's anti-drilling demonstration followed the newscaster's lead-in: "A large number of demonstrators camped outside a Payton drill site on South Adams this afternoon in Lamar. Their leader, Charles Unsel, declared that his group would not stop until the city council brought a halt to gas well drilling in the city. Our channel 3 crew was there."

He sat up as the scene depicted Unsel at the well site. In the background among several other workers, he saw himself, sweating under his broad-brimmed straw hat with a cloth draped from the hat and running down the back of his neck. Would the scene be shown in Dallas and would Ali recognize him? Ali had warned that he was not to be seen at anytime, anywhere, under circumstances, which might arouse inquiry from the authorities. Convinced his many weeks in Lamar had stamped him as just another of the many Hispanic residents, he found his face on TV alarming.

The words of Unsel, which he had heard in the afternoon, echoed again from the screen and were followed by a camera shot of the many marchers and their signs, which they waived as they trooped around the gate.

The announcer appeared again. "Mr. Unsel vowed that SCAD, or Sane Citizens Against Drilling, would appear at next week's city council meeting to continue their crusade. Attempts to obtain a reaction from the mayor were unsuccessful as his secretary said he was in a meeting."

He lay in his narrow bed, unable to sleep because of a growing concern. Ali had failed to contact him for over four weeks after outlining the grand scheme to destroy the electric grid. Ayazi had again driven to his assigned target. The large transformers and transmission lines quietly sitting near a neighborhood of small homes in West Fort Worth. North of the substation there were a large number of baseball and soccer fields filled with young children. Ali had promised to supply a detailed plan of the entire substation, which would direct him to the most vulnerable and effective location to cripple its operation. But Ali remained silent. Was the plan being abandoned? Had the brothers in Dallas and the audacious plot been discovered? He was more than ready to strap on the large explosives which would carry out the mission he had envisioned so many months ago in Pakistan. Did Ali think he was serene and calm, sitting each night in the small apartment with no friends or Muslim brothers to visit? With sixty pounds of explosives just a few feet from his body, he could only wait. The explosives sat quietly in the small closet, hidden by an old blanket. The assembled device closely matched those Ayazi had himself built in Pakistan. He knew the detonation would devastate everything around his exploding body.

Slowly his mind turned back to the afternoon's excitement. How had the television crews gotten to the drill site so quickly? While working there, he had learned at least three different routes leading from the center of town, and each required almost ten minutes' travel time, even in light traffic. Surely, the TV crews had been alerted in advance. Mr. Unsel must be a clever man, Ayazi thought. He was creating unrest, and anxiety and the media was eagerly assisting him. Omar had assured him that devil America was complacent and would someday collapse when its weak democratic government proved unable to cope with mass destruction that would erode that complacency. His time in Lamar was confirming that complacency. All its residents seemed unconcerned, well-fed, and without fear. They did not know the Nation of Islam was growing and would bring the wrath of Allah upon the unbelievers.

Yet here was a man in the city who proclaimed that death and destruction were imminent. Had Allah sent him as an ally? Was this a sign for Ayazi? The weeks spent at the drill site had engendered no dread of impending danger as the gas drilling was proceeding. Was the drilling really something to be feared as the demonstrators had warned with their many signs? Everyone working at the site was cheerful and relaxed. He remembered the tall dark-haired young man who had approached him last week. He had smiled and addressed him, "Mr. Sanchez, I understand you are the foreman of the Maladondo crew."

"Yes, that is true," Ayazi had responded, noting the man was not too many years younger than Ayazi.

"Well, I am Josh Powers. I am an engineer with the pipeline company, and I wondered if you and your crew could realign the first one hundred feet of the pipeline ditch about fifty feet to the east," indicating with his hand. "We have had to revise our plan. I would be very grateful if you could do that," he finished, again smiling at Ayazi. That was the first occasion Ayazi was asked by someone outside the company to direct the work of his crew, and he hesitated before nodding his head.

"I will talk to Mr. Maladondo, but it should not be a problem."

"Thanks a lot," the young man said as he turned toward one of the construction trailers that lined the drill site.

Ayazi had remained on the backhoe, looking at Powers back as he walked around a pickup. His mind's eye recalled another young man who looked very similar several years ago. Ayazi had been in the back of the pickup his father was driving as they rapidly rounded a blown-out mud building. In the middle of the street, a US Marine was walking away with his back toward them. For some strange reason, his helmet was in his hand as he whirled at the sound of the speeding engine. His eyes widened below his close-cropped dark hair. He dropped the helmet and raised his weapon, pointing straight at the truck's windshield, his finger already on the trigger. Ayazi aimed, squeezed, and watched at least three bullets hit the Marine's Kevlar-clad chest, knocking him flat onto his back. As the truck swerved, Ayazi again fired, this time hitting the Marine in the face. Was this Josh Powers a brother of that Marine, or was America filled with young men who had innocent faces and dark hair?

Ayazi finally dropped off to a fitful sleep, but not before he decided to attend the city council meeting on Wednesday night to learn more about the fear being exhorted by Mr. Unsel.

TWENTY-FOUR

"Chief, we'll have a full house on Wednesday. I talked with the fire marshal about opening the pre-council room to the public since I expect the crowd in the council chamber will exceed our fire code limit."

Mayor Fanning had known Chief Harold Knebler when he was a police sergeant in Fort Worth and was happy to support the city manager's selection of Knebler as Lamar's police chief four years ago. Knebler was a Lamar High graduate and had always lived in Lamar even while serving on the Fort Worth force. He knew most of the Lamar citizens, both the good and the bad, and his tenure as chief, thankfully, had been smooth and uneventful.

"I expect you are right, Mayor. The TV folks have enfranchised Mr. Unsel and his group. We have already assigned four patrolmen to keep things in line outside the main door on Wednesday, and I and two extra officers will be in the council chamber. Counting Jess and Sam, the regulars, that will make four of us inside."

"That's good, Chief. I hope Unsel doesn't go off the deep end, but you never know what those people might do. He was really pumped up on TV the other day with the cameras in his face." The mayor didn't appear very confident as he continued, "We've been contacted by two, and maybe three, television stations who want space in the chamber to position their cameras and reporters. It's gonna be a tight fit."

The chief frowned and his words were somber. "Why are they coming on Wednesday? I thought there were no gas drilling items on the agenda."

"Well, there is one," the mayor replied. "Estella Jiminez postponed that request for a gas pipeline crossing on Fifth Street last month because she was concerned some of her neighbors were not given enough information. So it is coming up again on Wednesday. Unsel and his crew don't care about the pipeline crossing really. They just want an excuse to address anything that has to do with gas drilling. I swear, I think they must pray every night for a gas explosion so they can be vindicated. We've had more than one hundred wells drilled in Lamar in the last ten years, and there is probably another two hundred wells drilled out in the county around Lamar. There has not been one mishap in spite of Unsel's dire predictions."

As the mayor paused, the chief spoke again, "Do you think anyone will come and actually speak against the pipeline crossing? There must be hundreds of pipelines and other utility lines that cross under the city streets."

"No, I don't expect there to be any opposition. Jiminez has said her folks are okay with it. There is always the chance, of course, that some citizen who is unhappy with Payton's gas leasing efforts or the actions of some other driller will use it as an excuse to mouth off, especially since everyone expects the TV cameras to be rolling."

"Well, we will be ready, Mayor. Just give me a sign if it looks like anyone is getting out of line."

"Thanks, Chief. I'm really sorry that we need to have so many of your officers on hand, but it's best to be safe."

* * *

Down the hall, Terry Leech and Alece Jackson were huddled in Leech's office and did not notice the chief walking by, following his session with the mayor.

"Alece, I understand why you are unhappy that the change in the financial policy has been postponed again, but you can count the votes as well as I can. Like it or not, the mayor will not support it and he has got Sanford, Jeffers, and probably Ramsey behind him. I'm not even sure how keen Jiminez is about it anymore."

Jackson frowned. His six-foot-two height, caramel skin, and graying hair gave him the look of a retired NBA star. He often carried his lean frame with grandeur when he rose to speak at any gathering. On the council for four years, he had succeeded in roundly defeating those who opposed him in the last two elections. His constituents were loyal because he addressed every concern they expressed to him by telephone, iPad, e-mail, letter, or voice on the street. But the battles were beginning to wear him down.

"Mr. Leech," he began, slipping into his old habit of formality when addressing matters in city hall, "I understand very clearly how our fellow council members fall out on this issue of justly providing for Lamar's less fortunate citizens. I understand that this council has responded to the needs of those citizens on some occasions, but the future will bring new persons to this council, persons who may believe that some who live here deserve their life of poverty, their life of hopelessness. Addressing community needs and assuring a fair distribution of federal and state grants is a constant battle for those I represent and many of those you represent. A clear statement in our financial policy directing future councils to pursue those goals will prevent some members from seeking excuses to ignore those in need."

Terry Leech was nearly prompted to stand up and salute, so beguiling and stirring was the speech. But he refrained, remaining in his chair, nodding his assent, and saying, "Alece, I have never doubted your motivations, and I applaud your effort. But you need to convince the mayor and others. I think some of them are simply leery of any attempt to control the actions of future councils by any kind of a policy statement. Anyway, I'm not so sure the law would require a future council to take or not take any action. You know, they could just amend the policy statement again."

"That may be the case, but I would hope that you could visit with Bobby Sanford and ask him to at least consider the amendment. I think you could be persuasive." Alece pursed his lips, giving his face the mien of a minister addressing his congregation. He was not happy with the thought he might have another confrontation with the Reverend Benjamin or the brothers in the coalition.

Leech nervously replied, "I tell you what. I will visit with him if I get a chance, but don't expect too much."

As Alece rose to return to his own office, Terry asked, "Do you think that Unsel fellow and his gang are really going to come and demonstrate on Wednesday?"

"Yes, I do. Public demonstrations have proven to be effective means of conveying public sentiment. Numbers get multiplied and carry a loud voice."

Terry nodded, remembering the days of Martin Luther King and the transitions brought about by his marches and demonstrations. He had no doubt Alece would have been in those marches had he been a little older back in those days.

TWENTY-FIVE

T he bankruptcy case was finally moving forward, and Bobby was due to appear with his client before the federal bankruptcy judge in Fort Worth in two days. He was still worrying over the creditor's schedule, however, when Karen, his longtime secretary, came into the office.

"Bobby, before you came this morning, Dave Mellon with the *Star Telegram* called and asked if he could meet with you tomorrow morning here in your office."

"What does he want to talk about?"

"He didn't say exactly. Just said he was working on an editorial that you might find interesting."

Bobby thought a minute, remembering several occasions when the media had taken license to inform the public that the councilman was unavailable or failed to return a call. What was it this time? "Okay, call him back and tell him that ten o'clock is fine with me."

Pushing sixty, Dave Mellon had worked a number of years at Dub Fanning's insurance agency before landing a job at the *Star Telegram* in the early '90s. Sharp and curious, he rose through the paper's ranks to become assistant manager and then the chief of the editorial board. Still with a full head of dark hair, he was one of the more photogenic of the paper's staff still clinging to the ever-shrinking numbers at the old print media. Bobby had little contact with the paper until Bobby was elected to the council. So far, Mellon had proven to be a straight shooter among the media that followed the few newsworthy stories emanating from Lamar.

"Thanks for seeing me on such short notice, Bobby. I want to get your input on a matter that we hope to cover in a series of editorials. I assure, you will not be quoted on anything you say and there will be no attribution to you in any of these articles."

"Well, I appreciate that, but depending on what we talk about, I may not care whether my name appears in print or not." Bobby smiled.

"Good point. These editorials will explore the widespread problem of unfunded public employee pension funds, and we want to compare the situations the large Texas cities are facing with what is going on in smaller but growing places like Lamar. You know Lamar has grown so much since I used to work for Fanning I can hardly recognize it."

"That's very interesting Dave, our budget director, presented a review of our pension at the last council meeting. He is very concerned that our present plan is heading for trouble, and he is proposing that we modify it. Like most cities, I guess, we spend more on employee wages and benefits than anything else, but I don't think our retirement costs are like the problems that have arisen in Houston, Dallas, and Fort Worth and elsewhere." Bobby hedged, waiting to hear more about Mellon's angle before offering any substantial comment.

Mellon laid on Bobby's desk several charts, explaining, "These show the last five years' trend of unfunded liabilities which those big cities are facing. The Government Accounting Standards Board issued their recommendation over two years ago that all governmental entities, including cities, clearly show on their annual financial statements the level of their pension liabilities. No one yet knows what those revelations will do to cities' ability to seek bond financing, but it has really gotten everyone nervous, especially elected officials."

"Yeah," Bobby responded, "I read an article on that last year in one of TML's issues. It looks like we may have the same problem, or will have, if we don't change our plan. When Lamar became a home rule city in 1998, the retirement plan was set up like it is in most other cities, and it has been improved, from the employees' standpoint, over the years. Any employee who retires is given a fixed annual income for life. So the city's liability is measured by each employee's matrix, and the city is on the hook to pay it."

Dave nodded his head. "Right, that's what most cities have done, and they are liable for millions of dollars they don't have because each employee is guaranteed that pension for the rest of his life."

"I know, that's what the TML article was about. But how are we going to get the money to pay off what we owe?" Bobby asked as if Mellon had the answer.

"That's exactly the point, Bobby. We are asking the same question in the series we are going to publish."

"Hey, Dave, don't expect me to supply an answer," Bobby retorted, raising his hand to ward off such an inquiry. "But seriously, the sixty-four-dollar question is, will the council and the employee representatives sit down and solve the problem? Lamar is not immune, but so far, the council seems stuck in a rut when it comes to fixing the problem. No one smiled when the budget director proposed a possible solution."

The discussion continued, with Bobby's suggestion that Dub Fanning might supply more insight regarding Lamar's quandary.

As the clock moved past eleven thirty, Bobby proposed that they walk over to Maudie's for a bite of lunch.

TWENTY-SIX

"Hey, Maudie, how about a table in the back room?" Bobby smiled, confident Maudie recognized that a council member in the company of a media guy might wish a little privacy.

Mellon seemed surprised he had been recognized outside the paper's offices.

Settled with very few others nearby that early, Bobby directed his blue eyes at Mellon.

"Dave, I really appreciate your visiting with me in person. A private face-to-face discussion with a newspaper guy is pretty rare these days. Seems a quick telephone call and leading questions is the standard modus operandi."

"Yeah, I know what you mean. I don't understand what they're trying to teach in journalism school anymore. Ever reporter wants to be an editorial writer, and we editorial writers are lucky to get out and visit the real world anymore. And that is not even touching what passes for news on television."

Bobby glanced quickly at Mellon and ventured a thought. "You know, I sometimes think the world is going crazy, the way it comes across on television. Last week I heard more spins than hard facts. Why a black congressman was even complaining that the weather service was somehow discriminating against African Americans because no hurricanes were given African names, and the hurricane reports were not broadcast in the kind of language African Americans could understand. It is unbelievable. And last year there was a report complaining that a disproportionate number of professional baseball players were white or Hispanic, with very few African Americans in *America's Game*. Why doesn't someone complain that there is a disproportionate number of black guys playing on basketball and professional football teams? Are the white guys being discriminated against? What ever happened to the idea that talent and ability should determine who succeeds?"

Mellon laughed out loud and shook his head. "Oh come on, Bobby. You and I know that good journalism motivates those stories. The free press in this country can only survive if it makes money. Boy, do we know that at the paper!"

"I understand that, Dave. But what about most people in the country that read little and rely on these crazy TV stories to educate themselves about the larger world they don't come into contact with? And what about the black people who are eager to believe the slavery era has not passed long ago and that they deserve some form of restitution from everyone else? When is all this going to stop? Is there no truth anymore, or are we just tired of looking for it? What happens when you can no longer enforce laws against a criminal because his skin color says it would be discriminatory to put him in prison?"

"Have you seen that in Lamar, Bobby?"

"Well, can I talk about that without being quoted in the paper?"

"Sure, we're off the record. But I'm interested in your view of how all this shakes out here."

"Okay, let me give you a case in point, as we lawyers sometimes say. At a recent council meeting, a black man from Dallas came to urge us to spend more city dollars in the underserved areas of the city. Now we address needs everywhere in the city constantly and respond to pleas from Alece Jackson and Estella Jiminez made in behalf of their constituents, and by that I mean African Americans and Hispanics. But this guy from Dallas decided to come over here and lecture us on how we should spend substantial money for a program to teach neighborhoods how to obey those in authority He wanted us to pay him a $1,500 honorarium for his service in bringing the program to Lamar. You used to live here, Dave. Do you believe we have a racial problem that requires us to hire a self-appointed black leader from Dallas?"

Mellon demurred and said, "I'm listening."

"Well, the implication was clear. He had spent several days talking in the Camp, and we maybe should expect some problem with people obeying authority if we didn't sign on for his program. In other words, if we don't have a racial problem here, he will find one for us."

"What did you do, Bobby?"

"We declined his offer. But not before Carl Jeffers raked the man over the coals! But my point is, there are unfortunately a lot of people in this country who want to prolong the memory of slavery to line their own pockets. They want to promote racism and identify *victims* as long as it gets them what they want. It seems like our free enterprise system is creating a racial capitalism."

"Wow, Bobby! Do you really believe that?" Mellon asked, his eyes slowly widening.

"I know that may sound a little far-fetched, but come to some of our council meetings and listen to Alece and Estella preface each of their complaints or opinions with a plea for more diversity, meaning more appointments, more committee members, more employees with a certain skin color. Race first and ability a mere second. And of course, they are implying that a lack of diversity is evidence of bias and racism in favor of white folks. The race card is alive and well even though it is supposedly buried in subtlety."

Bobby continued, "I have been to the courthouse many times, and I have seen how the use of a word, a term, can turn one's opinion quicker than honest candor. One more point. The use of the term *diversity* is carefully reserved for the meetings of the council, the pre-council meetings, and the other public meetings because that's when the media is listening and watching, that's when the voters can monitor what the council member is doing for them.

"Now, Dave, don't you think that all that would be good fodder for a *Star Telegram* editorial? Don't answer. I know the answer. That kind of honest discussion would serve no purpose other than raising the charge that I am a racist, a bigot. There's the problem. We do not have enough people of guts and goodwill who will openly and candidly address those issues, so instead we amuse ourselves with the silly pronouncements that the naming of hurricanes is evidence of continuing racism in our country."

* * *

Dave Mellon drove back to his office with more in his head than he had bargained for. What would the owners of the paper think if Sanford's views were explored in an editorial? Did Alece Jackson really believe that benefits assigned on the basis of race, or diversity, were the answer? Had Alece even read the recent *Star Telegram* article extoling the hard work and business success of Leon Harris, the black football star from Lamar? Harris had once been called Leon the Loper by a sportswriter who thought Harris resembled an African gazelle loping across the Serengeti Plain. Dave smiled. How politically incorrect such a reference would be in the present world.

TWENTY-SEVEN

Calling the council session to order on Wednesday evening, Mayor Fanning announced to the large crowd that additional seating and a TV was available in the pre-council room and warned that the fire marshal was prepared to pare the crowd if they did not thin out, particularly those standing around the walls.

Fully a third of the two-hundred-plus seats were already filled with old people, young people, and those in between, all wearing round stick-on yellow badges declaring SCAD Stop the Drilling in bold black letters. A few still carried the signs they had used in the six o'clock march in front of the city hall, but most had been removed after the mayor suggested that the signs were blocking the sight lines of others in the room.

With everyone finally seated, they all stood while the invocation was intoned and then the mayor led all in the Pledge of Allegiance. With eyes on the flag, no one seemed to notice the tanned man in the back row who stood but kept his hands to his side during the pledge, his mouth closed.

In unison, the council and audience sat after the pledge was completed. Ayazi had learned of the flag ritual from Omar but was surprised to hear it from so many voices.

One nation under God? What God and what nation? He knew without a doubt that this heathen country did not constitute a nation under Allah, the only true God. Every action every day in America was an insult to Allah. No praying, women in public practically unclothed, a universal consumption of alcohol. The teachings of Muhammad were so foreign to the infidels that their pledge was a mockery, a blasphemy, begging for punishment. The destruction of America was the true pledge, a pledge by which he was bound. Surely Ali would soon give him the signal to strap on the bomb and destroy the Americans' electric grid.

The matters before the council proceeded smoothly through the docket. The pipeline crossing item was read out by the city secretary, and Estella Jiminez moved for approval, but the mayor interrupted to state that a number of cards had been signed by some citizens, asking for the right to speak on the proposal before a vote was taken.

The first speaker, Charles Unsel, rose and approached the lectern in front of the council dais. Ayazi was surprised when a lady seated to his left leaned over and asked, looking directly at Ayazi, "Do you know about Mr. Unsel? He has been a hero, standing up to fight against these awful gas companies. They are going to destroy our city."

Finally gaining the courage to reply, Ayazi whispered, "Yes, I have seen him on TV," as the lady smiled her approval.

Unsel had begun his speech, so the conversation with the lady halted. She appeared elderly and was conservatively dressed, except for the round yellow badge on her shoulder. Ayazi's mind was running. Did the old lady, a grandmother maybe, really believe the drilling of gas wells was going to destroy her and others? If her fear was real, what would she and the rest of those in Lamar do if a well should actually explode? Maybe the infidels were not as comfortable and assured as they wished the world to believe!

Persuasive though he might sound, Charles Unsel's ten minutes at the lectern echoed the same message he had repeated many times before the council and recently before the TV cameras. Again, he closed with a plea that the council adopt a drilling moratorium. This time, however, his army of supporters cheered, whistled, and applauded, causing the mayor to sharply rap the gavel and warn that further such conduct could result in the expulsion of the people from the room.

Most quieted on the third warning, but two men persisted, becoming louder with each rap of the gavel.

"Chief, please have your officers escort these two men out of the chamber and out of the building," the mayor instructed, pointing to the two miscreants on the back row.

As the men were directed out the door, most of Unsel's crew booed and hissed, clearly rallying to their plan to obtain as much TV coverage and notoriety as possible.

Unsel was followed by five other men, each repeating Unsel's dire warning that the city council was ignoring the safety of the city and predicting, momentarily, a horrible explosion or worse.

At last, Estella's motion was presented and passed, whereupon the Unsel group rose and noisily marched out, carefully watched by the chief and his officers.

Intrigued, Ayazi walked out and mingled with the crowd, listening to their remarks and continuing diatribe against the uncaring and unknowing council members. The old lady who had spoken to him came up and said, "I hope you were listening to Mr. Unsel. I cannot understand how our city council can give away our city to those greedy gas companies. To make a dollar, they are willing to risk the lives of little children and everyone in the city. I was so impressed by Mr. Unsel I am going to a meeting he is having next week. It is at the Elks Hall just off the square. You should come too." With that, she turned and walked over to a small group, their heads bobbing as they reviewed the evening's events.

Ayazi carefully avoided the TV cameras that were roving through the people and walked two blocks to find his pickup where he had left it in the twilight before the meeting. Darkness had fallen, and he was happy for the nighttime cover. Traveling to and from work and excursions for groceries and gasoline had kept his presence to a minimum, he hoped. Exposure of his immigration from Mexico and his true identity was a constant fear.

TWENTY-EIGHT

A s a fifteen-year member of the Lamar Lodge of the Benevolent and Protective Order of Elks, Charles Unsel had earned enough respect among the brothers to advance to the governing board of the lodge. Reserving the hall for the Saturday meeting, however, had caused a rumble, especially among the members who viewed gas drilling as a positive activity in Lamar. To placate them, Unsel agreed to start the meeting with an announcement.

"I want to welcome all of you to this important meeting. It is very encouraging to see you here. But before we begin, let me state that this meeting and any expressions at the meeting do not bear the approval or sponsorship by this lodge and will express only the concerns and opinions of those individuals who speak here. I hope all of you have signed in at the table at the entrance. We would like to have your name and contact information as we go forward. We want your voice heard at city hall."

He then introduced himself as the president of SCAD and the chairman of Stop Drilling Alliance, the new umbrella group dedicated to preserving the health and safety of Lamar citizens.

Next, after introducing the leaders of two other organizations protesting drilling in the city, he outlined the history of drilling, both in Lamar and Fort Worth, and the efforts of SCAD to awaken the public to the destruction and dangers threatened to all.

Ayazi sat in the back of the hall. He had only pretended to fill out a card when he entered. The speeches went on for almost an hour, sounding much like Unsel's presentation at the last council meeting. Many predicted that gas wells like the one on S. Adam Street were only days from erupting and visiting havoc upon the city. Ayazi had seen nothing during his work with the excavation crew that foretold any such thing. Yet many seemed to genuinely believe that doom was lurking. How strange? Ayazi had seen, and caused, real doom and destruction in Afghanistan. How did these Americans, with their clean and neat neighborhoods, shiny cars, and peaceful days, expect such calamity? It would only come through the divine jihad conducted by him and his brothers. Their real Armageddon would surpass the predictions by the speakers when he and his brothers destroyed the electrical grid and brought their energy hungry life to a halt.

As the meeting closed, Unsel urged all to take a copy of the alliance report, which detailed the falsehoods and fallacies contained in the Fort Worth-sponsored air quality study made in 2011. The study was termed by him as a piece of propaganda funded by the gas industry.

Ayazi drove home, still awaiting the signal from Ali, a signal which would herald a real blow to the infidels who fretted over the drilling of gas wells.

TWENTY-NINE

To most of the Lamar citizens, Dub Fanning was Mr. Mayor. The gavel in his hand represented the law and the road the city was expected to follow. Most had little doubt that gas drilling in Lamar would not be halted by a moratorium or other council action so long as Dub Fanning was mayor. Charles Unsel and other detractors were waging a losing battle.

Bobby was keenly aware of Fanning's position about gas drilling but still disturbed that the mayor appeared so benign in the face of the ever-increasing drumbeat coming from Unsel. Thursday morning, following Unsel's latest appearance to demand that drilling be stopped, Bobby asked the mayor for a conference.

"Well, Bobby, what's on your mind this bright and windy day?" Dub asked cheerfully.

"Dub, I have practiced a great deal of oil and gas law, at least until I got on the council. I understand how oil and gas leases work, how exploration and production occurs. I've even spent some time on drilling rigs watching how wells are drilled. So I'm really concerned when people like Unsel are provided a public forum at city hall to spread lies and promote false fears. The people in this city deserve better. We should find some way to stop this demagoguery or at least present to the public the true facts. I've gotten calls and e-mails from people who believe that the sky is going to fall and that gas companies are an evil cabal seeking to destroy everyone. I think we should let everyone know that we are, in fact, looking out for their welfare and that Unsel and his like are simply off base."

Fanning chuckled before responding, "You know, I've sat in this chair for a long time, and I've seen a lot of Unsels come and go. Believe it or not, most of them strut their stuff for a while and are never heard from again. Somehow our folks seem to survive their lies and catcalls, and when election time comes, the voters pay little attention to those SAPs."

"SAPs?" Bobby asked, recalling Carl Jeffers's words.

"Yeah," Dub answered. "A SAP is a self-appointed prevaricator. Those are people who pretend to represent some constituency, and they present a series of false facts and figures to promote their cause. They believe that if they tell their lies often enough people will believe them. I'll bet I've seen dozens of them during the time I have been mayor."

Bobby smiled, wondering if this conversation had already taken place between the mayor and Carl.

"But, Dub, why do you let them get by with their so-called facts when you know they are simply wrong?"

"Well, Bobby, the city council is not a court of law. It does not swear each speaker to tell the truth and nothing but the whole truth. And even though the council members often sit as judges, they have to use their common sense to sort out which statements they hear are untrue. Maybe a court judge has an easier task if he can rely on a speaker's oath, but I can't imagine this council or any other council requiring its citizens to swear on the Bible each time they address the council."

"I don't know, Dub, maybe that would be a good idea," Bobby chimed and went on. "Charles Unsel sure doesn't hesitate to cite drilling mishaps which he knows are exaggerated or even false. And his statistics are just pulled out of thin air."

"Yes, but you and I know that and so we don't give him any credence. He is not going to win the day before this council!" Dub's hand chopped the air to confirm his pronouncement.

"Well, he must know that too," Bobby responded. "He has come before us seven or eight times this year and he gets nowhere. What's his point?"

"Aha! Now you're getting to the point," Dub laughed. "SAPs are not really trying to make a point. Their real interest is to embellish their appearance before TV or other media to establish their role as master or leader of their cause. In fact, they long to be anointed by the press as an environmental activist or some similar such title. The approbation, the public recognition, is the end which confirms their self-appointed role. While a win before the council would surely enhance that role, they obtain as much fulfillment from railing at the evil officials who continue to thwart them. Maybe it's a Don Quixote syndrome." Dub ended with a snort.

"But people like Unsel still create a false trepidation in the city because the press and TV give him more and more ink and time," Bobby replied.

"That may be true. But what can we—you, I, the council—do about it? Unsel has every right to speak, and the media relish anyone who can create the ever-needed controversy that sells newspapers, as they say. The press feels compelled to report every viewpoint in order to appear unbiased and, more important, to enhance their circulation. Any contrary view no matter how crazy or false is fair game. So freedom of speech and the press mean Mr. Unsel and his ilk will always have their say at our public meetings. If the gas companies don't like what Unsel says, they can do two things. They can make damn sure they don't cause any harm, and they can come to our meetings and present their viewpoint. In the meantime, we have enacted a fair gas drilling ordinance, and we are going to apply it fairly."

Bobby knew that Dub Fanning had fully expressed his views and that the conversation was at an end, unless Bobby had a different topic to toss on the table. He thanked the mayor for his time and took his leave. He hoped that Charles Unsel and his followers were rightly diagnosed by the mayor.

* * *

The next council meeting was almost two weeks away as Bobby wrestled with the task of presenting witnesses at the meeting to advocate, in behalf of gas drilling, human evidence to confirm the actions of the council. Was this just an exercise to support the continuing elections of the council members, or was it something larger, a reaffirmation of the democratic process by which crucial public decisions were placed in the hands of a few who act for the benefit of all? He knew that the media would be the conduit by which the public jury would sit in judgment.

So often the council sat as a court in judgment of the actions of its citizens. Now it was possibly going to be judged, and the mayor had appointed Bobby to be the council advocate, the one to convince Lamar that their publicly elected tribunal was acting effectively in their behalf. If it was not, how many of the citizens would abandon their faith in a republican form of government? Bobby stopped. Was he becoming consumed by his own musings?

His first call was to Maudie. Not only was she known and revered by many of the city's older residents, her restaurant was also a prime example of the economic flourish gas drilling was bringing to Lamar.

"Hey, Maudie, it's Bobby Sanford."

"Bobby, where have you been? I haven't seen you for almost a week."

"I know. The council and law practice have kept me hoppin' like a frog. Listen, Maudie, I need some help. You mentioned the other day that your business has been boosted by the gas drilling folks in town. We've got some people who want the drilling stopped and don't understand what a benefit it has been."

"Yeah, I saw that guy Unsel on TV. He's a real pain in the butt. He even comes in here trying to get his petitions signed."

"Well, that's the problem, Maudie. Not enough people hear about the other side. I would like you to agree to come before the council and tell everyone about what gas drilling has done for you. Everyone needs to hear something beside the constant doom and gloom from Unsel and his crew."

"Why sure, Bobby. I'll help any way I can."

"That's great, Maudie. I'll come by today or tomorrow and we can talk about it."

One down and four to go. He called two more business owners who agreed to tell how they were better off because of the Barnett Shale drilling and one of the foremen for a well-servicing company to talk about the money they received for work on wells in Lamar and the money their employees spent for food, gasoline, etc., in Lamar.

He explained that they would need to appear at the next time a gas matter appeared on the agenda, sign a speaker's card in favor of the item, and talk about how and why gas drilling was benefiting them as well as the citizens of Lamar. If Unsel was going to use the council meetings as a speakers' forum, certainly others were entitled to do the same.

Finally, he made an appointment to visit with the local manager for Payton Energy. He hoped they would agree to recite the amount of money they had paid Lamar citizens for lease bonuses and for gas production royalties. Those figures needed to be publicly aired if the advocacy was going to be effective in blunting Unsel's campaign.

THIRTY

"So what are you going to do when you graduate next spring?" he asked.

Libby put down her fork, gazing at Josh who sat across the table. "I'm not sure. Dad has very subtly hinted that I should think about law school. My grades have been good, and I've worked in his law office a couple of summers. I'm taking the LSAT this fall."

"What's the LSAT?" he replied with a slight grin.

"Oh, you know, the Law Standard Aptitude Test. You don't stand a chance of getting into a law school unless you have a high LSAT score," Libby said, peering at him. Surely he had heard of an LSAT.

Josh laughed, "I guess that's like the SAT I took in high school."

Sometimes Libby felt as if Josh enjoyed teasing her, and why? He was only four years older, but he was out of school and already employed in a profession.

This was the second time they stuffed themselves with Italian food at the new place on Crockett Street in Fort Worth, just a block from Josh's apartment, and it always seemed filled with people in their twenties and thirties.

"If it means anything, I think you would be a great lawyer. Every time we have a debate, you seem to win."

Libby blushed. Was he just teasing or what?

"Well, maybe it's in my blood, having a father who is a lawyer and now a politician," she announced with pride.

"I really like your dad and your mom. They have been very warm," he said. "I enjoyed the cookout last week."

"Thank you very much. How about your folks? Do they still live in Austin?"

His eyes clouded momentarily before he answered, "My dad, Brandon Powers, has lived there all his life. But Mom died my junior year in college. She had lymphatic cancer. It was very sudden."

He went on, unable to stop, "She was only forty. Very young, I guess. It was so hard on my younger brother and two sisters. They are still trying to cope."

"Oh, Josh! I am so sorry. I didn't mean to—"

"It's okay," he said, putting his hand over hers. "It's been hard on all of us, but Dad is a rock. He has pulled everyone through even though he has probably been hurt more than he lets on."

Libby squeezed his hand, wanting to comfort him. She could see the pain on his handsome face.

He shifted in his seat and pulled his hand away as if to signal a change in the conversation.

Libby sensed the change and picked up her fork to dive once more into the lasagna.

She was already receiving sly smiles from her sorority sisters at TCU every time she mentioned Josh's name. They never missed a chance to comment about her taking up with an older man.

It didn't bother her, though. Bobby and Becky had taken to him and that was enough for her.

THIRTY-ONE

In the last year of Bobby's studies at law school, Becky Cowan had seduced him, both mentally and physically, within five days of their first meeting. Her blond beauty was strangely matched by her common sense that repelled any action or thought that possessed no sound foundation. The youngest daughter of a rancher from Muleshoe, Texas, she rode a horse before she was five and feared nothing since. She did not hesitate when Bobby proposed the day he graduated from law school. She rode off with him to Lamar, never doubting that a failure to complete her last year of college was merely a minor consideration, a small loss balanced by lassoing a husband like Bobby.

"I had an interesting conversation with Libby this afternoon," Becky said as he entered the house. "She said you had lunch together, and she wanted to know if you have lost your mind."

"Yes, I mean no. I worry about her and I hoped she might find a little fatherly advice useful."

Becky glowered at him. "She was agitated a good deal. But I think she took it well when I backed you up and suggested that some things need to remain for marriage."

He couldn't help but smile. "Yes, Your Blondness, just like we did, right?"

"That's not fair, Bobby. You and I knew we were going to get married."

"Oh really, how come I wasn't told that?"

"I would have told you when you needed to know," she replied, moving close to give him a warm bear hug.

"But are you going too far by hinting Libby should find a boyfriend from TCU who is closer to her age?"

After supper, Bobby wandered into his study to again review his witnesses, Maudie, the guy from Payton Energy, and the others ready, willing, and able to rebut Mr. Unsel. The next gas-related matter on the docket could not be far off. The gas issue was taking far too much time. How would the council ever get around to tackling the upcoming budget, not to mention the ever-present pension specter?

Watson's June presentation to the council was sobering. The past three years, the UAAL had continued to increase and the city's annual contribution to the ERF was falling woefully short of what was needed to put the fund on a sound fiscal basis. The past indulgence by the council catering to the city employees' desire for larger and larger pension rewards was sacrificing the future stability of the city's revenue stream to meet other social demands, even the ambitious plans for a new library. The mayor seemed content to ignore the pension question, concentrating on the current task of balancing a new budget. There was never enough money to satisfy every cry for the next *need*.

The trustees of the pension fund, composed largely of current and retired employees, continued to maintain that the fund was sound and that the shortfall, if any, was easily cured by more city contributions. The POA was even lobbying for new amendments to the plan, which would place a larger burden on the plan's ability to pay future pensions. They insisted that the improvements were necessary if the city was going to assure the safety of its citizens by attracting the brightest and the best to new police cadet classes. Not far behind, the FFA were complaining that their retirement benefits were below the average provided to firefighters in the benchmark cities they annually threw into the budget discussions. Bobby wondered for years how the *benchmark* comparison proved anything. He never doubted that firefighters in each of the ten comparable cities sponsored the same argument. Moving any city upward toward the average only succeeded in raising the overall average, year after year, but none of the council members seemed to understand, or care, that this bootstrap ruse continually increased Lamar's cost of operation. Public safety and protection was sufficient cover for elected officials to gratify organized employees and, thus, to ensure their own reelection to office. Would the council ever address the question of what pension level was sufficient, or would it be content to deal with the short-term rewards and sacrifice the long-term health of the city?

THIRTY-TWO

He turned at the corner, on the way home at five thirty. Only a block from the office, he suddenly remembered that Carl had called that morning with an invitation to enjoy a beer at Mac's. Quickly reversing at the next corner, he drove the two blocks to the "Emporium" and parked next to Carl's car.

As usual, the beer was cold and Carl was already into his first schooner.

"What's up, Carl? You've been grumpy for a week."

"Well, have you ever heard that old song that was a big Arlo Guthrie song back in the seventies? I believe it's called 'The City of New Orleans.'"

"What? I don't think so. Why?"

"Well, the City of New Orleans is a train, and in the song, the train travels across the Southern part of the country and talks about the towns and people it sees on its journey. A line in the song begins, 'Good morning, America. How are you?' I heard that song this morning driving to work, and it made me think. America is not well. We are not what we used to be, what we were meant to be back when our government was formed."

Bobby laughed and asked, "Are you a beer philosopher?

"Oh, hell. You've seen it. A presidential election, and what is offered? On the one hand, an out-and-out socialist who believes the government should run everything and a woman who believes she is entitled and does not need to follow the rules and, on the other hand, a TV reality show host who delights in acting like a bull in a china shop and another freshman senator. We just had eight years of one of those, a community organizer. No one is goin' to vote for someone. Everyone is goin' to vote against someone. If a terrorist was to bomb our next president, half the country would cheer, like it was some TV reality show. And the pundits wonder why everyone is so disgusted with Washington."

"So you think our founders got it wrong?"

"No damnit! I mean it. When he wrote the Declaration of Independence, Thomas Jefferson said we had the right to life, liberty, and the pursuit of happiness. That's what we affirm when we recite the pledge to our flag and the republic for which it stands. But today we are throwing away our freedom and replacing opportunity with a search for security. No one wants to pursue happiness anymore. They just expect government to hand it to them like a lollipop! Federal health plans and minimum wages. The TV ads all say buy this, buy that 'cause you deserve it. Entitlements, entitlements! It's a little like our pension plan. Everyone's entitled to it, and the taxpayer has got to cough it up. No wonder the world is out rioting in the streets when governments run out of money because no one is working and paying taxes. And we don't seem capable of doing anything about it. Our conference with the mayor was a farce. He just cut off the pension conversation at the pre-council in June."

Bobby tried to suppress the bemused expression on his face and responded, "I know what you mean, Carl. Washington is so far in debt I don't think it will ever balance the budget."

"Washington hell! We're no better here in Lamar. We've had deficits for three years running now. Almost 80 percent of our tax revenue is committed before we even begin to set a new budget. Zero-based budgeting is a joke. And if that isn't bad enough, Jackson and Jiminez talk day and night about new programs and more spending we need to make for the underserved and the less fortunate. Everyone is afraid to call it what it is. It's just plain socialism."

Spurred by his training as a lawyer and the cold beer, Bobby launched into a rebuttal, "Yeah, every society is an exercise in socialism. That's what a government is for. If people are going to live together peaceably, you need to find a set of rules to guide their behavior. That's why we have city ordinances and police officers and code officers to enforce the ordinances."

"Come on, Bobby, I'm not talking about parking tickets. It's the fortune we spend to guarantee the economic well-being and physical health of every citizen—even those who can work but refuse to do so. Jefferson and Adams and those guys never promised happiness. They never intended for government to guarantee economic success. All they promised was the opportunity to achieve, not the guarantee of success. That's what free enterprise means—the freedom to use the opportunity to succeed. And government cannot ensure success. The more it tries, the more it discourages people to work and achieve on their own."

Carl was becoming agitated, waving his gnarled hand in the air. "There are now generations of Americans who don't work, who don't know how to work because our government has taught them to rely on welfare to put food on the table and a roof over their heads. And why? So the politicians can garner their votes at the polls. On top of all that, we've over 20 percent of all the employed people in the country working for some form of government. They are just dividing up the tax pie paid by the rest. They are not producing anything. As Lincoln once said, 'You cannot help the poor by destroying the rich.' What will happen when the wage earners, the investors, the entrepreneurs who pay the taxes decide it's not worth it anymore? Karl Marx thought a socialistic system would work. But the USSR is gone and China and Cuba are in the hands of dictators."

"So when I hear someone ask, 'America, how are you?' I say we are going to hell!"

Bobby watched Carl slump in his chair, an emphasis of the discouraging words.

"You sound just like a Tea Party advocate, Carl," Bobby said, shifting in his seat.

"Well, I'm sorry, Bobby. Sometimes it's just plain discouraging. Did you see that op-ed piece about the pension plan in the *Tribune* last week by Ron Blake and Alberto Estanza?"

"Yeah, I read it. Looks like the POA is already putting propaganda in the newspapers," Bobby offered with a grimace.

"Now that was depressing. I know that it can't be easy being a police officer, but we can't pay them more and more each year just because they have a hard job. The job doesn't get harder and the service to the city doesn't increase, but they expect a hefty increase in pay or pension benefit each year. It' got to change somehow. The POA article crowed that pension payments are spent in the city. I know that, but if that justifies a better pension plan, hell, we should just triple the pension benefits. Who cares what it costs!"

"You're right, Carl. But like you said, the mayor seems to look the other way."

Carl ignored Bobby's remark, and kept on. "You know, that guy Blake says anyone who wants to review the pension plan is an enemy of the police. I bet no one has ever fired a gun at Ron Blake, and he acts as if he is in mortal combat every day. I know a bit about that myself. Did I ever tell you about my uncle Leland?"

Bobby shook his head, waiting for Carl to continue.

"Leland Kenneth Jeffers was my dad's brother. Eight years older than Dad. I always looked up to him because he was a Marine. When I decided to enlist in the Marines out of high school, I asked Uncle Leland to tell me about his time in the corps because he never talked of those days. Boy, did I ever get an earful.

"My uncle said he had been on Iwo Jima, a lieutenant when they landed, and in two weeks he got a battlefield promotion to captain and became the company commander since no other officers were still alive. After three weeks, he said he only wanted two things. One, to kill more Japs, and two, to live one more day because no one expected to get off the island alive. He said he was not a hero, but only a lucky officer who was wounded instead of killed. He spent sixteen months in a Navy hospital where he was in a mental ward, listening to screaming all night long and regretting the fact he had lived. Afterward, he got a job as an engineer with the railroad until he retired at sixty-five. He told me he never married because he had nothing to give to any woman or family.

"He was not killed on Iwo Jima, but I got the point. He gave his life to his country. I shot at, and probably killed, a bunch of Iraqi soldiers in Desert Storm, but I never lived through what he did. He says they fought many Japs hand to hand where you could smell their breath and knew you would feel a bayonet go all the way through your belly if you gave an inch. And what did he get paid for all that? Barely enough to live on if he had been in the States. So I can't have a lot of sympathy for police officers or firefighters who think they can never be paid too much. Ron Blake sits in the POA office and probably doesn't run a beat more than two or three times a year. I don't see our country goin' in the right direction right now. It's headed downhill ever since we got back from Iraq."

"Wow, Carl. I never knew that about your uncle. We owe him a great deal, and you too." Bobby drained the beer schooner and set it on the table, looking at Carl in a new light, before he went on, "You know, I feel the same way about the pension plan. We've got to get a handle on it. But it's goin' to take a move to get everyone around the table and agree on what is fair and what we can afford. It seems like half the cities in the country have driven the car into a ditch, just as we have. If David Watson was correct, we may be looking at a bankruptcy in the future. I know the police and fire don't believe that, but business as usual is not going to work any longer."

Bobby leaned back in his seat and nodded slowly. Carl's views were not far from his own. The aborted proposal to change the council's financial policy was certainly a jab in the direction of socialism, if that was the proper term for it. If e-mails and text messages were an accurate indication, many citizens in Lamar had been taught little about government or civics while in school. Many of the messages complaining about city government were devoid of the simplest understanding of what the council's role was in their daily lives. To many, city hall was a complaint department and nothing more.

Waving aside Carl's suggestion of another beer, he rose.

"I've got to get home, Carl. Becky promised me a lot of honey-dews this evening. Here's a five to cover my tab."

"Thanks, Bobby. I appreciate you for listening to my complaints. I guess I worked too hard in the corps to sit by and watch some people just take a free ride. It's just not right!"

"I understand, Carl. Maybe we are getting too big for people to care anymore."

THIRTY-THREE

The Maladondo crew finished their work at the Payton well site by the middle of August, two weeks after the well was completed and began producing. Ayazi and his crew were moved to a building construction job on the east side of I-35. The blazing summer sun was fierce. Ayazi suffered in the heat until his body became accustomed to the typical Texas weather. He wished he still had his old turban to protect his head. The wide-brimmed straw hat seemed to only increase the discomfort of the radiant sunlight.

Friday's work was done, and he drove toward his apartment, grateful for a restful weekend but still agitated that he had not received further word from Ali. Repeated search on his cell phone produced no record of any attempts by Ali to contact him with more instructions. Such an attempt might have at least recorded a telephone number from which Ali was calling. But nothing! He kept recalling the mid-July meeting when Ali came to the apartment with the bomb and brave talk about the electric grid. It was puzzling and alarming. Was he being abandoned? Each day he found himself sinking deeper into the routine and easy life of the infidels—television, plentiful goods, cheerful camaraderie with the men working in his crew. How long would it be before he too became a contented lamb with no memory of the vow he had taken before bin Laden? Too many years had passed since that glorious day. The long hours of training and preparation were beginning to dull in the heat of Lamar.

Many years since 9/11 had come and gone and still no action by al-Qaeda in America. Was his jihad to be abandoned in the decadence of the Western world?

Lost in his despair, Ayazi did not notice the flashing lights in his rearview mirror and was startled when the siren was activated. Omar warned him such an event could occur, so he pulled his truck to the curb and waited.

The officer walked forward and leaned toward the pickup's open window. Looking at Ayazi, he inquired, "May I see your driver's license please?"

Ayazi's breathing quickened as he reached for his wallet and removed the Texas driver's license given to him in San Juan.

The officer glanced at the license, looked carefully at Ayazi, and said, "Mr. Sanchez, are you aware that your inspection sticker is out of date?"

"I…wha…no, sir," Ayazi stuttered, a look of confusion on his face.

The officer tapped on the truck's windshield. "This sticker expired in June, Mr. Sanchez. You need to have this truck inspected."

"Yes, yes, I will do that," Ayazi replied nervously.

"May I also see your insurance card?" By now, the officer was peering intently into the truck, where Ayazi's lunch pail rested on the seat.

Ayazi leaned over and opened the glove compartment. As instructed by Omar, he had checked the insurance card on his first day in Lamar. There it was, in the bottom of the compartment! He handed it to the officer with what he hoped was a steady hand.

"Thank you. This coverage is going to expire next month. You will need to get that renewed also." The officer returned the insurance card but still held Ayazi's license in his hand as he turned toward the rear of the truck.

"Please wait here a minute."

In the rearview mirror, Ayazi watched the unsmiling man look at the back of the truck and write something on a small pad he held in his hand before returning.

"Mr. Sanchez, I am giving you a citation for failure to have a current inspection sticker. However, if you will get your truck inspected and take your inspection receipt to the municipal court at city hall within ten days, the citation will be dismissed. Any questions?"

Ayazi remained silent. The officer tore a piece of paper from his pad and handed it with Ayazi's license through the window, saying, "I believe I have seen you before, Mr. Sanchez. Do you work here in Lamar?"

"Yes, I work for Mr. Maladondo."

The officer nodded, said, "Thank you," and returned to his patrol car.

Ayazi muttered, "Thank you" also, relieved but still uncertain of the meaning of his detention.

Behind the apartment, Ayazi stood in front of the truck and looked at the small inspection sticker glued to the windshield. The six and the sixteenth confirmed what the officer had stated. How could Ali have provided a truck that exposed him to detention by the authorities? Had Ali expected that the jihad would have been completed in June?

In the apartment, chewing on the last of the pilau, he studied the citation. It carried a cause number, an indication of the offense, also a number, his name, date, and vehicle license plate number. Would the police now make an effort to confirm the owner of the truck through a search of the auto license records? What if such a search failed to confirm his ownership or revealed that Ali or the Dallas group owned the truck or that the license plate had been stolen? He cursed Ali, the Yemen man of mystery.

* * *

Sleep eluded him all night. Years of survival in the mountains of Afghanistan had not depended on the whim of some man located in an unknown hideaway miles away. Even as a teen, his life was preserved by his boldness, wit, and self-reliance. Now the very existence and success of his jihad was compromised by the decadent lifestyle he was forced to endure and the failure of Ali and his brothers to carry forth their grand plan. He might be of no use to Allah if the authorities pursued the origin of his license plate. Ali and his cohorts themselves could be put in possible jeopardy.

Fear and terror was the path to the destruction of the infidels, and he could be an instrument in that destruction only if he would act before it was too late. As each hour passed, his fear grew. Not a fear of death, not a fear of pain. He had witnessed self-emulation before. He knew the explosion would send him to the afterworld without suffering. But he trembled at the thought he might fail to complete his pledge to Osama bin Laden, that he might confront Allah, his grandfather, and his father clothed in disgrace.

By dawn his resolve was complete. He could no longer put his fidelity to the test of more delay. He arose and removed the bomb from the closet. He carefully checked the ignition wiring and the trigger. He tested the battery. It carried a full charge. It was all remarkably similar to the devices he had assembled himself in Pakistan. He smiled as he envisioned how simple it was going to be. The fools had already spread fear throughout the city. Even the old lady was in a state of alarm, which he would spread like a wildfire!

He placed the bomb back into the closet before checking the drawer in the kitchen. Yes! The key was still there.

He knelt and recited Dhuhr, the midday prayers, with more than his usual fervency.

THIRTY-FOUR

Carl's angst echoed in Bobby's ears as he outlined the remarks he promised to deliver to the Fort Worth Rotary Club's next meeting. One of the largest clubs in the state by membership, the current president of the club had prevailed on Bobby to talk about democratic government in general and the role of the Lamar Council in particular as a component of local government. With a bit of personal introspection, he completed an outline which he hoped would do just that even though he still could not recall the City of New Orleans.

* * *

Having finished the usual business at the weekly meeting, the president approached the microphone and began, "I am confident many of you already know, or know of, Bobby Joe Sanford, our neighbor from Lamar, so he needs no long introduction. In addition to bring one of the best quarterbacks for the Lamar Lions, he is—he says—a very good lawyer and serves on the Lamar City Council. With four years under his belt, he has returned for another two years at that post. Please welcome Bobby Joe Sanford!"

The applause was genuine and loud. Probably because of the football success years back, Bobby thought, as he approached the lectern.

"Thank you very much. I am honored Harry asked me come today and share with you some of my thoughts about our democratic form of government. But I caution you that these thoughts are mine alone and not necessarily the views of the Lamar Council. In fact, it's for sure that some on the council would dispute much of what I am about to say.

"Like most people, I never spent much time thinking about city government before I got on the council. City governments pave the streets, collect the trash, and hire police officers. But I've learned it is a crucial part of our democracy and does much more just by its very existence.

"We've been very fortunate to live in this country, in this state. Government, and respect for government, is engrained in Americans, and for that reason, we all live together in peace. That is not true everywhere in the world as we have witnessed over the past five years on daily TV news reports.

"Living together in a common society is easy if you have strong family values and upbringing, assisted by meaningful religious institutions and effective schools. But where those values break down, or are lacking, a stable society demands more and more governmental input, more controls, and more laws. Time and again, we are seeing occasions, for example, when our council must consider, and sometimes enact, ordinances to address the behavior of a few citizens who tend to act in a manner not acceptable to most other citizens. Unrestrained barking dogs, automobiles parked in front yards, graffiti, and a proliferation of handmade signs placed on the city right-of-way are just a few examples of conduct that might have been restrained by family values or simple good taste and concern for our neighbors, but not today. So too we see more and more regulations issuing from federal, state and local governments. Is this just the natural result of a more populous, more dense, more mobile society in which we live? I don't know. But I do know that it means a loss of individual freedom, for every law is a restriction of conduct or a mandatory direction of certain conduct.

"And the laws reach far beyond an effort to curb barking dogs. We are seeing a long-term trend expanding the role and reach of government. Today, most people expect government to care for them economically and physically. Government now pays money directly to citizens in the form of social security checks, unemployment pay, retirement pay to government retirees, food stamps, and health-care payments. We expect and rely upon these receipts and never hesitate to demand that they increase. We are convinced that we are entitled to those payments. But what do these government checks do to the freedom of our citizens? Dependence upon government largesse erodes eventually the freedom to grow and learn and find success through self-sufficiency and the lessons of failure. Too many in our country now find that they have reached a state of dependency so overwhelming that their choices in life are controlled by government regulations. For example, you cannot earn in excess of a certain amount if you expect to receive government unemployment checks. The incentive to dig out of the hole is stifled by the hope of unending checks in the mail!

"Many government payees are now virtually slaves because their emancipation from dependency is forever lost. Too many are taught from generation to generation that they have no freedom or opportunity apart from that which may be granted by the government. The right of freedom and the pursuit of happiness called for at our founding no longer exists for them.

"Is this too harsh an assessment? When a large percentage of the citizens in this country pay no federal income taxes, how can that be explained to those citizens who do bear the federal tax burden? I do not suggest that some people do not pay any taxes. They do pay social security taxes, gasoline taxes, sales taxes, and such. But those taxes do not fund the general operations of government. How can we justify a federal tax system which collects the great bulk of federal revenue from a disproportionate percentage of society which bears that burden?

"How long will it be before the incentive to succeed, the desire to capitalize on a free economic opportunity, the desire to pursue happiness through individual effort, as Thomas Jefferson put it, dies out in this country and everyone looks to government to guarantee individual security and economic well-being? Who will pay the taxes then?

"If no one is paying the taxes and government has no revenue to make the payments on which everyone depends, will we have rioting in the streets? Will every town in America look like Athens?

"I don't have the answers to these questions. I only hope that people will start asking these questions. I hope that people will begin to look at what a responsible government can do and what it cannot do and should not do. History has taught us that political theories cannot and will not change the laws of economics because every human being will make the decision which will best serve his individual needs. Those decisions can only be restrained by laws which absolutely stifle that free choice, laws which lead to a totalitarian state. It has happened again and again in Russia, China, Cuba, and elsewhere. So think about it. Thank you very much."

The applause was genuine and bloomed into a standing ovation.

Had he gone too far in expanding on the concerns voiced by Carl Jeffers? He well understood that not every segment of the local populace was represented at the Rotary Club, but the audience's response was encouraging.

Bobby's eyes failed to notice the black man standing by the table to the left of the rostrum. He probably would not have recognized him in any event after so many years.

* * *

"Council Member Warns Against Socialism."

The Sunday news article in the *Lamar Tribune* quoted at great length from Bobby's speech but used the opportunity to report that "some critics believed Mr. Sanford had misunderstood the true vision of the county's founding fathers and therefore failed to recognize the great strides which the country had achieved by providing a society which cares for all and not just those who were heirs to a better time."

The critics were not identified so Bobby could not determine if they were merely the reporter's pawns to create a controversial piece or perhaps Alece Jackson's response to a telephone call from the reporter.

Becky waited until they had finished Sunday breakfast and were dressing for church.

"Well, Mr. Councilman, I see you made today's *Tribune*. It seems not everyone agrees with you though."

"Yeah. That's what the reporter said. The media doesn't always reveal who the other side is, if in fact there is another side. I already know not everyone on the council agrees with everything I said, but that's about par for the course."

"Well, I agree with you, sweetheart. But I am prejudiced as they say."

THIRTY-FIVE

osh double-checked his pocket to confirm that the tickets were still there. Libby had eagerly accepted when he called on Wednesday to ask if she would like to go to the Cowboy game in Arlington on Sunday afternoon. A preseason game of little consequence yet it provided a chance to see her again. But the call from the company manager late Friday almost derailed the plans however. The manager ordered him to go to the Payton well with the job foreman, Les Morton, and determine if the flange connections would be sufficient to mate with the new tank meter valve scheduled for delivery Monday morning. Not overly pleased himself, Morton finally agreed with Josh to meet at the well site early Sunday morning. Josh and Libby would still have time to get to the game before kickoff.

The traffic was almost nonexistent on S. Adams Street, except for a few early churchgoers headed toward downtown. At the gate, Josh got out, unlocked the gate, swung it open, and pulled his car onto the pad site. Les was nowhere in sight. He was bringing the rule and calipers they would use to check the flange measurements. Josh drove across the pad and parked near the ten-foot-high tank that contained the natural gas liquids produced by the well since it began flowing the last week of July. The tank was about half full, and

Payton expected to unload the tank with the pipeline when the new valve was installed on Monday.

* * *

Les parked his company pickup next to Josh's car and tumbled out with the instruments in his hand.

"Hey, Josh, how're they hangin' this early on Sunday morning?" A slight dig at having his weekend sleep cut short.

"I'm doin' well, Les. Already ran two miles this morning," Josh replied, knowing Les enjoyed a little banter. Conversation was his means of staying connected.

"Two miles? You got a guilty conscience or something? Can't sleep?" Les was not fond of declaratory sentences.

Josh laughed. "Thanks for coming out, Les. It won't take long to check that flange."

Fifteen minutes proved Josh correct, and Les tossed the instruments into his truck. They stood looking at the wellhead and the LNG tank, both neatly painted, with the Payton logo on the side of the tank.

"Well, Les, can you believe we got another well under production? It must gall that guy Unsel. He expects them all to blow up."

"Yeah. That's a strange one. You know he lives just three doors from me. He makes no sense. There are three thousand wells in the Barnett Shale and not one of them has had a problem. He even has a son-in-law, Jeremy, that works as a landman for one of the gas leasing companies. Jeremy and I play golf together. Hell, he even bought most of the leases that this well will be producing from. Talk about biting the hand that feeds you," Les expounded, shaking his head.

* * *

Ayazi parked his truck across the street from the town square park. Down Main Street he could see the cars beginning to arrive at the old church for Sunday services. He clutched the note in his hand as he stepped onto the sidewalk. It was Allah's will that guided him on the Christian's holy day.

Yesterday's effort to clean and again inspect his apartment had gone well after he returned from the business supply store. A writing pad and a cheap ballpoint pen was all he needed to complete his final message: "Allah's vengeance will come to infidel America. The crimes of the unbelievers will soon stop by the hand of the Nation of Islam."

He walked across Wood Street to the front door of the city hall, hoping to slip the note under the door. The door sill was too close, and he stood quietly. What if the note was seen as a mere scrap of garbage and thrown away? Returning to his truck, he noticed the door to Maudie's over the front hood. He and some of his crew often ate an early breakfast there, and he remembered that Maudie unlocked the front door promptly at 6:00 AM, except on Sunday. The note slid easily under her door. The final commitment was now in place.

The bomb vest lay on the floor by the passenger seat. His silent cell phone rested in his shirt pocket as he drove away from the town square, following his old route to the well site. Allah's hand surely had caused him to throw the gate key into the kitchen drawer and forget to return it to the Maladondo office, he thought, murmuring another prayer to the Great One.

A block away, he pulled to the curb and carefully wrapped the bomb around his upper body. The bulk and weight forced him forward against the steering column, but he carefully adjusted the seat, calmly noting the quiet houses which lined both sides of the street. What would the scene be when it happened?

Approaching S. Adams Street, he could see the well site, a half block to the south. The gate was standing open! Another sure sign from Allah. Near the tank there were a car and a truck. Two men stood nearby.

Without hesitating, he turned into S. Adams and sped toward the open gate that lay almost one hundred and fifty yards from the wellhead.

Through the gate, he pushed his foot down on the accelerator, with his left hand firmly clutching the steering wheel. Ten feet from the wellhead, the front of the truck lifted as it passed over a shallow rut in the graveled surface. At that moment, Ayazi shouted, "Allahu Akbar!" and pressed the switch on his chest.

* * *

The roar of the motor caused Josh and Les to turn their heads. "That looks like Sanchez," Josh uttered.

The small blue pickup gathered speed while they watched, bewildered.

"What the hell is he doing?" Josh asked.

As the truck leaped into the air, there was a loud crack, with a blinding flash of light. The concussion wave struck the two men just as flying debris overwhelmed them. One of the truck's front wheels, with part of the axle attached, slammed into the tank above their heads, rupturing its skin. The escaping LNG flowed out and quickly ignited from the shear heat which engulfed a circumference of two hundred feet from the wellhead.

THIRTY-SIX

T he Lamar Fire Station 4, only three blocks away, was quiet before the explosion startled the crew, and an engineer and two firefighters were already on one of the engines, with the diesel turning over, when the dispatcher's call came in. They had donned their bunker suits in two minutes after they heard the station windows rattle in the wake of the blast. They still held their boots in hand as the engine left the bay.

The fire call came from Mr. Markum, the lone gas lease hold-out, whose house sat 525 feet from the wellhead. "The well has exploded!" he shouted to the 911 operator. "We're all going to die!"

As the engine gathered speed, there was no need for an address as the rising column of smoke clearly pinpointed the location. Nearing the gate at the pad site, the engineer called over the mike to the dispatcher, "It's the Payton well. Everything's on fire. Send out another alarm. It looks like two or more vehicles are involved."

A shaft of yellow flame towered almost 30 feet above the ruptured wellhead. The fire at the tank encircled 360 degrees, contained in the earthen berm surrounding the tank. Black smoke rose ominously into the blue morning sky.

* * *

For the people of Lamar, the hot August Sunday morning would always be a day marked indelibly on their personal calendars—a day recalled by the question, "Where were you when the explosion happened?" It was their own December 7 and 9/11 rolled into one.

Bobby and Becky, like most who were awake, looked at each other quizzically when the sharp report rolled over the town.

"That doesn't sound good," he exclaimed. His call to the central police station was finally answered after a number of rings.

"Mr. Sanford, I wish I could tell something. All we know at the moment is there was an explosion at the Payton well on Adams. We have three units on the scene, and Chief Knebler is on his way there. I will contact him and ask him to call you as soon as possible. Mayor Fanning has been alerted and is standing by."

Two more engines responded on the second alarm, the bright red trucks roaring with their sirens and flashing lights. The first two police officers began to roll out the yellow tape and called for assistance to block off all traffic from the scene.

The ranking fire department engineer confirmed the assessment by the men on the first engine, noting the scattered debris from the shattered blue pickup, the charred bodies near the burning tank and battered vehicles. Everything bore an eerie resemblance to pictures beamed too often on TV from Iraq and Afghanistan. Little remained of the pickup, save the blackened frame, still bearing two wheels and little else. The well could not have possibly caused the horrific destruction.

"A bomb of some kind," one of the firefighters remarked to no one. Well trained in responding to a possible gas well mishap, the firefighters quickly concluded that a suppression of the wellhead fire would require a special team even though the tank fire could be monitored as it burned itself out. The chief concurred and a call was directed to a well-known outfit in Houston which had a worldwide reputation for successfully fighting well fires. Chief Knebler was briefed when he arrived and wasted little time in contacting the mayor and the other council members. Together, the two chiefs and the mayor came to the conclusion that the calamity was not an accident, and the mayor placed a call to the ranking FBI agent in Fort

Worth. The agent, fearing the worst, asked the mayor to arrange for a dozen hotel rooms.

"Mayor, if this is the result of a deliberate bombing, we will need to have the CIA and the Department of Homeland Security accompany our folks to Lamar. I would expect them to be there by tomorrow afternoon at the latest."

Bobby was shocked. Surely the chief was wrong. A bomb! As rabid as he was, Charles Unsel and his group could not have done such a thing. And two bodies! Why was anyone at the well on Sunday morning?

Hanging up the phone, he turned to Becky.

"This makes no sense. The chief says someone deliberately blew up the well."

"What? Why would anyone do that?" she replied, laying aside the dress she had intended to wear to church. She had no doubt Bobby was going to be very busy soon as the news spread throughout the city.

All of the four local TV stations in Fort Worth and Dallas interrupted their broadcasts by noon, reporting the explosion with on-scene news. The excited reports were sketchy and conflicting, with only two of the stations suggesting the suspicion of a bomb. No mention was made about the bodies discovered by the firefighters. Mr. Markum was interviewed several times, complaining with gestures that "the gas companies will not rest until we are all killed by their greed!"

* * *

Becky called Libby on her cell phone after one o'clock.

"Libby, have you seen the TV today? We've had a big explosion here."

"No. What happened? I'm waiting on Josh. He and I are going to the Cowboy game this afternoon. And he is late!"

When Becky completed her report of the turmoil, Libby said, "I'm going to call him. We'll miss the kickoff if he doesn't hurry. Maybe he knows something about what happened. You know, he and his people worked on that well."

THIRTY-SEVEN

T he goats were everywhere! Salih was chasing after a kid that had run from its mother, and behind came his two brothers. The stones in the field caused him to stumble, bringing forth loud laughter from the brothers who called after him.

"Wake, wake, Ibrahim." A hand shook his shoulder.

He looked into the eyes of Khalia bending over his bed and realized he had been dreaming. He dearly loved Khalia, but it was considered rude for a Muslim's wife to forcibly assail her husband's body, and he glared at her.

"What is it, woman?" he growled

"It is on the television. A large explosion in Lamar, that town south of Fort Worth. They say it may be a suicide bomber. Allah save us. It is just like 9/11."

With that, Khalia ran out of the room, wringing her hands over her head.

Still wrapped in his robe, Salih sat transfixed before the screen, trying to comprehend the conflicting reports, one saying the gas well exploded, the other insisting that only a bomb could have caused the destruction, fully evident, even from a television camera stationed a quarter of a mile away. His anxiety rose as he remembered that the Afghan had worked several weeks at the well site. Surely he had not betrayed the careful plan which was almost ready to be launched in a few days.

After thirty minutes before the TV, he could no longer torture himself with the dire thoughts of what might come if the Afghan was involved, and patting Kahlia's hands with assurances that all was well, he left the house and drove to the PRO office.

By dusk, all the reports were confirming that a bomb was suspected and that federal investigators were due to arrive overnight. Airports were put on high alert, and the DHS elevated their terror alert to the maximum. In desperation, Salih repeatedly dialed the cell phone he had given to Sanchez, but he got no response. Tempted to drive to Sanchez's apartment, he soon realized the FBI, or others, may have already traced that connection if Sanchez was believed to have caused the explosion. His presence at Sanchez's apartment would be incriminating, to say the least.

At 9:00 PM, he called Khalia and said he would eat supper out and would be home much later. Her anxiety had lessened slightly, but she begged him to return quickly.

Now with only one light shining in the office, he began the task of assessing his next actions, if all this meant a suicide bomber had acted in Lamar.

THIRTY-EIGHT

The home of Ibrahim a Salih nestled among large oak and pecan trees in one or the upper-class areas of North Dallas. His family's contacts with their neighbors was cordial, but distant, as was the case with most of those who had acquired financial success that enabled them to afford homes boasting four or five bedrooms and spacious lawns.

Salih's children attended the Muslim school near the local mosque each Saturday morning to study the Koran, a study Salih felt was essential to counter the Christian culture they experienced in the private American school a few blocks from their home.

Khalia hardly slept Sunday night following the explosion, fearing that the event would bring back the suspicion, the glaring stares which followed her whenever she appeared in public with the traditional Islamic head covering. The anxieties had been ushered in by 9/11 years ago. Her concerns elevated when Ibrahim failed to call home again after the message that he would not return for the evening meal on Sunday.

Late on Monday afternoon, she was relieved to hear his pickup pull into the drive. Her greeting and smile were met with a dark scowl, however, and his first words were directed at the children who were watching a television program.

"What is this? You should be in your rooms reciting your evening prayers. Is this what you learn at the mosque? Is Allah to be ignored while you waste your time gazing at the television?"

Khalia was astounded. Ibrahim was very loving to his children. What caused such an angry tirade? And where had he been all day?

* * *

The twenty-four hours in the PRO office compounded Salih's frustration as it swelled and turned into anger and despair. The message from the Palestinian charity office, relayed from Zawahiri himself, was unmistaken and so direct that Salih feared the elaborate codes would be proven vulnerable to signet of the CIA. Zawahiri learned of the explosion in Lamar, Texas, within minutes of the first national news report. His anger was unchecked as he heaped blame upon Salih and ordered the electric grid plan halted. He demanded that Salih explain how the entire American counterintelligence community had been mobilized, with only two deaths credited to such a miserable jihad. He reminded Salih that, from the beginning, he had feared that Salih's plan lacked the ability to inflict a large and dramatic number of deaths which would strike terror. His final message, coming at noon, Texas time Monday, forbad Salih from taking any further action which might jeopardize the existence and location of the other three agents. Salih's plea to redirect the plan with only three agents was met with more anger and recriminations. The rebuke was clear and, in Salih's mind, totally wrong.

The ignorant Afghan tribesman was a mistake. Why had they not sent a reliable Arab, like the other three? Did al-Qaeda really believe that Taliban sheep herders were truly committed to any action beyond the Afghan borders? He had even warned them in May after he had delivered Sanchez to Lamar. His doubts had now been proven correct, so why was he being blamed? Did they expect him to board Sanchez in his own house with his children? Zawahiri was so consumed with the killing of individuals. There simply were too many Americans. It was the American way of life that must be killed. The sources of energy, food, and water must be put into jeopardy if America was to perish. That is why he spent two years developing the grid plan, a plan that was now abandoned because of one apostate Afghan who lacked the discipline necessary to bring about a jihad, who was blinded by his own egotistic quest for personal glory.

Without a glance to Khalia, Salih strode into his study at the rear of the house and slammed the door. He pulled out a notepad from the desk drawer. His engineering training directed him to compile a careful list of the steps necessary to dismantle the aborted plan. The remaining three bombers must be contacted. They must be told the plan was being postponed and the bombs they held must be recalled and placed in safekeeping. It would be necessary to communicate with the two men responsible for constructing the bombs and direct them to dismantle their facilities lest the FBI somehow trace the Afghan's bomb to its origin. And what about Maladondo's cousin? He was a direct link to the smuggling and placement of Sanchez, a liaison held true only by the payment of money. His very existence was now a threat that must be dealt with, sooner rather than later. Finally, at the end of the list, how would he explain to Khalia and the children that their holiday to Damascus was cancelled?

THIRTY-NINE

The pre-council room was no more than a spacious area adjacent to the council chamber The oversize mahogany table in the center was wired for microphones at each council member's chair so that the pre-council sessions, like the chamber sessions, could be accessed by the closed circuit television within the city hall and, more importantly, for the purpose of preserving the verbatim record of the public meetings held in the room. Over twenty chairs lined the walls of the room, seating for staff members and the public. But on Monday morning, only the mayor and the six council members occupied the room. Bobby had not been surprised when the mayor had called at 9:00 PM Sunday.

"Bobby, I am asking all the members to meet with me at nine tomorrow morning in executive session. Please don't be late."

Dub Fanning's face could not hide the fact that he had only three hours' sleep since the explosion. Each member waited silently as he began.

"Thanks very much for being here this morning. We have a very serious situation on our hands, and I want to bring you up-to-date. But first, a couple of housekeeping matters. The city attorney is concerned that we are meeting without posting a public notice. The government code says we must give seventy-two hours' notice before meeting as a body, even in executive session. I don't think the code ever contemplated such an event as we have here, so I told the attorney that we would worry about that later. Our citizens don't want us to sit on our hands at a time like this.

"Next, I ask each of you to please turn off your cell phones, iPhones, Blackberries, iPads and put them on the table in front of me. I don't want to be interrupted, and I don't want any communication going out of this room. All the microphones have been turned off."

With the devices stacked in front of him, the mayor proceeded, "George Wiseman, one of the FBI agents out of the Fort Worth office, has been appointed by Washington to act as agent in charge here in Lamar. He and I will be holding a public press conference in front of the building at eleven this morning. I want each of you to be there. But you will need to know some things before then.

"Mr. Wiseman, the Police Chief and the Fire Chief all agree. Yesterday's explosion was caused by the deliberate ignition of a bomb or some other type of explosive. A suicide bomber! I have been to the well site and the evidence is quite clear. A twenty- or thirty-foot pattern of the explosion is evidenced by the spray of the gravel pad site and by the debris from a vehicle which was almost entirely obliterated by the blast. Only a three-foot-high piece of well tubing remains above the ground in the bottom of the crater. A few scattered human remains have been found in the explosive pattern. A Texas license plate, apparently part of the debris, is being checked with the vehicle records in Austin this morning.

"Just an hour ago, Mr. Wiseman told me that our police department turned over to him a handwritten note, which may have been written by the bomber or someone connected to the bomber. Maudie Walton found the note on the floor of her restaurant when she opened the door this morning. She carried the note to Chief Knebler's office. Mr. Wiseman Skyped the note to the CIA in Virginia. It was written in Arabic, and a translation was returned to him just before he called me."

The mayor paused and pulled a piece of paper from his pocket. "This is what the note said: 'Allah's vengeance will come to infidel America. The crimes of the unbelievers will be stopped by the hand of the Nation of Islam.' It was signed by someone named HasI-Ahmed Ayazi."

The council members looked at one another in shock, and a few started to ask questions before being halted by the mayor's raised hand.

"I know. It's hard to comprehend. Why would any terrorist want to blow up something in Lamar? The Department of Homeland Security, the CIA, and the FBI are working on that question. That's about all we know so far. I want each of you to go to your office in this building and stay there until eleven. You've seen the media camped outside, and it's important that none of us speak to them before the press conference. Please, please do not discuss this meeting or what I have told you with anyone before that conference."

Carl's hand shot up and he asked, "Mayor, the news reports mentioned two bodies were found. Do we know who they are?"

"Not yet. The fire was so intense there was no way to identify them by any personal effects. However, one of the vehicles near the bodies was an Infiniti G35 coupe, and the other was a large GMC pickup. On the side of the pickup, away from the explosion, they found a company logo of the outfit that did the engineering work at the site. Mr. Wiseman is contacting the company manager at their office this morning, and the license plates on the car and the truck are being checked in Austin along with the other plate I mentioned."

* * *

Bobby sat in his office and picked up the phone with dread in his heart. Ignoring the mayor's admonition, he called Becky.

"Where is Libby?"

"She is still asleep. She is so worried that she hasn't heard from Josh, she was up almost all night."

"Well, I don't know any other way to tell you this, but they say that one of the cars at the well site is a G35 coupe, which is what Josh drives, and they also found a pickup with his company's logo on the door. I don't know how we can prepare her for this, if it was Josh. I have to stay here for an eleven o'clock press conference. Try to keep Libby asleep, and I will come home right after the conference."

"Oh my god, Bobby. Surely that's not true," Becky cried and almost sobbed.

"They are checking the license plate on the car, so we should know for sure today. I'll get home as soon as I can."

It was almost an hour before the press conference. Bobby stared out the window. The world was falling as he realized Libby had probably lost a friend and he would soon see his daughter plunged into despair.

The ringing of his phone interrupted.

"Bobby, this is Dub. I just got a call from Mr. Wiseman. The Austin reports are in, and the G35 was owned by Josh Powers. I know your daughter was dating him. I am so very sorry."

Bobby sank further into his chair, unable to respond.

"They have also identified the driver of the company pickup, but his name is being withheld until the next of kin are notified this morning. The exploded truck was apparently owned by a man named Juan Carlos Sanchez. The FBI thinks he may have worked for the Maladondo company. They don't know yet if Sanchez was the one driving the truck or if he is the Ayazi guy who signed the note or both."

"Mayor, I already knew that Josh drove a G35. But it's hard to know it was him at the explosion."

"I'm sorry, Bobby. If I can do anything to help, let me know."

FORTY

Xavier Maladondo was not pleased to be spending an hour in his office on Monday afternoon while an FBI agent peppered him with questions in a very accusatory tone. Another agent was pouring through the meager personnel records which had been brought in from the back room. Maladondo's face had registered genuine shock when the agent revealed that that Sanchez's license plate had been found at the bomb site.

"Mr. Maladondo, this file says Sanchez came to work for you in May, but not much else. It doesn't even show a social security number for Sanchez."

"Yes, I know. He said he was going to furnish it to us. We've withheld social security, medical, and those things from his paycheck."

The room was seeming to grow warmer.

"And where is Mr. Sanchez? Your clerk says he has not reported for work today. When was the last time he was here?"

"Well, I think he worked Friday on that building construction job over by I-35. If he hasn't come in today, maybe he's sick." Maladondo gazed at the agent, wondering if he should call his attorney.

"Tell us again. How did you happen to hire Mr. Sanchez?"

Maladondo rolled his eyes. Was this a trick? He told them that thirty minutes ago.

"Like I told you already, my cousin in Dallas knew I needed some help, and he called me in early May. He said Sanchez was coming to Lamar, so when he showed up, he looked strong and able and we put him to work. He is a good hand. He even got promoted to foreman on that job at the Payton well site."

"And what was his address?" the short blond agent asked.

"Well, I showed you. He had an apartment at that address on his paperwork when he was hired."

"No, I mean what was his address before he came to work here. Was he from Mexico? The file doesn't show that he had a green card or anything." The agent was starting to become annoying.

"Hell, I don't know his life history! I'm Hispanic, been here all my life. Never even been to Mexico."

The grilling finally concluded, but not before they demanded the name and address of his cousin in Dallas. After they departed, Maladondo wasted no time in calling his cousin and warning him that he could expect a visit from the FBI.

* * *

By five o'clock on Tuesday, the agents had visited with almost everyone in Lamar believed to have had any contact with Sanchez, who himself was still among the missing. The agents were almost certain he was the one scattered over the gravel at the well site. Maudie Walton knew nothing except for the fact that the note was on the floor by the door when she came in on Monday morning. She had never heard Sanchez speak but a few words when he ate at her restaurant, if he was, in fact, the man who seemed to guide the few men who came in with him. None of the neighbors near the Sanchez apartment recalled anything other than seeing him go in and out, always alone. Even those who worked with him knew nothing beyond the time they spent with him on the jobsite.

On Wednesday, the FBI obtained a search warrant from the federal court in Fort Worth, empowering them to enter Sanchez's apartment. The door opened to a master key they had with them. Almost immediately, a trained dog sniffed out a presence of explosives in the closet. A worn prayer rug and well-used clothing completed the sparse inventory which was carefully bagged. Because both Sanchez and his truck were missing and the Austin report tied to Sanchez, the agents were convinced that he had triggered the bomb and was probably the man Ayazi who signed the note. What they could not understand was why an apparent Islamic suicide bomber was blowing up gas wells in Lamar, Texas. Why would al-Qaeda, if it was al-Qaeda, send an apparent illegal immigrant to kill just two people?

* * *

The Wednesday evening council meeting was called to order and immediately suspended on a quick voice vote until the first Wednesday in September. All agreed that the conduct of any orderly business was almost impossible, with SCAD and others demonstrating out in the hallway. The media presence in Lamar was growing daily as reporters, TV cameras, and correspondents from all over the world overflowed every motel on I-35 and crowded out the regulars at Maudie's. Some of the reporters insisted that Maudie point out the exact spot where she found the note. NBC, ABC, CBS, Fox, and many others were reporting daily on the latest developments while speculating that suicide bombers were eminent throughout the country. Police were being alerted by anxious callers in many cities upon the slightest suspicion of unfamiliar characters acting strangely. One talking head opined that Lamar was probably just the beginning of a planned jihad across the country by many sleeper cells which were lying in wait.

But not everyone believed those tales of foreign terrorists. Charles Unsel had wasted little time in convening and haranguing his SCAD members on Sunday evening.

"Maybe now the council will listen! It is time to march on city hall. Ed Markum is with us. The explosion blew out all the windows on the side of his house. He was lucky the Barnett Shale did not kill him. We will go to city hall on Wednesday evening. Please be there and bring your friends who will now understand. The city is trying to cover this up with the tale of a suicide bomber. They would not even let me get close enough to see it. This danger has been there all along."

It took the media only one day to find Unsel and put microphones in his face so he could repeat his messianic call. Uncaring gas producers or terrorist bombers? Both messages were rapidly agitating everyone in Lamar and far beyond. As the fear spread, many terrorized citizens in Lamar, Fort Worth, and throughout North Texas called for their state, county, and local governments to suspend all gas drilling and post armed guards at every well site. Ayazi's single act was spreading a sense of alarm much like that seen right after 9/11. The DHS raised its alert to its highest level, not yet clearly understanding the full significance of the Payton bombing and what it might portend for the rest of the country.

Perhaps Ayazi's pledge to bin Laden had succeeded.

FORTY-ONE

Outraged by the council's postponement of the Wednesday evening council meeting, SCAD and their followers left city hall and marched repeatedly around the town square, lending the specter of a Halloween parade in the evening dusk. Their signs and placards denounced equally the council and the gas producers. As darkness descended, many of them planted their messages in the soft earth of the park and announced their intention to remain all night. The square had not witnessed such a display since the Occupiers' encampment in 2011. Images of the demonstration appeared on every national nightly newscast, again featuring Charles Unsel, who, by then, was becoming the recognized spokesman for those offended by the failure of their government to protect their safety and welfare.

* * *

Dub Fanning was exhibiting the strain. The city was in turmoil, and everyone expected their first and only mayor to restore the peace and tranquility which had vanished on Sunday.

The noise of the demonstrators in the town square filtered through the windows of Fanning's office, distracting his review of the report on his desk. With full knowledge that the explosion was a deliberate work of one man, a suicide bomber, he struggled over the task of communicating to the residents and to the world that the gas drilling activity and the council's approval of that activity were not the cause of Sunday's event. He read once more the report he had requested from the city's engineering department, reflecting the information contained in the state comptroller's sales tax files. Lamar was the home to 32 public gasoline service stations, which, together, contained over 130 gasoline and diesel fuel pumps, more than the number of gas wells in the city. Those pumps were open to access and visited by the public 24-7. If a ban on gas wells was a solution to public fears, should not the city also ban the operation of fuel pumps which supplied everyone's daily transportation needs? How would Charles Unsel answer that question if he carried the responsibility of the Mayor's office?

He sighed. He knew the answer. Unsel was one of those who was rapidly becoming an extremist as attested by his escalating pronouncements to the swarming media. He remembered a treatise he once read, which defined an extremist as "an ardent proponent of a particular viewpoint who possesses a paranoid fear of any contrary position, a person lacking the ability or desire to present an argument relying upon objective facts and rational persuasion. Such people would rather use fearmongering through mental or physical threats to advance their viewpoint."

Fanning smiled to himself. Unsel fit the mold entirely. He was irrevocably dedicated to hearing only his own words. He would not foreswear any allegiance to his position even if he were rational enough to consider facts he had so far chosen to ignore. With resignation, Fanning dismissed his earlier thought of meeting with Unsel to convince him that the city would be better served by allaying the fears stoked by Unsel's dismissal of the veritable facts.

Would the people of Lamar listen to the facts? Was it not self-evident that risk accompanied every endeavor to produce and consume hydrocarbons, that potential danger could be found in almost every aspect of daily living? Once more, he answered his own question. The wound was too fresh. The media thrived on conflict, discord, and danger. It would not allow the public to be assuaged by simple logic, at least until today's headlines were supplanted by more compelling and newer events.

The afternoon interview with the *Tribune* reporter had revealed to Fanning that a memorial service for Les Morton would take place at the Pentecost Church on Friday, and a like memorial service would be in Austin at about the same time for Josh Powers. He rose and pulled his coat off the rack next to the office door. He needed to go home and tell Sue Lynn that they were expected at the Morton service on Friday and must meet personally with Morton's family no later than Thursday evening.

Down the elevator, through the chute, and out to his car, he stepped out into the parking lot and was relieved to see no reporters were lying in wait near his car. In truth, he had nothing further to add to the almost constant interviews and public statements he had handled since Sunday.

FORTY-TWO

The dark circles under Fanning's eyes the next week remained a testament to the fatigue that dogged him from the moment he heard the explosion. The council still had not adopted the new budget due, in part, to the cancelled council meeting in late August. To meet the September 30 budget deadline, it was becoming apparent that no progress would be made on the pension plan question. Like the council, the entire city was moving at a lethargic pace as people struggled to find some reason why the terrorist war had landed in their city. Fanning, dismissing those dreary thoughts, extended his hand, waving George Wiseman to a seat.

"Thank you for coming, Agent Wiseman. I know you and your people are very busy."

They both sank into chairs that bordered the table in the mayor's conference room, a small alcove next the mayor's office.

"Mayor, I am happy to share with you what I can, but we know far less than I wish even after two weeks. So far, we believe that this Ayazi, who wrote the note found by Maudie, is the same man who worked for Maladondo using the name Juan Carlos Sanchez. Some of the analysts in Washington are convinced Ayazi was an Afghan based on what we found in his apartment, but we can't be sure. If he was from there, chances are he was somehow smuggled into the country by al-Qaeda.

"Al-Qaeda has not made any public statement about the explosion, so we can't confirm their involvement. The bomb was too powerful and sophisticated to have been something simply put together by Ayazi acting alone. It's possible al-Qaeda was behind the bomb, but Ayazi may have targeted the well site without the knowledge or approval of al-Qaeda. That kind of attack, with few fatalities, just doesn't fit their mold."

"However, I think we can take comfort in the fact that any further attack in Lamar like that is very remote." Wiseman paused to take sip from the coffee cup at this elbow.

Fanning frowned and replied, "I wish I could convince our folks of that, Mr. Wiseman," as he wiped his hand over his drawn face.

"Whatever the motive, the bomb has terrorized us and everyone in the Metroplex. I don't think anything will be normal here again. Have you any idea why that man came to Lamar in the first place?"

Wiseman set his cup down, swiping the back of his hand across his lips.

"Well, we're trying to run down Maladondo's cousin, who supposedly asked Maladondo to hire the guy, but the cousin's whereabouts is a question at the moment. Because Ayazi looked and acted like a Mexican and spoke Spanish, he may have been brought across the Rio Grande with other illegal immigrants and then was somehow directed to work in Lamar like many other immigrants. But obviously, he was not your run-of-the-mill wetback."

Dub's eyebrows rose, a little surprised at the FBI agent's cavalier comment about the long-simmering immigration controversy.

Wiseman went on, "In any case, we are continuing our investigation, along with the CIA and the DHS. At this point, we don't believe Ayazi's action was part of any concerted plan because there have been no similar incidents in the country, and we've detected no change in the electronic traffic which is monitored here and around the world."

"You say he may have been directed to work in Lamar. Who would have directed him and why?"

"That's a crucial question, Mayor, and one we are still pursuing. If al-Qaeda sent him to America, they may have wanted him to simply blend in somewhere until he was later called on to carry out a specific mission. They may have linked with someone outside the country that relocates other immigrants coming across the border. We hope we can find that link, if that's what happened. You know, we refer to these people as terrorists for a reason. Their sole rational seems to be to create terror in the hearts and minds of Americans, Frenchmen, Britons, or whoever in the West they hate. They kill people they have never met, so it is not a case of personal revenge or hatred, and it doesn't seem to be a campaign to seize or occupy a country's government. It has no explanation and no end purpose, except to express and execute some religious mandate, which most of us consider insane. The note the bomber left seems to confirm that, but we have yet to understand why he, or anyone, would believe that the destruction of a gas well would serve that end. He worked there. He must have believed no one would be there on a Sunday morning. So the motive here is not clear. We may never know." Wiseman halted, waving his hand to signal he had no further comments.

The mayor was not satisfied that he was receiving the full story.

Either the FBI was running up a blind alley or Wiseman was not telling all he knew. Any kind of link between al-Qaeda and immigrant smugglers surely warranted a vigorous investigation. Realizing he could gain little more, Fanning ceased his questions.

"Well, again, thank you for coming, Mr. Wiseman. I certainly hope you are correct in thinking that this was not part of a plan to disrupt us here in Lamar."

"You are most welcome, Mr. Mayor. I know how disturbing this is to everyone."

They both rose as Fanning, again, held out his hand to the tall, lean agent.

"Mr. Mayor, I hope you will understand that I have covered some things that are still not public knowledge. Please keep our conversation confidential, at least until we are ready to make an official public statement after we have gotten further down the road."

"Yes, or course, I understand," the mayor responded, wondering how much solid or privileged information he had actually received. What if al-Qaeda was complicit? That thought was not useful in allaying the anxiety hanging over the city, a miasma which would not dissipate with the bland assurances from the agent.

Watching the agent amble down the hall toward the elevators, Fanning turned and walked into his office. He sat behind his large desk and reached a decision. Fifteen years was enough. This would be his last term as mayor of Lamar.

Still engrossed in the deathly saga of the bomb and the investigation, he was interrupted by his secretary.

"Mayor, while you were talking to Mr. Wiseman, Ron Blake called. He would like to visit with you tomorrow. He said he has some new figures about the performance of the pension plan."

"Okay, tell him to come over in the morning, about ten."

FORTY-THREE

Domingo "Dom" Larranago glided his new Chrysler 300 into the drive of the darkened clapboard house on N. Calhoun. He rubbed his hands over the wheel, caressing and smelling the black leather. The black sedan with chrome high wheels would command a lot more respect than his old car. His mother had actually purred when he visited her earlier that evening, calling by for his usual Sunday dinner.

"I'm so proud of you, Dom," she said, gazing out the window at the shiny auto and almost missing his plate as she served another enchilada verde.

"Yeah, Ma, you tell Aunt Rita that Xavier may be a big business-man, but he ain't got no car like mine."

Looking down the street, where the old streetlamps long ago ceased shedding any light on the row of houses, he could make out only two homes that had lights showing in the late gloom. Garbage pickup was due with the morning sun, and both recycle and garbage bins, resting on their small wheels, lined the curbs, one with a calico cat scratching at the lid, intrigued by the leaking odors. It was one of the reasons he had taken a lease on the house facing his car. It was dark and quiet in the deserted neighborhood. It had served well as a perfect drop house location for the marijuana and cocaine that he distributed in the Metroplex. Dallas was a large market, but a small dilapidated house in North Fort Worth was a far safer place to conduct his business since the DEA's roundup in Dallas last year. Only two blocks off North Main, the house provided a quick in and out route for his clients who moved the stuff all over Dallas and Tarrant Counties. As a wholesaler, he could not command the high street prices, but the volume keep his yearly income in the six-figure bracket.

It was already 2:00 AM and still the man had not arrived. At last, the final payment. All the others, in cold cash, had not been late. Three smuggled from Mexico had been so easy he almost felt guilty taking the money. Moving drugs and people across the Rio Grande was a seamless job with the cartel in Mexico, and he had demanded a handsome price from the camel jockey who had contacted him six months ago. The man was very careful, refusing to tell Dom how he had learned of Dom's border connections. But money was money, and in Dom's business, too many questions from either side were unwise.

The radio was playing a tune from his younger days, a mariachi band from Guadalajara. When Xavier called last week, Dom was pleased for the opportunity to tell his cousin about the new Chrysler, but Xavier had been more interested in discussing the FBI.

"Listen, Dom, the FBI just left my office an hour ago. They are asking questions about that guy Sanchez you sent to me in May. They think he was the guy that bombed the gas well here. What's goin' on?" Xavier was exercised.

"Sanchez? He was just a bracero I ran into who was looking for work. Didn't he do okay?" Dom replied.

"He was a good employee. Quiet but smart. But they wanted to know how he came to me. So you may be hearing from the Feds about it."

"Well, I don't know nothin' about him. Have they talked to him?"

"Talked to him? No one's seen him since the explosion, and the FBI says there were pieces of him all over the place and what was left of his truck. He won't be talkin' to anyone."

"Did you tell them where I live?" Dom's voice took on a new tone.

"Hell no. I don't know where you live. I just gave them your name and told them you live in Dallas. I guess they can find you. Just don't send them back to me again. I only hired the guy."

"Don't worry, Xavier. Like I said, I didn't know him. Just knew he wanted a job."

A week had passed and he heard nothing from the Feds. Maybe they couldn't find his address or his cell number, neither of which were widely known except among his business associates. But he still worried that they might have a plant buried in the product pipeline who could ID him before too long. This final payment could fund a little underground vacation for a while if necessary. He didn't need to be answering any questions about the three wetbacks he helped relocate. The man he had contracted with was not interested in relocating Mexicans wanting to send earnings back to Mexico.

The black pickup moved slowly down the block with lights out. Dom would not have noticed it even though he looked north toward Northside Drive where a police car was speeding, lights ablaze and siren blaring. The truck pulled to the curb behind Dom's car before Dom knew it was there. At last, the money was coming!

The tall balding man with the black mustache stepped out from behind the wheel, carrying a small canvas sack.

Dom lowered his window as the man approached. "About time, man. I was getting ready to leave."

"Ah, my friend, I am a man of his word. Step out and you can count it if you wish."

Dom accepted the invitation and carried the sack to the front of his car to examine its contents in the glare of his headlights. "Yeah. It better all be here You got what I promised you, right?"

Stopping in front of the lights, he quickly began counting the packets of $1,000 bills in the sack. He smiled as the total mounted.

He felt the jab at the back of his skull just as the count was finished. It was the last thing he ever felt.

The large man picked up the sack and the scattered money and reached into the Chrysler and turned off the headlights which bracketed the body on the driveway. The silenced pistol hardly disturbed the quiet night.

He returned to his truck and drove away, placing the pistol and silencer in the glove compartment. With any luck, he would be back in North Dallas by 3:00 AM, even with a short stop when crossing the Trinity River. The weapon would never be found in the dark water.

FORTY-FOUR

Glancing at his watch, Bobby realized he was running late. He had promised two clients he would finish the outline for each of their cases by the end of the week. What had happened? It was Friday morning and he would be pushed to get to the law office by nine o'clock.

Finishing a second cup of coffee, he turned to the next page of the newspaper, wondering why last night's *retreat* at the council had failed to pull together a comprehensive approval of the budget. It was going to be a struggle to overcome the $12 million shortfall which must be closed by October 1, but the session had floundered around with meaningless presentations from several department heads, who seemed more interested in crowing about their accomplishments and the needs for more funds in the coming year. The question of how to address the pension mess was never even mentioned by Art Isham, the city manager. Both Bobby and Carl had hoped that David Watson would elaborate on his suggestions to revise the entire pension plan. But for some reason, he was not at the meeting.

Halfway down the second page, his eye caught a short story titled "City Budget Director Dismissed."

Citing the city manager, the story declared that Watson had undertaken several steps in the budget office which were detrimental to the efficiency and morale of those working under his supervision, and he was asked to step down after serving less than five years as the city's budget director.

"Unbelievable!" Bobby muttered to himself. Facing one of the toughest budget gaps Bobby had seen in his four years on the council, the city was now without a budget director? The shock soon gave way to anger. Three hours of budget discussions and neither the city manager nor the mayor even mentioned that Watson was out the door. Was Bobby the only member who had been kept in the dark, or was the entire council to be surprised by reading the paper? Apparently, someone believed the media was entitled to more information than the elected officials.

He pulled his iPhone from his pocket and pressed the speed dial for the mayor's office. He was put through.

"Dub, this is Bobby. What's goin' on? I just read in the paper about David Watson."

"Hi, Bobby. Well, it's a long story. Isham didn't want to divert everyone's attention last night from the budget questions by getting into this issue, so he said nothing about it."

His agitation still rising, Bobby asked, "What do you mean *issue*? I thought Watson was one of our rising stars. He has worked very hard to get our finances straightened out, and Isham just up and fires him?"

"I know, Bobby. But it's not that simple. Isham's the city manager, and it's his prerogative to hire and fire folks. He said he has been receiving some serious complaints from longtime employees who documented some of Watson's actions that were directly affecting the employees."

"Well, this is a shock to me, Dub, and to be frank, I'm disappointed the council was not advised about this or whatever the issue is that has left us without a budget director."

"I don't disagree, Bobby. But Isham says he and the staff members have got it covered. I'm hoping we can get the budget wrapped up at our next meeting. He says he has found some funds that should help us close the gap with only a small reduction of certain expenditures."

"I sure hope you're right, Dub. This is not going to be an easy budget, but I suppose there never is an easy one."

* * *

By two o'clock, the client outlines were completed, notwithstanding the lingering news about Watson, and sent by e-mail to their offices. Turning to a court opinion which one of the associates had copied and placed on his desk, Bobby was interrupted by his secretary, Karen.

"Bobby, Mrs. Ramsey, your new colleague, is on the phone and would like to speak with you."

"Okay, put her on."

Bobby had encouraged her to run for a seat on the council. He and Becky knew her socially, and her track record in the real estate business was impressive. Her past experience as a CPA was an additional qualification in his mind.

"Hey, Paula, how are you? I hope the council work has not soured you so far."

"Not yet, Bobby. And by the way, thanks again for your help during the campaign. I'll get to the point, I know you're busy. If you have a few minutes, I would like to come to your office and discuss some city business."

"Sure. I've got no one coming by this afternoon. When do you want to meet?"

"I can be there in ten minutes, if that will work," Ramsey replied.

"You're on, if you don't mind sitting in a messy office."

* * *

Dressed as though she were attending a posh cocktail party, Paula Ramsey entered and took one of the comfortable chairs flanking the tasteful coffee table near the far wall. Bobby supposed that glamorous attire was the standard work-a-day uniform in the real estate business. Self-assured, she wasted little time in getting to the subject.

"Bobby, even before I decided to run, I spent a good deal of time reviewing the city's finances and the last three budgets. I also spent several hours swabbing David Watson who knows the finances better than anyone. I guess I can't get far from the fact that I used to be a practicing CPA. It came as no shock to me in June when David tried to tell the council that the city's pension plan was in big trouble. Anyone who bothers to read the newspapers knows that public pension funds across the country have turned into a disaster. Cities, counties, and states are piling up debts that are going to cost somebody a helluva headache just around the corner."

Bobby laughed. "Paula, you are the preacher, preaching to the choir! I agree. You know Carl and I applauded Watson's efforts to address that problem, but I'm not so sure anyone else on the council believes it is a problem or maybe they just don't give a damn."

Ramsey responded, "You may be right. I asked to come see you because I got a very strange call this morning before I even finished breakfast. It was David Watson. He said he had been fired. I was shocked and asked him what was the reason. He suggested I read the morning *Tribune*, but he said the article in the paper was a lie. He said that two women he supervises had complained to Art Isham. Both were longtime employees that he hardly knew, and they had never complained to him or anyone else about him as far as he knew. I said that unhappy employees don't always have the honesty to tell you. He just laughed and said, 'Yes, but what if I tell you both women are married to members of the city police force?'"

She was getting Bobby's undivided attention. "What kind of complaint did the women make? Was it some kind of sexual harassment claim?"

"No. David said they told Isham that he had been high-handed and was destroying office morale."

Bobby nodded slowly, recalling his earlier conversation with the mayor. "Paula, I was shocked when I read the paper this morning. I called the mayor because I found it strange that we discussed the budget last night for three hours and no one was told that the budget director had been ordered out the door. The mayor simply said there were issues and that it was Isham's job to hire and fire his staff."

"Something doesn't make sense," she replied, crossing her long legs and tossing her close-cropped auburn hair.

"I met with David the week after the election and asked him point-blank about the pension debt. He called it a fiscal disaster in the making, and he told me about the council presentation he was going to make in June. I haven't been here very long, but I couldn't believe it when the mayor practically cut him off at the knees by suggesting that the plan be *tweaked* by changing a few things that only applied to new employees. That's not going to do any good. How did the council let the city get into this mess?"

Bobby winced, knowing the question was probably on the mind of half the taxpayers in the city. He had spent many hours hoping to find the answer.

"Paula, I wish I had the answer. I don't think we arrived here through any evil intent. But almost every governmental body is run by elected officials who worry first about bring reelected and second about where the ship of state is going next year. You sat in that pre-council meeting when Watson presented his ideas. With one or two exceptions, everyone in the room was a city employee, an employee who wants and expects a pension someday from the city. Not one of them was ready to applaud Watson's idea, and not one of them was eager to see any council member adopt his idea. It is them against the taxpayers. The council members, who are supposed to represent the taxpayers, find it easier to keep quiet and let things slide for someone else to address after they are gone."

"Boy, am I getting a quick lesson in politics," Paula responded, shaking her head. "Do you mean the council has just sat back and sold the taxpayers down the river?"

"Oh no. In the past ten or fifteen years, the pension fund investment returns have been very good, so it was easy time and again to amend the plan. The council could do that in good conscience and without any significant cost to the taxpayers. But the problem is, investments don't always go up, and with the market's turndown, here we are with a big problem, which the taxpayers will have to pay for."

"This just doesn't make sense to me. Why should public employees be guaranteed future retirement payments when the rest of the world has to suffer when the economy turns down? I mean, anyone retiring under a 401(k) plan, or a similar program, must ride the investment market both up and down."

"I know, Paula, but this not a simple accounting equation. It is overridden by politics."

Paula was undeterred. "Well, explain that. How can a governmental system ignore economics and any downturns simply by saying it's just politics?"

Bobby was fascinated. At last, someone was digging to the core of the dilemma. What was the answer? He gave it a shot.

"All I can do is give my view from spending four years on the council. The city, or any republican form of government, elects officials who tax and spend to achieve certain societal goals. The goals change from time to time due, in large part, to the officials' perception of what the voters want. If they don't respond to those wants, they will no longer be government officials. When you have more and more voters who are employed by the government, you have more pressure on the officials to satisfy the wants of those employees—that is, more wages, more pensions and other benefits paid out of the public treasury. And who pays for it? The remaining voters that don't work for the government." Bobby stopped.

"Well then, what is the answer? How is this process stopped before it grinds to a halt?" She was still digging for a solution.

"I'm not sure, Paula. Some cities in California and elsewhere have taken bankruptcy. But that doesn't change the game. It just lets them holler King's X and start over by laying off a lot of employees and maybe creating a smaller city that no one is eager to call home anymore. Here in Lamar, we are going to have to change our pension plan or change how we do business by cutting out some city services or maybe go to the bankruptcy court. None of those choices are happy ones. Not for our taxpayers or our employees."

Paula shook her head and said, "Well, the council has got to come to its senses, Bobby. It's got to turn this charade around and explain to the taxpayers what's going on. If not, the city may end up in the bankruptcy court, or worse."

Bobby smiled. Paula made three. If they could find one more stalwart recruit, maybe something could yet be done.

FORTY-FIVE

Sgt. Alberto Esparanza, Bert to his friends and many of his fellow police officers, was born in Lamar and had never lived anyplace else. A longtime member of the Lamar Police Force, he enjoyed a solid reputation as a competent and loyal city employee, and as the vice-president of the police officers association, he had become a sounding board for many of the officers who frequently believed Ron Blake's role as president had taken a wrong turn. Blake's article in the *Badge*, implying that sworn council members were miserable people for even discussing the pension plan, was only one example of his actions which some called high-handed or worse. Blake had simply dismissed those concerns as disloyalty and continued to harangue the POA members at each meeting.

Esparanza was not surprised when Blake walked into the POA office with a broad smile on his face.

"Hey, Bert! Did you see that article in the *Tribune* this morning? Seems that budget director and his sharp pencil got sent out the door."

"Yeah, Ron, I saw that. Too bad. I thought he was a nice guy," Bert replied.

"Come on, Bert. Watson was hell-bent on taking away our pension. Your pension, my pension. I'm gonna hit twenty-five years in a few years from now, and that bastard wanted to throw out our pension plan and put us on something that would cut a big piece out of my retirement. He deserved to get his ass canned."

Blake kicked the trash can by his desk to emphasize his disdain and glared at Esparanza, daring any disagreement. He went on, "Everybody that works for the city is going to be hurt if the council listens to someone like Watson. Believe me, those folks in the budget department were happy to see him go."

"Well, I guess so. But what if the city is not able to cover the pension liability someday? There are cities where they have gone broke for that reason, and they've laid off a lot of employees, including a lot of police and fire."

Blake flopped into his chair and threw his feet up on his desk. "That's a bunch of bullshit propaganda put out by the chamber of commerce. That's not going to happen here. The city has promised to pay the pensions, and the city is gonna have to pay up. That's the city's problem, not our problem. We went to Austin back in '06 to push through the constitution amendment that says the city can't reduce our pensions. If the council can't get their budget in shape, they sure as hell can't take it out of our pocket!"

Esparanza sat silently. Debating with Blake was useless. It was Blake's way or the highway. But Esparanza's review of the city budget and actuarial predictions were painting a different picture. If Lamar was forced to cut back other expenditures to pay the growing pension debt, layoffs could happen as they had in California and Pennsylvania. The more recent police hires in Lamar included a number of Hispanics. How would they benefit by keeping the old pension plan if they were turned out on the street?

Blake rose from his chair and ambled over to the soft drink machine resting against the outside wall. Popping the tab on a can of Coke, he turned to Esparanza, still on the same subject.

"Old Isham was not very eager about dumping Watson, but I reminded him that our contract talks were just around the corner and they would go a lot smoother if we didn't have police officers and their families fretting over this pension scare. He's been here a long time and has always worked well with us."

Esparanza sat up and frowned. Was Blake trying to lean on the city manager as well as the POA members? Isham was due to retire soon. Maybe he had little worry about the city's budget in the years to come.

"Speaking of the budget, Bert, I hope you will get together with the trust fund's actuary. You need to get your ammunition ready for those contract negotiations. I'll bet the council will drag out this pension red herring as an excuse to cut down our compensation. The damn council always talks about the importance of public safety and then turns around and tries to get our pension rights."

FORTY-SIX

Bobby walked through the chute and stepped out into the bright parking lot. The late September sun graced the fall season, the best of the year in Lamar, highlighting the red and yellow leaves drifting downward in the slight breeze. He carried with him the docket book for next Wednesday's council meeting. Summoned by the need to review some correspondence received at his council office, he took the opportunity to collect the docket book from the secretary's office and relieve the police department of the chore of delivering it later that evening to his home, as was the custom.

Nearing his parking space, he noticed Alece Jackson's car backing toward him. He waved.

"Hey, Alece, what brings you to the hall on such a beautiful Friday?"

Alece stopped, turning his head to the left as Bobby came alongside his car.

"What's up, Bobby? I had to check on some e-mails that came in yesterday from some unhappy constituents."

Bobby laughed, noting the gloomy expression on Alece's dark face.

"Yeah, Alece, I know about that. I think half the folks in town are unhappy about something, and they are always the ones you hear from. I've just been doing the same thing."

Alece snorted and said, "The e-mails I got are from people who believe more gas wells are goin' to explode. They want every well shut down." He shook his head.

"It's amazing," Bobby replied. "I guess they don't believe the FBI and the CIA. They don't believe anything except what they want to believe."

Alece shrugged and lifted his hand in a parting salute.

"Say, Alece, I was just on my way to Mac's to have a beer with Carl. Come join us."

"Aw, man, I don't know. I'm pissed at Carl for the way treated Reverend Benjamin back in May. He had no cause to disrespect that man."

"Well, come on, Alece. Carl's got no beef with you," Bobby exclaimed, extending his hands in supplication.

"All right, I'll come, but I don't want to hear no speeches about Reverend Benjamin."

* * *

Bobby and Alece walked in together to find Carl sitting at a secluded table in the far corner opposite the bar. Carl's large hands were wrapped around the stem of one of Mac's fourteen-ounce glass schooners. Mac was no fool. He learned years ago that draft beer served in a frozen schooner moved much faster than beer sold in a can or bottle.

Carl gestured to the other chairs at the table. "Park yourselves, men. I think there is more beer where this came from."

Alece pulled out a chair on the far side of the table without taking his eyes off Carl. "How you doin', Carl?"

"Not bad, Alece. How 'bout you?"

Bobby nodded at Carl while waving at the nearby waitress who was carrying four schooners to the next table.

With beers in hand, the talk quickly turned to speculation on the fate of the Dallas Cowboys. Halfway through the preseason with only one loss, a long-awaited trip to the Super Bowl was possible. Bobby's opinions regarding the quarterback's performance carried some weight, and he opined that the boys would go far if they could finish the year with only two or three losses.

With the second schooner, the conversation soon wrapped around issues, past and present, before the council. Bobby briefly offered his regrets that the budget had been passed without any meaningful discussion about the pension mess, but neither Alece nor Carl seemed interested in the topic. Alece saw an opening as the talk came to a pause.

"Say, when are we goin' to get that financial policy rewrite back on the table? Lamar is growin' fast, and we need to make sure everyone grows with it, not just some parts of the city."

Bobby glanced at Carl before responding, "I don't know, Alece. That citizens' committee the mayor appointed is still workin' on the question. Have you checked with the mayor lately?"

Carl's face was becoming animated. Bobby feared a mini speech might be forthcoming as he steered the discussion back to Alece.

"What do you think about those proposed changes, Alece?"

"What do I think? I'll tell you what I know for sure. The east side needs help. The folks that live there don't have a supermarket, they don't have no Walgreens or a CVS, and the one or two filling stations sell cigarettes, soda pop and do dope. People have to drive for blocks to buy groceries or stuff from a drugstore, and if they don't got a car, they got to ride the bus for hours to do any shoppin'. Why do we want to brag about a city that's got that kind of life goin' on?"

Carl leaned forward and responded, "Alece, I know all that. A part of my district is on the east side. But the city can't pass an ordinance requiring Walgreens to spend $750,000 to build a drugstore. They're in the business to make money and they're free to take their business wherever they want. And the city can't get in the business of buying a car for everyone who needs one but can't afford it. Even if the city believed that was a proper city task, you know our budget can't afford something like that."

Carl took a long pull on his schooner, eyeing Alece and waiting for his reply.

"You may be right, Carl, but the city sure seems to have no trouble when someone wants a tax abatement to start a new business or build a new building on the west side of I-35. So why is the east side gettin' short-changed all the time?"

Bobby jumped in, hoping the debate would not escalate. "Alece, you know that we direct HUD funds to the people on the east side and a lot of the city's housing trust funds. I think everyone on the council knows how important it is to have the entire city prosper. But the concern I have with the proposal on the financial policy is that it seems to require this council and future councils to direct city revenues toward a certain goal, a goal that may or may not be one that can or should be achieved from year to year, depending on what other fiscal needs the city may have. For that matter, I don't think we can dictate what a future council should do about any city expenditure. That will be up to the people who sit on the council." Bobby glanced at Alece to see if he was getting his point across.

Alece paused and looked toward the ceiling, apparently collecting his thoughts. "I understand your point, Bobby. What you are sayin' is that you and Carl, and maybe others, like the way things have gone, so let's not rock the boat. But I'm tellin' you, things can't go on like they have in the city and in the state and in this country. I think some of the others on the council believe that too. So we will see!"

Bobby held up his hand, palm facing Alece, an unconscious gesture to deflect Alece's words.

"Alece, this is really a matter of economics, not us versus them. Carl and I both believe that everyone has equal rights here. Hell, the best man I ever played football with was Leon Harris. He saved my bacon on the football field, just like Jim did with Carl when they were in Desert Storm. This isn't about who you are. It's about how you perform. Jim Grant has not complained about how the city operates."

"Yeah," Alece said, "Jim Grant has a big house, big backyard, and a family car. He has nothin' to complain about."

"Whoa," Carl blurted out. "Jim Grant has a four-year-old Toyota. If it looks good, it is because he knows the automotive business and he takes good care of it. What he's got is what he's worked damn hard for. Nobody gave him a hand either."

Bobby again jumped in. "Hey, enough politics. Like the man said, religion and politics don't ever get resolved." Carl and Alece nodded, and as Carl beckoned the waitress, he asked, "Have you driven to the bomb site lately? It looks like Payton is fixin' to move a rig in and drill a new well. You can hardly tell there was an explosion. New fences, the works."

Carl's face dropped as he suddenly remembered and turned toward Bobby. "Gee, I'm sorry, Bobby, I forgot about Libby's loss."

"Oh yeah," Alece said. "I heard last week that you knew one of the men killed by the bomb. I'm sorry too, Bobby."

"That's okay. We'll get over it in time. But it sure was a shock."

They sat silently when the waitress asked, "Another round?"

Bobby and Carl nodded, but Alece said, "I got to go. I got a meeting this evening." He rose and held out his hand to both of them. "Thanks for the beer, Bobby. Next time it's my turn."

As Alece rolled out of Mac's parking lot, headed for his meeting with Reverend Benjamin and the brothers, Bobby and Carl sipped slowly on their third beer.

"Well, maybe we know where Alece is coming from, nothing new," Carl mumbled.

"Right, and I suppose he has no doubt where we stand," Bobby answered and then went on, "It can't be easy when your great grandparents were slaves, and everyone knows it."

"What? What the hell is that supposed to mean? I don't know that Alece's grandparents were slaves." Carl's voice rose.

"Just an observation. But you do wonder, don't you?" Bobby said, taking another sip of the cold beer.

FORTY-SEVEN

The office of Alece Jackson, Agent, normally was not open on Saturday, but Alece was seated behind his desk, gazing at his nephew. Elisha was in town and asked on Friday if he could come by and continue the discussions with Jackson about political science.

"Say, Elisha, how's it goin' with your political science class? Do those folks teach you anything?"

"It's okay, Uncle. We're into the Constitution and how our governments are formed. We even talked last week about how city government works."

"Well, that's good. What did they say about runnin' a campaign to get on city council?"

"We're not that far yet. I think they want us to understand how governments are formed, and then we'll talk about elections and political parties."

Alece laughed and said, "Hey, maybe I should come and lecture to your class. I could tell your professor a few things about elections." He rocked back in his chair and smiled, remembering last night's meeting and how he had told the brothers his story of lambasting Sanford and Jeffers, especially Jeffers who was so dense he couldn't show respect to Reverend Benjamin. Lost in that thought, he barely heard Elisha rattling on.

"That's a good idea, Uncle. You might like to sit in on our class. It is amazing how the US was formed and how it works."

Alece sat straight up and tilted his head. "How it works? How it works is that black folks are kept on the outside lookin' in. All the slaves were freed in 1864, but we're still pushed to the side while the white folks run the country like they always have. The pledge says liberty and justice for all, but we ain't never been included in the *all*."

Elisha was startled. This was almost verbatim from the last meeting with Uncle Alece. Why was he so agitated?

"But, Uncle, we elected Barack Obama to the White House and you on the city council. A lot has changed."

Alece grimaced. "Barack Obama! He ain't no black man. His momma was white and his pa was a free man from Kenya. He may be an African American, but he is not one of the black brothers. His grandpa was not put in chains and hauled across the ocean as a slave. His family was not turned out into a country run by white folks who would not let him vote. They wouldn't even allow a black man to serve alongside a white man in the Army until after World War II. The only equality was the right of a black man to get killed. Obama is a joke. He is just a token to make the white folks think they are givin' justice to all."

"But, Uncle, you told me last time that I should get into politics and maybe run for office someday."

"That's right, and when you and a lot more get there, maybe we can make the government serve up some justice to replace all that was taken from us for over three hundred years. The government serves who runs it so the day will come when we control that system to serve the black man. We've learned how the system works for the ones who have the power."

Alece's eyes bored in on his nephew. "You listen to me? You ain't gonna hear the truth from those professors over there, so don't believe 'em when they tell you how the US government has worked all these years. It has been built on the back of the black man!"

* * *

Elisha drove home, unsure of the political *education* imparted by his uncle. His mom and dad had never talked that way. Had something happened to Alece that was not even known to his mom. He puzzled over how he might ask her about Alece's background. Maybe the brothers were infecting him somehow.

FORTY-EIGHT

As usual, Thanksgiving and Christmas were looming, only two weeks away, and Bobby began to think about what was different or unusual he could gift to Becky. He sometimes wondered what remained that might please her after twenty years of marriage. A sneak side trip to Niemans in Fort Worth might provide a prize when he was there. With that settled, he turned back to the chore of reviewing the files of a new client that lay strewn across the large oak table in his office.

The cool fall air and the rising excitement over the coming holidays had somewhat soothed the lingering alarm which dogged Lamar since the late August explosion.

An announcement in the *Star Telegram* in September about the death of an Hispanic man in North Fort Worth had no impact in Lamar, except for Xavier Maladondo, who was yet trying to understand why his cousin was found with a bullet hole in the back of his head. But deep down, he knew the less he understood, the better off he was. The FBI spent another hour with him and asked the same questions although the agents did not share with him their rising suspicions that the murder was at the hand of al-Qaeda or a Mexican drug cartel or both. Dead or alive, the FBI continued to pursue the few leads they obtained from tracing the cousin's movements before and after the bomb.

Nationwide fear of subsequent suicide bombings had proven false, at least so far, and security lines at airports and elsewhere continued as before. A relative tranquility seemed to be flowing into Lamar, much like a returning friend that had strayed. Few people bothered anymore to drive by the blackened well site although it would soon be in operation again. Tempered by the impending holiday and the pervading belief that the explosion was no fault of the well or its owner, even Charles Unsel and SCAD had lessened their clamor at city hall.

"So," Bobby asked himself while he loaded his briefcase for the court visit, "why am I becoming more tense and anxious each day?"

The answer was not difficult. The death of Josh had not erased the swirl of emotions yet plaguing him over Libby's lingering grief. The bomb had solved in a very cruel manner the quandary about the budding romance between Josh and Libby.

FORTY-NINE

"Sue Lynn and I really enjoyed and appreciated the dinner at your house the other night, Bobby," the mayor said, leaning back in his large chair. "Becky is a grand cook. You must be very proud of her."

"We were honored to have you, Dub," Bobby replied, watching the mayor rock in the swivel seat. "Becky likes having company, and she thinks Sue Lynn is just like her mother. Besides, she was very flattered to have the city's First Lady as a guest."

Dub smiled, remembering how his wife always reacted with a scowl whenever she was referred to in that manner.

"Well, thank you. And thank you for agreeing to meet with me this morning. You know, it's been a tough few months since that damned terrorist blew up the well, and I believe it's a good time to touch base on several things. This job has gotten a lot more complicated because of him, and it's not eased off much."

Bobby listened, his mind open to whatever was coming. Dub was not a garrulous man, but he was clearly leading up to something. He seldom invited anyone to his office on short notice without a goal in mind, a request, or a plan.

"Why do you think you and I and the others spend our time working on this council?" Bobby was surprised. He was not ready for a Socratic dialogue.

"Oh, I guess somebody's got to take care of the people's business," he lamely replied, looking somewhat sheepish.

"No doubt about that," said the mayor, nodding his head. "People have to complain to somebody, somebody to blame for what they don't like. But there's a lot more to it than that. People want stability, they want to wake up tomorrow morning and know they can go to work, their children can go to school, and at the end of the day their home and the city will still be here. That bomb put a big dent in that stability, but it's getting better."

Bobby sat up in his chair. This was obviously going somewhere.

The mayor proceeded, "The real reason we are here is to maintain the system, to keep government wheels turning so people can get on with their lives."

Perhaps a bit prosaic, Bobby thought, but undoubtedly true. He smiled and waited.

"That's exactly what we swore to do when we took the oath of office. We swore to preserve, protect, and defend the Constitution and the laws of the United States of America. The same oath taken by almost every public official in this country. And you know what, we reaffirm that at least twice a month when we recite the Pledge of Allegiance before our meetings." Dub turned his head and cast a penetrating look at the American flag siting in the corner of his office.

He went on, "That pledge does not say we swear allegiance to the United States of America. It says we pledge allegiance to two things—the flag and the republic for which it stands. I don't believe many people ever think about what that means. The republic is that unique form of government established here in the 1780s, and it is our duty to act so that our form of government, our system, is not compromised or weakened or destroyed. And no one can destroy that system quicker than we can."

Bobby could sense Dub's animation, and he quickly agreed, "I understand, Dub."

"I know, I know. Everyone on the council feels the same way, I'm sure. Only our obligation goes far beyond reciting the pledge every two weeks. When we pass an ordinance, when we spend the taxpayer's money, we need to ask ourselves what our policies do to the founding principles of our government. The Congress, the Texas legislature, and all our governing politicians need to do the same thing. How often do we casually toss out the term *unintended consequences* and then have to duck when some of the consequences come back to haunt us?"

Bobby suddenly thought of Jackson's proposal to amend the city's financial policy to direct future expenditures down a proscribed path. He said, "Like that financial policy change we delayed."

"Exactly, Bobby. Alece believes that his policy will enhance the lives of many citizens, but I'm not sure he has considered or cares about the effect it would have on the operation of our budget or our city government." The mayor folded his hands in front of him and glanced at Bobby to see if anything was sinking in. Bobby was one of the smartest ones on the council. Was he ready to hear more?

"Bobby, do you remember that fellow Benjamin who came over from Dallas last May?"

"Yeah, the one Carl tried to chew on?"

"That's the one. I had a little visit with Carl about that."

Bobby laughed out loud. "Carl said you leaned on him a bit."

"Yes, I did. Not because I disagreed with Carl's assessment of the situation, but because Carl dragged it out during the council session. Not every thought needs to be expressed in public, you know, in front of the media. The point I'm trying to make is there are things going on in this country that are going to cause big trouble." He paused and then went on, "Two or three years ago, someone put a name on it, a name I never really understood at first. Have you ever heard the term *moral hazard*?"

"Is that something like a road hazard?" Bobby asked, thrown off-balance by the term.

"Could be. But it means that the moral or correct path of our government is being put at risk. The term has been used to describe the effect of government actions which cause or perpetuate fiscal policies that are not sustainable in a republican, democratic form of government. The term was coined, I think, in late 2008 when the federal government decided that an economic bailout was needed for AIG, Goldman Sachs, General Motors, and others because they were too big to fail, otherwise our economic system would go down the tube. There's another example. Allowing our federal tax system to force more and more taxes to be paid by fewer and fewer productive citizens so that the government can continue larger and larger entitlement programs to those who pay little or no federal taxes. That is a huge hazard."

The mayor was now on a roll. "Look at our own budget and the huge proportion of our tax revenue we must spend to support our growing employee retirement fund. And we are just a small part of that runaway problem that exists across the country. How much longer can we afford to hire more and more government employees while there are less and less private industries paying in the tax revenues?"

Bobby could only nod at the lecture, knowing it had not reached the end.

"Our government is teaching and encouraging people every day to abandon self-reliance and depend on government security for their well-being. This not what Thomas Jefferson meant when he wrote about the right to happiness. There's a big difference between happiness and pursuing happiness. No one can possibly guarantee happiness, not even the government."

Bobby had never heard this many words from Dub Fanning. Why was all this being pitched to him?

As if reading Bobby's mind, the mayor grinned and said, "I guess you want to know why I'm telling you all this?"

"Yeah, it did cross my mind," he answered.

"Well, we talked to you Saturday about Sue Lynn's cancer treatments. They are going well, but you never know what the future will bring. And I'm getting a little worn down myself after eighteen years in this seat. So she and I have decided that I will not run again after the end of this term. Filing for this seat will be a little over a year from now, and I hope you will think about doing that." He stopped, carefully watching Bobby's reaction.

"Dub, that's a surprise. I think everyone believes and hopes you'll be here a long time to come."

"No. That won't be." He returned to the point, with persistence. "You must think about this. You've got the experience and political support to make a fine mayor. I would, of course, give you my full endorsement if you decide to do it."

"Dub, I am very, very flattered. I'll have to consider a lot of factors. The loss of my daughter's boyfriend has put a different spin on things at my house."

"Sure, Bobby, there is no hurry. But I hope you will keep quiet about my decision to step down. I would want to wait until next year before I make a public announcement. In the meantime, I will just act coy." He smiled with what he hoped was a coy expression.

* * *

As Bobby drove home that evening, he turned over in his mind the newfound development. Was Dub feeling that he had failed Lamar, allowing a terrorist bomb, witnessing widespread fear? He speculated on how Becky might react to the prospect of becoming the First Lady. And what about the moral hazard Dub feared. Was it really that bad? Dub was seldom wrong, but maybe the bomb had been too much for him to weather.

FIFTY

A heavy snow in early January was uncommon in Lamar, and after lunch, Bobby began to consider that he might close the law office and send everyone home while the streets were still navigable. He was making little progress anyway with the revision of his client's contract as the minutes dragged by. Lost in thoughts of the past year, he was fearful that the new year held small promise of resolving the lingering and troublesome issues. The city's pension plan, police and fire negotiations, Charles Unsel, and the ever-looming memories of the terrorist bombing hung on. As the unresolved concern about Libby crept into his mind, Bobby finally concluded that the day held little promise.

Mesmerized by the snow falling steadily on the street outside, he didn't hear the first ping on his iPhone, which lay on the desk. But the second one alerted him to a short text message: "Bobby. Can we meet? Leon Harris."

He stared at the bright screen and scowled. Leon had left Lamar, what? Twenty-five years ago? Why was he calling?

Picking up the intercom, he paged Karen, "Karen, can you check the Fort Worth phone directory and find a number for Leon Harris? Yes, I believe he lives in Fort Worth and has a business there also."

Sending text messages was not Bobby's favorite way of communicating. The shorthand expressions and hidden motivations were not an acceptable means of conducting a law practice in his estimation. Moreover, they offered nothing but quicksand in discharging his duties as a council member. Even e-mail, with its eternal records in cyberspace clouds and servers, continued to remind him of last year's newspaper articles which dogged an Austin council member who was careless with his personal messages sent via a city issued iPad.

The phone was answered on the second ring. "This is Leon."

"Hey, Leon. Bobby Sanford here. I got your text. What's up?"

"Bobby! Thanks for callin'. What's goin' on down in Lamar besides the snow?" The deep chuckle was the same as Bobby remembered from their days in the Lamar High locker room.

"Well," Bobby replied, "not much except politics and unhappy law clients."

"Yeah, that's why I sent the text. I need a good lawyer. Wonder if I might come down there and visit with you."

"Don't tell me there are no good lawyers in Fort Worth. There must be hundreds of them."

Leon paused and sighed before he answered, "Yeah, that's true, but I've got me a problem that's a little out of the ordinary, and I think you are the man to handle it."

"What kind of a problem?"

"I think we better talk about it in your office if you've got some time soon."

"Sure, Leon, but you know I'm just a general civil lawyer. I don't handle criminal or family matters."

"It's not like that, Bobby. Don't worry."

"Okay, how about nine o'clock on Thursday? You know where my office is, near the city hall?"

"Thanks, Bobby. I'll see you then even if I have to come on skis."

Neither Bobby nor the other three lawyers in the firm accepted new clients without a candid discussion of fees and the execution of a written engagement agreement. A later suit by a disgruntled client, who misunderstood the nature of the case and its possible results, was a problem they didn't need, especially in a small city like Lamar. But Bobby was intrigued. Leon sounded very mysterious.

FIFTY-ONE

The snow in the well-traveled roads had melted and run off by Thursday as Leon moved to one of the chairs in the conference room, pulling it closer to the large table dominating the space. Dressed in slacks, a wool sport coat, and tie, Leon's appearance surprised Bobby. Added pounds, a balding forehead, and scattered gray in his dark hair had replaced the quick and lithe figure from years past. The dark mustache and fashionable goatee would have completely fooled Bobby if they had met on the street. Only his dark bronze skin and deep brown eyes looked the same.

"You have changed, Leon."

"Oh come on, Bobby. I bet you can't wear the old Lions jersey anymore."

"No, I mean, where did you get the professor's disguise? You look like something from a Hollywood movie!"

"I know, my Clara thinks it's cute, and it makes people believe I'm an acute businessman. I don't turn down money in the bank."

Bobby grinned, stood up, and walked to the sideboard. "How about some coffee?"

With cups in hand, the ex-classmates got to the point of the visit.

"I've been sued for $2 million, Bobby. I need your help."

"That's not pocket change, I guess. What kind of business are you in, Leon?"

"Well, this is not about my business. I run a large warehouse on the east side of Fort Worth. Lease out space to a lot of small businesses, distribution stuff mostly. If this was a business problem, my lawyers in Fort Worth could handle it."

Reaching for the small briefcase he had at his side, he pulled out a sheaf of papers, laid them on the table, and looked dourly at Bobby.

"I've been accused of defamation, whatever that means."

He handed Bobby a summons, with an attached petition, and had the good sense to sit quietly as Bobby began reading.

A full ten minutes passed before Bobby carefully placed the papers in front of him, but within reach. Frowning, he gazed at Leon, who was beginning to fidget with his tie, as if it were too tight.

"These are serious claims, Leon. This man Benjamin says you wrote a piece calling him a slave master, a blackmailer, and a threat to the city council of Fort Worth! Obviously, he doesn't appreciate that, and he wants $2 million for damage to his reputation."

Leon stared back at Bobby, shaking his head. "That's what he says, but this man is a badass. But he's not the first one who is trying to suck blood from the black people in this country."

"You mean you think that what you wrote about him is true? Then you've nothing to worry about. All you have to do is prove it."

"Okay. What he said at the council meeting is on the record, don't you think? It can be proved."

"Sure, what he said can be proved. The question is, have you just repeated that or have you said something different? What is this piece he says you wrote?"

Leon reached into his briefcase and handed two typewritten pages to Bobby. "This is what I wrote."

RESLAVED: The Fate of The Dependents

It is time for the African American community in the United States to come awake. Constant complaints about human bondage existing 250 years ago and cries for restitution and atonement are subjecting our community to a new and insidious role in society. A role of incompetency and incapability. A role destined to rob us of the individual freedom promised by the Emancipation Act of 1864.

Too many of our men, women, and children are being cast into a subculture of economic dependency by government and other apologists who salve their own conscience through affirmative action programs and other devices which destroy the freedom and opportunity of the individual. A willingness to rely upon the goodwill and largesse of others is creating a new slavery and obedience to serve those who promise atonement, only to gain the economic and political power of the country.

It has become so rampant that many of our own have joined forces with the *politically correct* crowd. Only last month, at a meeting of the Fort Worth City Council, I saw an African American named Rev. Jeremiah Benjamin. He implored the city to establish a program of welfare and aid to black communities in the city. He was selling a plan to educate black youths to respect authority. He cleverly implied a threatened disobedience if the program was not adopted. The program included a healthy honorarium, payable to him and the Dallas-based coalition which he represents. The Reverend Benjamin is not unknown in these parts. He travels far and wide in his efforts to profit from the affirmative action mantra which the country has embraced, but only if he can be personally enriched as a modern-day slave master, living off the victimization of our own people.

But he is only one example of those, both black and white, who profit from the slow erosion of the black man's individual responsibility and freedom to succeed or fail in his own right.

It is time to wake up!

Leon the Loper

The rise and fall of Bobby's eyebrows paced his reading, punctuated by grunts and sighs. He again looked across the table and spoke in measured tones. "Leon, I know this Reverend Benjamin. He came to our council and made his pitch. I don't think most of our members appreciated it. But why did you write this diatribe about slavery and send it to him?"

"Whoa! I wrote it, but I didn't send it to anybody."

"Well, how does he know about it? And who else knows about it? He has no claim if you didn't publish these thoughts to other people."

Leon was already pacing around the table, and he began a roving dialogue, "Hell, I don't know. All I can say is about a month after I wrote it, it started showing up on blogs, Instagram, and the whole damned internet. It is all over the place!"

Bobby was shaking his head. His only prior case involving a defamation claim was between two brothers who were eager to carry a long-standing feud to the courthouse.

"How does he know you are Leon the Loper if you didn't put this out to someone?"

"Good question. That's why I need you. I don't have any answers. It's all a shock to me."

Bobby slowly sipped his coffee, trying to organize his thoughts. Benjamin's lawyer, Malcolm Colter, was a well-respected black attorney in Dallas, a vice president of the Dallas Bar Association. Benjamin and his lawyer were seeking more than a redemption of Benjamin's so-called reputation. $2 million was serious money.

"I haven't had a lot of experience with these kinds of lawsuits, Leon. Maybe we can find a better lawyer for you." The wave of Bobby's hand seemed to signal a dismissal of the idea that he should join in the fray.

"I'm not here because you and I played football together," Leon retorted." I came because you understand what I was talking about when I wrote this." Leon stabbed the two pages with his forefinger.

"Do you remember that talk you gave at the Rotary Club awhile back? I was there and I recorded that speech on my iPhone. You said many government payees are now virtually slaves. Did you believe what you said? I don't need some lawyer who thinks that two black litigants need two black lawyers!" Leon's dark eyes were jumping, reminding Bobby of their days as one of the best passing duos on the football field.

"Okay, okay. Calm down. Let me do this. Benjamin is not going to settle for a few peanuts. He's probably already in for a few thousand dollars. His lawyer is not cheap and is not some fly-by-night just out of law school. Let me walk this through Oliver Roberts, one of my partners. He has handled several defamation suits, and his help will be needed. I'll visit with him and then let's go over this again on Monday, talk about fees, and let me try to understand how this whole thing has come about. I've got the feeling that something else is going on here."

"Sure, Bobby. But I think my answer is due in about two weeks. It's all a mystery to me."

Watching Leon walk out of the office, Bobby thought about the many previous clients who had passed through the door, leaving their legal problems for him to solve or at least shepherd to some conclusion. But Leon's case struck a different cord. He had never represented a black person, and he knew little about the ambitions, desires, and motivations that guided their actions, and he certainly had no knowledge of the life Leon had developed after their last day together at Lamar High. He was glad Roberts was close by to offer another opinion.

FIFTY-TWO

Oliver Roberts, a graduate of the Oklahoma University School of Law, joined the Sanford firm after getting his belly full of practice in a large city. A few years over fifty, he had welcomed the opportunity to put his experience to work as the office manager of the Sanford firm, whose founder was spending more and more time at the city hall. During Oliver's tenure of more than five years, Bobby had come to rely more each day on Oliver's wise counsel and ability to analyze potential clients.

Oliver listened silently as Bobby related his recent meeting with Leon.

"So what do you think, Oliver?"

"What I think is Leon the Loper is not making sense or he is not telling us everything. But that's about par for most guys who get sued."

"Hey, Oliver, I've known Leon since we were kids in school. He's not gonna lie to me."

"Maybe so, but why does he write something like this, call a man a slave master, and then says he didn't show it to anyone? And now, it's all over the internet. It's not rational. Ha, maybe he typed on his PC and accidentally pushed Send. In any case, we shouldn't take this on and just wait for the plaintiff to explain how Leon published this thing. God knows, the internet has made it public, maybe all over the country. No wonder this reverend fellow is claiming his reputation has been smeared."

"Yeah, I understand. But Leon's coming back on Monday, so I hope you can join us. But I have to laugh at the thought that Reverend Benjamin has a reputation which could suffer any reprobation, especially among those that know anything about him. In my opinion, he has already exposed himself to public contempt."

"You think? Well, all we need to do is get you on the jury. I'm telling you, this could be a real dogfight between two black dogs!"

* * *

The driveway in front of the garage was still covered for the most part in snow. The tire ruts from the Jeep and Becky's car identified the only traffic in front of the house.

The cold hung in the garage, and Bobby welcomed the heat as he passed through the laundry room. He unzipped his leather jacket, a Christmas gift from Becky, and hung it on the row of pegs lining the wall.

"Is that you, honey?" Becky greeted.

"And who were you expecting?" he replied, wrapping his arms around her warm body, his mind slipping away from thoughts of Leon and the ongoing pension discussions from Wednesday night's council meeting.

"Libby called this afternoon. She was rattling on about Josh. You know she has said very little about him since the funeral. I think she is finally putting it behind her. But she didn't shed much light on the nature of their relationship. I may have to prod her a little bit."

Bobby frowned and simply acknowledged with, "Go carefully, Becky. Speaking of mysteries, a ghost from the past was in the office today. A black guy in my high school class wants me to handle a lawsuit for him. He's been sued for two million dollars, maybe more."

Becky smiled. "That would be interesting. What did he do to stir up that kind of money?"

"I'm not sure yet. Come with me into the den. Maybe I can show you."

Bobby sat at the PC, and after a false start, an outlandish website blossomed onto the bright screen with the comment, "Check this out! Slavery rides again!" The full text of Leon's message followed.

Becky scrolled down the page, shaking her head. She turned. "Who is this Leon the Loper?"

Bobby snorted and replied, "That's my classmate, Leon Harris. He got that nickname when we played on our high school football team."

"Bobby! You're not going to get mixed up with this, are you? If it's made the internet, it could get nasty."

"I don't know. Oliver and I have talked it over, and I am going to meet with Leon on Monday. He knows plenty of lawyers, but for some reason, he insists that I should defend him. You remember that Reverend Benjamin, don't you? That man who tried to lean on the council last year."

"Yes, I remember how upset you were." Becky turned back to the screen once more and scrolled through the blog again. "What's all this talk about slavery? We've never had any racial problems around here. Your Leon seems to be provoking a revolution that could hurt a lot of people. That terrorist bomb still has everyone on edge."

Bobby shrugged. "I know, Becky. I'll try to find out what's at the bottom of all this before we make any decision. The suit against Leon is in Judge Welton's court in Fort Worth. We've had good luck there."

The piercing look from Becky was not lost on Bobby. She knew quite well that his last remark meant he was seriously considering the assignment.

FIFTY-THREE

Monday morning promised a mild day, with the sun removing the last trace of the snow. Bobby and Leon gazed silently out the window of the conference room as Karen set the coffee carafe and cups on the table. She turned to Bobby. "Do you need anything else, Bobby?"

"No. Thanks, Karen. Just hold any calls for a while."

Leon slowly smiled, baring his even white teeth, which had amazingly survived his days on the football field.

"Well, Bobby, are we ready to get on with this lawsuit?"

"I'm not too sure. I can't make sense out of it, and Oliver and my wife have been less than enthusiastic about me jumping into it. I don't understand why you wrote this thing." The petition rattled as Bobby waved it in the air. "How did it get spread all over the internet? Why would Benjamin take it to court, and I don't understand why you believe I should get into a squabble between you, Benjamin, and Colter. I'd be the only white face in the ring!"

Leon listened stoically, his eyes unblinking. He moved his chair closer to the table before he responded, "One reason I wrote this manifesto, if that's the right word, was because I'm fed up with people treating me like I'm part of some tribe, a black tribe, that I think and believe like someone else because my skin is black. After I moved out of Lamar, I spent two years in the Army, then I went to Abilene Christian and majored in American history. I started my warehouse business almost fifteen years ago, and I've made a good living. So why do I and why do you have to listen every day to people who tell me that I am incapable, that I can't compete, that I am not a part of this country because one of my ancestors may have come off a boat with chains on his ankles? Why does anyone let themselves be cowed by an idiot like Benjamin?"

Leon paused, then laughed. "Yo, I guess that's a mouthful. But it really hit home last month. I sat down at my PC and typed this thing after my daughter, Dee, came in to show me the letter she got from the University of Texas. It's no secret that the university won't accept first year students unless they rank in the top 10 percent of their high school class. Well, Dee is very smart she makes only As and Bs at Paschal High, but she's not close to the top 10 percent. But she insisted on sending her application to Austin anyway, and they wrote to say she was accepted, that the Texas University system was proud of their affirmative action program which made room for minorities and others in order to, and I quote, provide a balanced student body beneficial to all."

Leon signaled a pause with his hand before he continued, "Well, I have grilled into Dee and her brother, Leo, that the only way to get ahead here or anywhere in the world is to work hard and prove your own worth. You should earn your way, not depend on someone else to hand you anything. I've pointed to my business and our home, an old restored house in the Ryan Place neighborhood, as proof.

"So my reaction to Dee's joy in receiving the letter from Austin was not what she was hoping for, and she ran off in tears to her mom. That's when I sat down and typed this, what Benjamin calls a defamation. Then a couple of days later, I heard your talk at the Rotary Club, and I knew that you, an elected official, understood that self-sufficiency is being lost in this country, especially in the black community."

Bobby shifted in his chair, remarking, "At least that explains why you wrote it. But how am I going to speak for you when our only relationship has been on the football field? I don't think that I can convey what you or any other black man feels about these things. I've not had to live through what black people have endured, and race relations are still far from being perfect. Ferguson and Baltimore have proved that."

Leon rose and refilled his coffee cup, glancing sideways at Bobby.

"That's another reason I want you to defend me, Counselor. I didn't cause my skin to be black any more than you caused yours to be white. Our parents fixed that. The only thing you and I are responsible for is what we've done since we got here. Maybe you don't know if one of your great-great-grandfathers was a slave owner, but who cares? A man can't be held responsible for someone else's actions that happened years before he was born. Hell, the US Constitution prohibits Bills of Attainder, the infliction of penalties for prior actions that were not condemned by law at the time. How then can you be held liable for actions taken by prior slaveholders even if they were your ancestors?"

Bobby stared. What was Leon talking about? Was he now a constitutional expert?

"But what do we see every day? All around us, a society that preaches mea culpa and pretends it is making amends for history by treating black people as professional victims, like people who just walked off a plantation. How can we enjoy the right or ability to use the freedom this country has promised when we are all buried under pity and pandering?

"This political correctness is becoming insane. Awhile back, I saw an article in the *Wall Street Journal* reporting a student movement at Harvard Law School, demanding the school's crest be changed to remove the likeness of a family seal attributed to a wealthy nineteenth-century slave owner. Do those students think they will get an A on their next exam because of their outrage over slavery? No one in their right mind today believes that slavery was a noble or moral institution. What about George Washington's face on the dollar bill, he owned slaves? As a matter of fact, let's just tear down the Washington Monument in DC and we all can be politically correct."

Leon was making his third circuit around the table as Bobby worried that the coffee could be spilled. Leon sat, took a breath, and concluded, "Well, that's why I liked your talk and why I want you to be my lawyer. The lawyers that represent my business are very good, but I don't believe they have the guts to make my point."

"I admire your point, Leon, but don't forget that the goal of Benjamin and Colter is to take $2 million out of your pocket. This suit is not about providing a soapbox from which you and I can orate."

"Yeah, I know, I know."

Bobby pulled the petition over to his side of the table and leafed slowly through the pages. Dropping it on the table, he looked at Leon.

"I'll take the case. But we'll have to agree on a fee arrangement and sign an engagement agreement, like I do with all clients."

"Benjamin has got to prove his case, meaning he must show that you wrote this statement, that you published it, that is, you made it public so that it damaged his reputation and caused him monetary damages."

Bobby laughed. "It will be interesting to see how he has been exposed to public contempt or ridicule since he has made no secret about his campaign to extort money from some local governments. But a mystery still remains. How did your work get out of the house and onto the internet?"

Leon frowned and replied slowly, "I think I have that figured out, but I'm not sure yet. I printed off several copies and showed one to Clara the next morning as she was headed out the door. She was late and jammed it in her purse. She teaches advanced algebra at Tarrant County College. When she came home that afternoon, she couldn't find it in her purse."

"Are you saying someone at the college or somewhere else may have gotten their hands on that copy?" Bobby asked, leaning across the table. "If that's so, Benjamin may not be able to prove that you published it. Maybe someone else did. We'll need to do a little investigation on this."

"Okay, I get it," Leon replied. "But isn't truth still a defense, no matter what? I saw and heard Benjamin at the Fort Worth Council meeting. He did ask for money personally paid to him, and he was trading off the needs of black people. In my opinion, he is a slave master no matter what he says."

"I don't know, Leon. But we'll put every defense in our answer, and do whatever discovery is needed to prove those defenses. It's not going to be cheap, and neither is $2 million."

"My bank account can handle it. The legal fees, I mean," Leon responded. He had blocked his mind from considering how he might cough up $2millon.

FIFTY-FOUR

In her mid-forties, Clara Harris was still blessed with a bright face and ready smile which engaged her students at Tarrant College every day. Fortunately, her math classes were finished by 2:00 PM, and she was waiting at Paschal High on Monday for Leo to exit the school. Dee had texted Clara at noon to advise that her last class was going to be finishing late for some reason and asked Clara to give Leo a lift home.

Coming out of the school, Leo recognized the Lexus SUV and quickly jumped into the passenger seat. "Hi, Mom. Where is Dee?"

"She's got to stay late, so I am your chauffer today, Baby."

"Mama! Don't call me that. Someone might hear you."

"Okay, Baby," Clara grinned.

The drive from school to Ryan Place was less than a mile, and as they turned onto Rosedale Street, Leo posed a question, "Mama, Dee was still acting sore this morning about her talk with Pappa. I don't understand what he told her or why she is bein' so huffy. It's been almost six weeks ago. Why is she so upset?"

Waiting at a stoplight, Clara turned her head toward Leo and said, "Your Pappa has worked very hard all his life to make a good business so he could give you and Dee a big house and the good things to enjoy life. He knows the effort it takes, and he wants you and Dee to understand that. He was not happy when the university offered to enroll Dee because she is black and not because her grades meet the standard set for white folks. He believes the university is sending the wrong message, and you should not be fooled by it."

"The wrong message? What does that mean?"

"Well, I guess it means that if your Pappa and me and you and Dee are goin' to be equal citizens in this country, we have to be free to succeed or fail just like everyone else. He doesn't think we should be put in a special class that will be looked down on or that will be treated different because we're black. You know, Leo, when I grade the math tests in my classes, I don't look at a student's skin color to set his grade. How would you feel if your history teacher gave you an A just because you are black? Would that make you feel proud if you knew you had not answered the questions correctly?"

"No. But why did the university say they would take Dee in?"

"Now that's a good question, Baby. Oh, excuse me, Leo. The university and lots of other people believe they need to feel guilty because, years ago, black people were slaves in this country. So they think they must prove they are innocent, that slavery was not their fault, and somehow if they give black people something, they will feel better about themselves."

"That doesn't sound right to me," Leo replied. "Why do they feel guilty about something that happened a long time ago? Does everyone believe that?"

"I can't tell you what everyone believes, but there's lots of them, and some of them are black, who say every day that white folks should feel guilty. But I do know that handin' out something to someone because they are black is a way to make that black person feel inferior and not a full person. I know because it's happened to me before. That's why Pappa got upset about Dee. He loves her very much, and he does not want her to act like some poor victim who must be pitied all her life. He wants her and you to be proud and not depend on anyone to give you a handout. He wants you to be respected for what you do, not because someone else wants to make themselves feel good.

"Now I know you and Dee get treated wrongly sometimes, but you just get in there and work hard. Most people in this country will respect you for it. Condoleezza Rice, Barack Obama, and that Dr.

Carson, who ran for the Republican nomination, worked hard and they are respected for what they've done and not because they are black or white."

Turning into their driveway, Clara glanced at Leo. He nodded and said, "Okay, Mama, I got it. But boy! Dee is still not happy."

"So, Leo, why don't you explain it to Dee on the way to school tomorrow?"

FIFTY-FIVE

T hree hours of discussion and the review of recent court decisions had not removed the deep frown from Oliver's brow.
If anything, his reluctance to take up Leon's defense seemed
to be increasing as he and Bobby drafted their client's answer.

A general denial of Benjamin's claims was standard and necessary to put the burden on Benjamin to prove his allegations. They
agreed that the proof of Leon's authorship would be simple since
Leon had no basis to deny his creation. How Benjamin and his lawyer learned that Leon the Loper and Leon were one and the same was
yet a mystery, but Leon was not going to deny he wrote it.

Proof that the statements were false was Benjamin's problem,
but Bobby would have to prepare evidence to counter on that point,
hoping that the official records of Benjamin's statements at the council meetings in Fort Worth, Lamar, and elsewhere would convince the
jurors that Leon's opinion of his actions was accurate. The term *slave
master*, however, was going to be a challenge, which Oliver viewed as
the best reason to steer clear of the battle.

"How does one prove the truth of such a statement?" he asked,
shaking his head. "Bobby, Leon really has only one defense. If we can
persuade the jury to believe Leon when he says he never published
those two pages. I know he says he gave Clara a copy, but if that is all,
I don't think Benjamin can make his case."

Seated across the table, Bobby nodded. "I agree. That question must bother Colter also unless he's been able to trace how it all got on the internet. Even then, he'll have to prove that it was Leon's negligence which let it get out. We'll have to talk with Clara. Maybe she can tell us how it got out of her hands."

Oliver clasped his hands on the table, leaning toward Bobby. "I don't see how Colter can prove large damages here. In the first place, we can show that Benjamin is a public figure. He certainly has promoted himself all over North Texas and never misses a chance to get in front of a TV camera. And given his bombastic style and demands, Colter may find it problematical when it comes to showing that his reputation has been diminished to any significant degree. Finding creditable witnesses to prove that he is an upstanding and respectable citizen may be tough."

"I hope so," Bobby replied. "But don't forget that the NAACP and their cohorts are well versed in putting a noble spin on the so-called plight of the black people in this country. I'm sure Benjamin knows those folks very well."

With the answer completed on Oliver's office computer, Bobby assured Oliver that he would have Karen finalize it and e-mail it to the court clerk by Thursday, well ahead of Monday's response deadline.

FIFTY-SIX

T he *Star Telegram* runner, proud of his reputation as a blood-
hound, had checked the clerk's office daily, waiting for the
answer to be filed. He eagerly obtained copies of Benjamin's
pleading and the answer and lodged them in his battered briefcase he
toted every day.

Several blocks south, on Houston Street, he entered the paper's
offices and placed the filings on the city desk. A staff reporter had
already drafted the article based only on what was in the pleading.
Slave master caught his eye initially, and he awaited the answer before
putting the finishing touches to the article.

* * *

"Bobby, Judge Welton's clerk called. The judge wants you and
Malcolm Colter to visit with him in his chambers tomorrow at ten."

"Okay, Karen, but you'll have to cancel my eleven o'clock meeting with Mr. Peterson. I can't get back here by then."

The *Star Telegram* story Monday morning about Benjamin's
lawsuit reached the court's attention very quickly, Bobby thought.
Already he had listened to Becky's response. Certainly, the judge
could add little. Becky was not pleased that in just two days Bobby
was trumpeted as the intrepid defender of a litigant's cry for freedom.

Entering the main door of the new Civil Courts Building, not a hundred yards from the old 1898 Tarrant County Courthouse, Bobby was impressed. It was a far cry from the utilitarian arenas he was accustomed to in Fort Worth and Cleburne. The ad valorem tax collections in Tarrant County must certainly be on the rise, he mused, as he located the elevators leading to the fifth floor and Judge Welton's court. Over six months had passed since a client's business had called him to a Fort Worth court, and he had not seen Judge Welton in more than two years. He knew the visit would prove interesting and maybe unsettling.

Malcolm Colter, dressed in a dark-blue suit and expensive tie, stood alone near the rail fronting the judge's bench as Bobby entered the empty courtroom.

"Well, Mr. Sanborn, it's nice to see you," Colter greeted, holding out his large hand. "I believe the judge may have found our case interesting." He smiled broadly, perhaps signaling that he, or his office, may have had some earlier communication with the court.

Bobby grasped the offered hand and replied, "Nice to see you, Mr. Colter. Does the judge know we're here?"

"Well yes, but his secretary says he has someone in his chambers. Only a few minutes though."

Bobby nodded, surveying the large dark man who looked exactly like his pictures Bobby had seen in the media and in the *Texas Bar Journal*. He exuded charm and confidence, well suited to courtroom litigation.

The door at the side, near the judge's bench, swung open and the secretary announced, "Gentlemen, the judge will see you now." Not a grant of permission but an instruction, which both attorneys quickly heeded.

Judge Welton, the resident of the court bench for over twelve years, waved from behind his impressive desk, bidding the two attorneys to the two chairs facing him.

"I appreciate your coming to see me on such short notice. I know you both must be very busy."

Colter hurriedly replied, "Not at all, Your Honor. We know the court must be pressed for time also."

Bobby smiled and nodded. Was Colter going to represent both parties in the case?

The judge returned the smile and, wasting no more preliminaries, got to the point.

"This lawsuit you have filed, Mr. Colter, has reached this court by luck of the draw and, I am sorry to say, has reached the press almost as quickly. I find that the exchange of opinions between the litigators has gone viral, and now we find ourselves in a dispute which is apparently engaging hundreds, maybe thousands, well beyond this city."

The judge raised his hand, a Stop sign, as Colter began to reply.

"Just a moment. These observations are not made idly. The gist of the lawsuit revolves around a topic which may encompass much more than the personal dispute between your clients. I don't intend to turn my courtroom into a national debating contest, so there are going to be some rules—or guidelines if you prefer—governing the conduct of this case. Is that clear?"

Colter and Bobby both nodded, yet unsure what rules were being contemplated.

"First, to the extent that I am lawfully able to do so, I am going to restrict media presence at the trial. That is, no cameras and only a limited number of print reporters at any one time will be allowed in the courtroom.

"Second, I am requesting counsel to instruct clients and witnesses to refrain from talking to the media outside the courtroom. That will be difficult to monitor and enforce, I know, but I'm asking your cooperation, which will be greatly appreciated.

"Third, I ask you, as counsel, to likewise refrain from communicating with the media which, in any way, purports to present your client's claims or defenses. Those presentations must be made in court and under the rules of evidence. I do not need to be reminded of the Bill of Rights, freedom of the press, or freedom of speech. The case must be tried in that courtroom next door and not anywhere else even though many may try to do so.

"Finally, the jury will be carefully instructed, as always, to refrain from personal contacts outside the court which might influence them in any way."

He stopped, looking first at Colter and then at Bobby. "You first, Mr. Colter, since you represent the plaintiff."

"Well, Your Honor, certainly no one can disagree with your characterization of the case and its far-reaching implications. I assure you that I and my client will abide by your instructions as fully as possible." Colter's voice projected a deep resonance that seemed to echo off the walls.

Judge Welton's face creased in a smile. "Thank you, Counselor. I do hope you and your client find that possible."

Turning to Bobby, he said, "And you, Mr. Sanford, I haven't had the pleasure of you in my court for sometime. What is your view of this case?"

Taking the judge's apparent cue, Bobby responded with a smile, "Judge, I am honored to be here, but as you might expect, my client is not too happy about it. But I will indeed inform him of your instructions."

With that, the judge moved on. "Gentlemen, given what we have before us, I am asking that we put aside the standard discovery order and get this case ready for trial in just six months. I know you have busy schedules, but the longer this drags on, the more likely we are to have this one morph into a three-ring circus. Our justice system does not need or deserve that. My clerk will soon send you a proposed discovery order setting out deadlines for depositions, evidence discovery, and pretrial motions. If any of that gives you heartburn, let me know and we can meet here and discuss it. Thank both of you for coming."

With that, the lawyers rose, said goodbye, and exited.

Waiting at the down elevator, Colter inquired about the current affairs in Lamar and concluded the short conversation, "Bobby, I'm sure you understand that my client wants nothing but the best for his people and is deeply hurt by this charge which is bouncing around the internet. Surely there must be some way to resolve this without a court battle."

Bobby hesitated before he answered. Was the man a pitching for settlement? "Malcolm, if it can be resolved, I am all for it. But it is a little early in the game, don't you think? Two million dollars is a lot of money. I've never heard of a reputation worth that much."

Colter tossed back his head and laughed. "Touché, Bobby. Let's see where this leads us."

An exchange of goodbyes summed up their ride down the elevator and departure from the building.

FIFTY-SEVEN

The second January council meeting was uneventful although Bobby thought he detected more glances directed at him than normal. After Dub banged the concluding gavel, he motioned to Bobby and said, "Have you got a minute? I'd like to visit in my office."

"Sure. That was a short meeting. I've got plenty of time."

Waving to a few of the departing citizens and a couple of remaining staff, Dub led Bobby down the hall and into his office.

"Grab a seat, Bobby. Sorry I don't have any coffee to offer."

In their seats, Dub proceeded, "Bobby, I'm sure you know that most of the people in Lamar subscribe to the *Star Telegram* and maybe the *Tribune* also. And so your case in Judge Welton's court is not a secret."

"No surprise there, Dub," Bobby responded, already hearing what he feared when he determined to take on Leon's case.

"And," Dub went on, "even though most people may not remember Leon Harris, hell, most people didn't even live here then. Even so, that recent writeup places Leon squarely in the middle of Lamar, and I would expect that most people here will follow the suit very closely."

"Sure, the squabble is already on the internet. The judge is concerned about the ripples that are spreading."

"Yes, well, you remember our conversation awhile back about you running for mayor next year?"

"Sure, of course."

Dub shifted in his large chair and pulled a Kleenex out of a drawer. Wiping his forehead, he plunged on, "This suit could have a major influence on your campaign. Might help, might hurt. I'm not talkin' about whether you and Leon win or lose. I'm just sayin', bein' knee-deep in a racial controversy may resonate strongly with the voters, good or bad, I can't say. We've been fortunate that we've had no such squabble here. We have a diverse council, and I believe everyone is treated fairly in Lamar."

Bobby nodded, wondering if Dub had ever sat down and talked with Alece Jackson.

"Come on, Dub. I know it's more than my possible campaign you're concerned about. If it comes down to it, I'll forget about that. I have an obligation as a lawyer to represent Leon as best I can. I can't let any personal concern of mine get in the way."

"I understand that, Bobby. But you're right. It's more than that. Leon is being sued by that guy Benjamin. He was very upset that last time he came before the council, and I wouldn't be surprised if he comes back. If he does, I've got to ask you Bobby to sit out that meeting. I don't see how his appearance before you, sitting as a council member, could be good for Lamar or good for Leon."

There it was. Dub was not going to let Bobby, as a council member, kick up any dust in his city. Bobby agreed silently. It was something he had wrestled with before the second meeting with Leon. But the die was cast. His undivided devotion to Leon's case was essential.

FIFTY-EIGHT

The Harris House was not difficult to find. Occupying several acres on the east side of Riverside Drive, the thirty-foot-high warehouse seemed to sprawl back from the street. Bordered by broad driveways down each side, it easily accommodated a number of semi-rigs that were backed against the loading docks.

Bobby turned the Jeep into the small area in front marked Visitors. He had asked to meet at Leon's workplace in order to get a better feel for Leon's daily life and routine. It was obvious that Leon's long absence from Lamar had created a man who had evolved into a character unknown to Bobby.

Inside, the large space was filled with many colors and sounds as motorized loaders and carts moved in and out of long aisles and carried cartons, crates, and boxes to and from the loading docks and the tiered racks in the brightly lit arena. Bobby stood and watched a few minutes before Leon walked up and grabbed his arm. "Hey, Bobby, come on into the office. You could get flattened out here."

"Not a bad idea. Is it always like this? All this hustle and bustle?"

"Yeah, business has really been good since I got that big loan last year from the bank. We handle about twenty different customers now," Leon boasted, ushering Bobby into a group of offices off to one side.

Inside Leon's office, he was directed to a steel chair. As he sat down, Leon said, "It's a little quieter in here. Thanks for coming, Bobby. Well, how was the meeting with the judge?"

"Judge Welton has never been one for much small talk. He wanted to let me and Colter know that he is going to keep a tight rein on our case. I mean, he doesn't want either side talking to the press. He is not happy that your manifesto is bouncing around the internet. I'm not surprised, but some of your comments extend far beyond the specific remarks about Benjamin. It's not going to be easy to conduct this suit just as a defamation fight."

Leon nodded. "You got that right. I want to show you something I copied from the internet sometime back. It's about the Supreme Court's recent rehearing in that action Abigail Fisher filed against UT because of the program that caused my daughter to get so mad at me. The NAACP filed a brief with the court supporting the university. Here's what they said."

Leon held out a piece of paper to Bobby and sat back as Bobby began reading aloud, "Race is merely a fraction of one factor that admission officers may consider when looking at an applicant as a unique individual. UT's constitutionally permissible holistic review process recognizes the simple truth that race is still relevant in American society and that race may help shape and inform individual perspectives and experiences."

Bobby looked up and glanced at Leon, then returned to the page which stated that the NAACP brief had continued. "The long history of racial segregation in Texas creates a compelling interest for the university to seek racial and ethnic diversity in its student body."

Again, Bobby looked at Leon, who remarked, "What did I tell you, Bobby! My daughter was offered admission not because they considered her qualified under the standards set by the school for others. What happens to black boys and girls when they get in because of their skin color and later fail to get a degree because they can't make the academic grades? How do they feel when they are branded with failure just so the university can crow about how tolerant and understanding they are with their holistic view that dispenses pity for the plight of the blacks?"

"Okay, okay, Leon. But this talks about a unique individual and individual perspectives and experiences, doesn't it?"

"Bobby, that's bullshit, and you know it. UT never even interviewed Dee. All they know is she's black. All they know is her individual perspectives and experiences are presumably the typical perspectives and experiences of all blacks. The university wants only diversity of color, not diversity of individuals. It's only to satisfy its own self-gratification."

Bobby nodded, unsure how to respond to Leon's fervor, and said, "But what if the Supreme Court rules that the university's admissions program is lawful?"

"So what? That won't mean it's right. That won't mean my kids have to buy into the affirmative action game! And," Leon continued, "what about the diversity on UT's football team? By far, a majority of the players are black. Why not more white players to make the team holistic? I'll tell you why. It's because the football team is filled with players who have proven their individual ability. The players who have proven their own talent. No, sir, the coach doesn't put anyone on the A team because of the color of his skin. Why do you think every NBA team is filled mostly with black basketball players? Same thing."

Leon stared at Bobby, his mouth open, his eyes fixed.

"You have a point," Bobby warily replied. "I can see why you were upset at how Dee was treated. Has she come around? Does she understand?"

"Oh, she is speaking to me again. But how can I send her and Leo out into a world that wants to smother them in affirmative action? That crap doesn't affirm anything but the desire of some people to brag about how far they have come, how enlightened they are. They are not ready to look at a black man as an individual. It's just too easy to put him into a class characterized by the color of his skin."

"I know. I've seen the diversity game played at our city council. Not to mention, of course, Mr. Benjamin." Bobby was now recalling the concerns of Judge Welton, and he ventured a thought to Leon, "The judge, I think, has recognized the complaint in your manifesto, Leon. That's why he's worried about the other people jumping into this case. He's serious about us, you, me, Benjamin, and Colter keeping our sights strictly on the defamation claim."

"Well, good luck. My words have traveled far and wide. There's no way to take them back."

"Maybe so, but Benjamin wants the $2 million out of your pocket. No one on the internet is going to reach into his own pocket. Don't forget that."

Leon made no reply. He sat staring at the page that bore the remarks from the NAACP brief.

"Leon, we've got to get the case ready. The judge has issued a discovery order, and we don't have a lot of time. Colter and I are trying to work out a schedule for your deposition and Benjamin's deposition. To pull our case together, we will have to review the minutes and records of every council meeting that Benjamin has attended for the last several years to see what he said. We need to depose the officers of Benjamin's coalition in Dallas, and we need to find people who can tell us more about Benjamin and his background—does he have a good or bad reputation, have your words hurt his reputation. He already has the advantage of your words which brand him as a slave master. This is not going to be easy."

"I've never thought this would be easy, Bobby. Don't sell me short. Over the past forty years, black people have been happy to take everything the government and liberal white folks have offered. Government handouts for each child born to black mothers who didn't care about having, or keeping, a husband, social programs based on the past guilt of slavery. All bought and accepted because too many have been willing to trade their dignity and individual worth. I've never done that, and I don't want my children to do that. I have a successful business which I earned. No one gave it to me. It has brought home to me that so many black folks have sold out. They have let themselves become dependents, people who must rely on the guilt and actions of others to survive. Now that a black man has been elected to the White House, maybe even that guilt will go away and blacks will be left with nothing—no freedom and no opportunity."

Bobby was moved by a new emotion and angst as he left and headed south to Lamar. Maybe Judge Welton had seen more in the lawsuit than Bobby. Leon's manifesto was posing a confrontation between a movement that had put Obama in office and an unknown force that feared the growing fallout from the Johnson Civil Rights era. If Leon was correct, the Obama years had served only to propel the trend which Leon obviously feared. Did the manifesto really get out to the public by mistake? How was he going to prepare for such a battle? Had his own meager statements around city hall merely been hollow bombast? Was he capable of leading Leon's charge?

FIFTY-NINE

The depositions of the two opponents, Harris and Benjamin, were completed by the end of April. Neither was pleasant, seasoned with anger, objections, and threats to take motions to the court. Each litigant's education, family history, and life's travails up to the modern day filled the long days. Bobby was pleased that Leon's path reflected the story of hard work and success in contrast to Benjamin's career as an activist, closely associated with appearances before eager television coverages of every racial slight occurring in North Texas, whether real or perceived. Yet the question remained, how would a jury of the litigants' peers view each of them? What black jurors would be seated, and what would be their take on this racially charged tug-of-war? And how would white and Hispanic jurors approach the case?

All these questions rolled through Bobby's head at the Wednesday-night council session, competing against the city's business. The presentation of next year's budget carried ominous concerns about the employee's pension plan, still unresolved.

At the close of the meeting, Carl Jeffers rose and walked over to Bobby's chair. "Bobby, you got a couple of minutes to talk?"

"Sure, Carl. Let me get my stuff together, then let's go to your office."

Rain splashed on the windows of Carl's office, lending a somber mood, as they each took a seat.

"I don't mean to meddle in your affairs, Bobby, but Jim told me something this morning that you ought to know. He said he ran into Alece Jackson last week, and Alece started rambling about a meeting he had with that Benjamin guy you're in court with. Alece had gone to a meeting of that coalition group in Dallas back last winter, I guess, and this Benjamin started spouting off. He was mad about someone called Leon the Loper who was circulating lies about him. Alece began laughing and told Jim that he said to Benjamin, 'Yeah, I know him. He's a dude that used to play football in Lamar.' Anyhow, Alece told him all about Leon and what a big star he was in high school."

Carl stopped and looked at Bobby as Bobby slapped a hand against his forehead.

"So that explains that," Bobby cried. "We never knew how Benjamin figured out who to sue. That's very interesting. Maybe I need to talk to Alece. I didn't know he was a friend of Benjamin."

"Oh yeah. Jim says the two have been working together for a long time. The coalition has even contributed pretty strongly to Alece's campaigns."

Bobby waggled his head, reflecting his chagrin at the news after laboring in the lawsuit for months and not being aware of that information.

"I hope that Leon's case is goin' okay, Bobby. That Benjamin and his kind are not doing anyone a favor, except him. If he ever shows up again at our council, I'll just walk out. I don't care what the mayor thinks."

"Thanks, Carl. It's a tough one. That news article in the *New York Times* last week was bad news. Seems like liberal activists are on the war path, and I wouldn't be surprised if they try to influence the trial somehow. Judge Welton thinks so. He called me and Benjamin's lawyer in to talk about it. Frankly, he raised hell about the *Times* reporter's suggestion that Al Sharpton might march to Texas to support Benjamin and his good work for the Civil Rights Movement."

"I read that article, Bobby. Seems to me that they are mustering the troops to defeat Leon. You know the NAACP didn't pull any punches in that article last month in the *Dallas Morning News*. What are you going to do if someone like Sharpton shows up here?"

"I don't know yet. Leon has given me the names of several black writers who share his views. Maybe one of them would be willing to speak for Leon. But I've got to be careful. As I said, the judge is not happy with the publicity that is growing. It wouldn't be much help for Leon if I got thrown in the pokey."

"That would be something. Think of the headlines that would create."

SIXTY

Walking back to his office, Bobby was lost in thought. Amazing! Leon was being sued because of the off chance of Alece and Benjamin discussing the mysterious Leon the Loper. What if the conversation had never taken place? Would Benjamin ever have learned the identity of the man who called him a slave master? But now, Leon's authorship was not an issue. His recent deposition had crystalized the fact that Leon was eager to have his views touted to the world. Was a copy of the manifesto deliberately placed in Clara's purse with the hope it would fall into someone's hand? That was a question he did not intend to pursue with Leon. But Colter would not hesitate to toss that suggestion into the jury box. As Bobby pondered whether he should engage an internet expert to rebut Colter's inevitable effort to trace the manifest's route to the internet, a shout greeted him.

"Hey, Bobby! Whatcha doin', roamin' around this late?"

Alece Jackson, with a broad smile, waved from his office door.

"Hey yourself, Alece. I was just goin' to my office to collect some stuff and head on home."

"Me too. But you got a minute? You know that amendment to the financial policy is still floatin' around, and I hope you've come to where you can support it at our next meeting. You know the folks in the Camp deserve to share the growin' economy here in Lamar. That's just right."

"I don't know, Alece. We've already got in place the MWBE program. You heard that report tonight. Over 20 percent of our capital projects are employing minority and women contractors, most of them black-owned businesses. How far can the city go in directing taxpayer money to a particular group?"

"Come on, Bobby. That's not goin' to build any grocery stores in the Camp. That MWBE program only puts money into the contractors, and all the projects are on this side of the of I-35. That's no help to my folks."

Standing in the doorway to Alece's office, Bobby could almost hear Benjamin shouting amen as the words flowed from Alece. He responded, his voice rising, "Alece, handing out city money just because someone's economic situation is less than someone else's will not solve anything. Socialism is not the answer."

"Yeah, I've heard that before. Sounds like your client, Leon Harris!"

Bobby flushed and then retorted, "Well, Alece, why don't you talk to Leon? Maybe he can explain it better than I can."

As Bobby pushed off the doorjamb and turned to the hall, Alece fired back, "Yeah, Leon will find that some people don't appreciate him actin' so high and mighty."

In the Jeep, with the wipers rhythmically sweeping the windshield, Bobby reflected on the debate with Jackson. Was he merely repeating the mantra of Benjamin and the coalition, or did he really believe his remarks? And what about the MWBE program? A deliberate policy of the city to direct capital funds into the hands of blacks and women, supposed minorities who were unable to participate in the construction of city projects because of past and lingering prejudices? Was the program helping them or just condemning them as a class of incompetents and underachievers? There was no doubt about Leon's view of that question.

SIXTY-ONE

As Becky prepared rice and shrimp for the next day's supper, Bobby sat at the kitchen table, watching the 10:00 PM news on channel 5.

"Anything interesting happen at council this evening?" Becky asked, slipping the food into the refrigerator.

"No, just more talk and concerns about our new budget and—"

"And what, Bobby? Bobby?"

Becky turned to see Bobby staring at the small television screen on the kitchen counter. A number of people appeared to be marching in a tight circle, waving signs, and shouting, right fists clenched and thrust overhead.

Bobby cautioned, "Quiet, Becky. Look at this!"

The signs were crudely lettered and read Black Lives Matter and We Will Succeed. Bobby frowned as one black man turned and flashed a sign stating, Leon Must Go.

"Hell, they are marching in front of the courthouse in Fort Worth," Bobby cried, rising from his chair. Just then, the scene shifted to the news desk at the studio as the man facing the camera commented, "Well, Laura, it seems that the lawsuit filed by the Dallas civil rights activist has caught a few people's attention."

"That's right, Roger. More than two dozen activists were at the courthouse this afternoon, and our Don Long was there."

The screen was again filled with signs and marchers, showing a reporter approaching a large black man who held the sign referring to Leon.

"What is it that you and your fellow marchers are protesting, sir?"

"This man Leon Harris is not one of our brothers and he is malignin' our folks. Black lives do matter, and we deserve better treatment!"

"Are you referring to the man who has been sued here in this court?"

"Yeah. He sold out, don'cha know?"

"Where are you from, sir?"

"I come from Dallas. We don't appreciate what he is sayin'."

The scene shifted once more to the studio.

"This doesn't look as though it's going to be a quiet battle, does it?"

"No. It has already been the subject of news articles in the paper, and it is still a couple of months before the trial starts. We will have to keep an eye on it."

The news commentators turned to another subject. Bobby sat, staring at Becky. "This is exactly what Judge Welton warned us about. He won't be happy to see it has landed at the front door of the courthouse."

Becky frowned and shook her head, flinging her blond hair in a whirl. "Did you see that sign? The one that man was holding? What does he mean that Leon must go? Are they making a threat? Are they going to hurt him?"

"What? Oh, that's just a lot of bluster. Leon's diatribe has stirred up a lot of talk."

"Well, I don't like this, Bobby."

The vibrator on Bobby's iPhone signaled him, and he looked at the screen, nodding to Becky.

"Hello?"

"Bobby, have you seen the evening news?" Oliver's voice shot forth in a strident beat.

"Yes, we were just watching it."

"This is not good, Bobby. The judge is going to be madder than hell. If this goes on, how are we going to get a fair jury? Most the black folks in Fort Worth are gonna want to hang Leon. The $2 million won't be enough."

"This won't help us. I agree, Oliver. Defamation might not be the only issue."

"Bobby, let's get together in the morning. I think we should ask the judge for a mistrial."

"A mistrial? Benjamin won't just go away, Oliver. Colter will only file again."

"Well, if that won't work, surely the judge will order a change in venue. How can we pick a jury with a mob marching outside the door?"

"Maybe. But I don't know where the case could go. The news media is just going to follow us. At least Leon is a Fort Worth man with a business. He would be a stranger in another town."

"Okay, okay. You may be right. But we damn sure better find some way to counter these sign toters, these people the TV likes to glorify as activists. I'll bet that guy from Dallas was recruited by the coalition. Benjamin has been in the business a long time. He was happy enough to brag about it in his deposition."

* * *

Bobby was not surprised by the 10:00 AM call from Judge Welton's clerk. He and Oliver were promptly seated in the judge's chamber at 2:00 PM as the judge strode in, a scowl marking his visage. Dressed in a dark-gray suit and red tie, he wasted no time.

"Gentlemen, as often as I admonish my juries to ignore the news media and television while discharging their duties, it may surprise you to learn that I do not practice what I preach. I was viewing the ten o'clock news last night, and I witnessed a spectacle at the courthouse door yesterday afternoon. Do you know what I am talking about?"

Bobby and Oliver and muttered, "Yes, sir," glancing at Colter to see him also nod.

"Good. But not everything appeared on the TV screen. One of my clerks was on her way home, and as she came out of the building, she observed a man viewing the scene from across the street."

The judge turned his gaze on Colter. "It was your client, Mr. Colter."

Colter sat silently.

"As you may recall, Counsel, we discussed this point several weeks ago. I find it very disturbing that a litigant in this court was seen at yesterday's disturbance. Since the Reverend Benjamin resides in Dallas, it is hard to believe he was in Fort Worth on a shopping spree."

Colter stirred, turning one of his hands. "Judge, I assure you that I have advised my client about your concerns and I have directed him to avoid the media. I certainly was unaware he was in Fort Worth yesterday."

"Mr. Colter, your client, no doubt, enjoys freedom of speech and freedom of travel, as do all our citizens, but I again admonish you and you other gentlemen. Picking a jury in this case will be difficult enough without the weight of issues best left outside of the court. I will take a very dim view of any efforts to detract from the case at hand, and I will take whatever action within my power to limit such activity, including sanctions against parties and counsel. Am I clear?"

Walking to Bobby's Jeep, Oliver ventured, "I take the judge at his word, Bobby. Maybe we should reconsider a motion to change venue. He's not happy with Benjamin."

"Yeah, he was sure upset. If Benjamin pulls another stunt, we may want to do that."

"I don't believe he will resist the temptation to stage another act," Oliver concluded.

SIXTY-TWO

On Capitol Hill, only a few blocks east of the Library of Congress, the "Shack" occupied the southwest corner on a quiet street that once claimed stately postbellum residences. It now served an ever-growing phalanx of federal agency buildings and boutique law offices. For more than one hundred years, the small restaurant had offered delicious crab meat, hauled from Chesapeake Bay and served steamed, diced, and covered with a special red sauce. Senators, representatives, their staffs, and out-of-town constituents claimed its tables for lunch every day.

It was business as usual when a black Lincoln Town Car cruised quietly to a halt before the restaurant's modest entry. A well-dressed, stately man unfolded from the rear seat, waved to the driver, and strode up the two steps leading to the weathered front door.

Inside, Caleb Fontaine beamed, seeing the man as he entered.

"Well, good day, Senator. We haven't seen you in sometime. Welcome."

The Senator returned the smile and extended his hand to clasp the hand offered by the maître d'. "How are you, Caleb? I've missed seeing you. Hope the crab is tasty as always."

"Yes, sir, Senator, only the best for you." Tall and black as ebony, Caleb wore his twenty-year tenure with erect posture.

"I expect you want your usual table, Senator. Let me get Jasper to seat you."

"Thanks, Caleb. Hope your family is doing well." The Senator nodded as he turned and directed his steps toward the small back room, lined with the portraits and photographs of past congressmen.

Seated at the table in the far corner of the imposing room, he glanced at his Rolex watch, confident that his dining mate would not be far behind. In the next moment, a balding man glided across the elegant carpet and nodded at the Senator before he sat in the single chair facing the wall.

"Sorry, Rick, the traffic was worse than I expected."

"No problem, Floyd. I just got here myself. DC is growing every day, a lot busier than when we arrived, what, almost sixteen years ago. In fact, I've got to be back at the Senate Building in an hour, so our lunch will have to be short."

"Sure thing. What's our agenda today?" Floyd Grimmer had known Senator Richard Harbaugh since they were in grade school together, and he was accustomed to every mood and desire which drove the Senator, both in Washington and on the campaign trail at home in Alabama.

Signaling Jasper to approach and take their order, the Senator replied, a scowl lining his brow, "I guess you saw that *New York Times* article the other day about that defamation suit that Benjamin filed in Texas. It may be a problem. Benjamin always jumps before he thinks, and now we've got a debate about the rightful place of African Americans. It is stirring up the media, not just in New York but in many places. I've seen a copy of Harris's deposition which was taken by Colter last week. If he is telling the truth about his motivation in writing the piece that upset Benjamin, his testimony at trial could ignite half the black people in the county."

Floyd squinted through his rimless glasses, a slight curl on his upper lip at the mention of African Americans, a term he and Rick had rarely heard during their school days. He replied in his Southern drawl, "Yeah, I read it. That Harris fella sure poked Benjamin with a sharp stick. But we we've heard it all before."

The Senator nodded. "True enough. But pronouncements from black professors and editorial writers don't get much attention after a day or two. This may be different. Benjamin, or someone, got a bunch of folks to demonstrate at the courthouse yesterday, and as usual, the media won't let it go."

The Senator paused to take a sip from his wineglass at his elbow and went on, as if on cruise control, "Harris's little blurb has gone viral on the internet. Some of my staff were talking about it yesterday. Floyd, being the party whip in the Senate means I've gotta pull every string I can to keep the African Americans supporting the party. If only 10 percent of them were to go the other way, we could lose a lot of congressional seats, including mine! Why do you think I support every civil rights push by Jackson and Sharpton and every bill that supports affirmative action programs to send money to the black communities? This crazy nut in Texas may be starting a crusade that could end up on our back porch." He stopped and raised the wineglass again.

"Okay, Rick, but what can we do about it?" Floyd asked, shifting in his seat with the discomfort of a man knowing what was coming next.

"I want you to get down there and find out all you can about Harris and his lawyer, Sanford. I have already gotten some of the civil rights crowd to send cash to Benjamin. You know that National Action Network and Rainbow Push Coalition aren't the only ones that bring us the black vote. But it's a two-way street. I must do more if I want to hold on to their support. So you need to check their history, their police records, and anything else that can be used to back Harris and his lawyer into the swamp. They could be very dangerous. We need to get under their skin somehow."

* * *

Before 3:00 PM, Floyd confirmed an evening flight to DFW on American Airlines. As an old pal and a longtime gofer for Harbrough, he was on the move every week. Tiresome but it made a good living for someone that had not been able to afford a college degree. The Senator's muted tone at lunch, designed to hide their discussion from other diners, had not dampened the agitation in his voice, and he clearly expected Floyd to garner information sufficient to put a stop to the Harris problem, as it was labeled by the Senator. Floyd had poured water on Rick's fires before, assisting the Senator's program of promising more to the blacks to assure their loyalty to the party's candidates. However, the latest outcry from Rick and his associates for new legislation to dole out restitution for the shame of slavery struck Floyd as too radical. How could anyone justify taking dollars out of Floyd's pocket when he and his ancestors had never owned slaves? Righting the scales made good press, yet why should he pay? He never tipped the scales. Rick had yet to answer that question or even to admit that is was a legitimate concern.

An hour into the flight, he pulled a pad from his briefcase and listed the public records he intended to review in Texas. Surely, Leon Harris had left behind tracks which he hoped would remain hidden from the public.

SIXTY-THREE

Samuel Franklin Madison, Professor Emeritus, was very pleased with his position as a Fellow at the American Policy Institution, but on occasion, he missed the give-and-take with the students at Howard University. At sixty-seven years, he felt as though his best days were yet ahead of him. After leaving the university, he finally concluded his book, and it was selling modestly, enough to supplement his salary at the Institution.

Race relations in the country were in flux, as always, and each year he was compelled to review and revise his signature course which educated, and he hoped, guided the black student body at Howard. That journey, coupled with his own life experiences, had inspired his book, *Where We Are*. Ongoing studies at the Institution, in Indianapolis, now offered the opportunity to fine-tune his thoughts and provided many avenues through which to observe current events which constantly confirmed the thesis of his book.

His daily review of news items had led to the story in the *New York Times* about the unique lawsuit in Fort Worth. The Leon the Loper diatribe struck a chord, and he was not surprised a week later to learn of the demonstration at the courthouse. Only a few minutes were needed on his office PC to ascertain the name, address, and telephone number of Leon's lawyer.

"Mr. Sanford, my name is Sam Madison. I am calling from Indianapolis. If I am not intruding, I would like to talk to you about your case involving Leon Harris."

Bobby heard the soft, high-pitched voice and wondered why anyone in Indianapolis cared about the Harris case.

"Yes, Mr. Madison. What can I do for you?"

"Well, Mr. Sanford, I am what is sometimes referred to as an African American, among other things, and I am a Fellow at the American Policy Institution. I have read the statement by Leon Harris, which is getting a lot of attention, and I am both impressed and curious. You see, the remarks by Mr. Harris are similar to some thoughts I have expressed in a book I recently published titled *Where We Are*. It is about race relations in America, then and now."

Madison halted, waiting for Bobby's reaction.

"Ah, I see. Do you think he may have read your book? He's not mentioned it to me."

"I guess that's possible. But the reason I am calling is because I am going to be in Dallas next week for a meeting. If possible, I would appreciate the opportunity to come to Fort Worth and talk to Leon and you, of course. Maybe I can assist you in preparing your case."

Bobby gritted his teeth as he replied, "Mr. Madison, I know Leon's words have gotten some attention, but this case is really about a defamation claim. You are not a lawyer, are you?"

Madison laughed. "No, I am not, but I taught a course on race relations for years, and it occurs to me that some insight on that question might be helpful to Mr. Harris."

"Okay, Mr. Madison. You are certainly welcome to come by, but we don't anticipate hiring any expert witnesses in this case."

"Oh, I'm not proposing that I present any testimony. In fact, any help I can offer would be without any charge. You'll merely have to decide if my thoughts are worth your time."

Bobby laid the phone aside. He would need to tell Oliver that a volunteer was arriving in a few days. Who was next? Al Sharpton?

SIXTY-FOUR

At the edge of the rear parking lot, Bobby stopped to check the passing traffic. Turning the wheel, his attention was captured by the melody of his phone. It was from Becky.

"On your way home, Bobby, will you go to the Walmart on I-35 and pick up some medicine I ordered at the pharmacy yesterday? You know the drill."

"Yes, Captain. Anything else?"

"No, I shopped this afternoon. That's all."

The parking lot was unusually crowded. Gazing for a parking spot, Bobby failed to notice the tall, slim black boy who was pushing a line of shopping carts toward the Walmart entrance. He was startled when the boy tapped on the Jeep's fender.

Bobby hit the brake and rolled down the window. "Wow, I am so sorry. I didn't see you." The boy grinned and walked over to face Bobby.

"Hey, Mr. Sanford. That's just part of the job."

"Well, it could have been bad. How do you know my name?"

"Oh, I've been to some of the council meetings in Lamar. My uncle is on the council. Alece Jackson."

"Your Alece's nephew? What a coincidence. I don't think Alece would be happy if I ran over you. How long have you been working at Walmart?"

"I'm a senior at Paschal High. I just work here on the weekends and some evenings. Usually in the stockroom, but as you can see, the parking lot has gotten backed up."

"That's for sure. What's your name?"

"My name's Elisha Freeman, Mr. Sanford. Alece is my mom's older brother. I'm savin' up so I can go to UTA next year."

"Well, I'll bet Alece is proud of you, Elisha."

"I hope so. But Uncle Alece is still not happy with some of my ideas. Says I'm not fightin' hard enough to get what is owed to me. All I want to do is get a degree and maybe go on to graduate school someday."

"Good for you! I'll bet you'll do it too. But be careful out here."

Bobby watched as the tall youth returned to his task and moved the long line of carts down the driveway, carefully avoiding the cars. Elisha and his schooling ambitions would strike a happy note with Leon.

SIXTY-FIVE

"I put the medicine on your vanity, Becky," Bobby announced, walking into the kitchen.

"Thanks, sweetheart. Did you talk yet to Leon about the demonstration at the courthouse?"

"No, not yet. He's still tied up with the contractor who is making some changes in Leon's warehouse. Maybe tomorrow. I'm sure he's heard about it. I've got to warn him away from any thought of trying to respond, whether or not Benjamin provoked it. The judge won't tolerate much more of that kind of stuff."

He opened the refrigerator and pulled out a beer, popped the cap, and sat at the kitchen table.

"You know, Becky, this case makes me wonder where we are headed. I mean, the whole world. Protest, marches all over the country, and now we've got a race dispute which has Dub on edge. You'd think our own problems at city hall would be enough in a small town." He swallowed a sip of beer.

"Oh yeah, I almost forgot. While I was at the Walmart, I came very close to running over a black kid working in the parking lot. It was a nephew of Alece Jackson. Can you believe that?"

"How do you know Alece's nephew?"

"I don't. But he recognized me and introduced himself. We started talking. A nice kid, tall. Doesn't look at all like Alece."

He tipped the bottle again and continued, "I got a strange call at the office today. A man named Madison. Says he's interested in Leon's case. Wants to come and chat with me and Leon. That thing Leon wrote is inviting a reaction from all over the damn country."

"Why does he want to talk to you?"

"I'm not sure. He said he wrote a book that somehow parallels what Leon wrote. Crazy. If he had written a book about defamation, I could see why he might be helpful. I guess we'll find out. He'll be here next week. He is in Indianapolis. Works for some institution there. A think tank, I guess."

Becky moved to the table and set a plate in front of Bobby.

"Here you go, Counselor, your favorite shrimp and rice."

He smiled and nodded, absently wondering if the lawsuit was moving into an arena far removed from his comfortable experience as a small-town lawyer.

SIXTY-SIX

The week passed quietly, with routine city business, small legal problems, and fortunately, no more demonstrations. The call from Indianapolis had almost been forgotten when the man arrived late Tuesday afternoon. Small in stature, with a trim figure, he stepped boldly into the conference room, a broad smile dominating his lined face. Grasping Bobby's hand with a firm grip, he thrust forward with his left hand a business card.

"Thank you, Mr. Sanford, for letting me come. Your directions were very helpful. I've not been outside Dallas before."

The open air of confidence surprised Bobby. Think tank Fellow was something his imagination had pictured as a stuffy academic sort.

"I'm happy you found us, Mr. Madison. Lamar is sorta hidden by Fort Worth and Dallas."

"Yes, I suppose so. But please, I hope you will call me Sam now that we have met. Informality makes for easier communication and more candid conversation, at least in my experience." Madison's face was split by his broad smile and even white teeth.

Bobby returned the smile. "Okay, Sam. And I am Bobby. Straight talk has always worked around these parts. But I have to tell you, Leon couldn't make it today. Tied up at his business. So I hope you can stay over tonight. I booked a room for you at the Ramada Inn."

"That's fine. I'm not going back to Indianapolis until the end of the week. I welcome the chance to visit with you and Leon. As I told you last week, race relations constitute a large part of my life, both personally and as an academic subject. I guess you might say I have seen the subject from all sides. I think Leon's case has thrust it onto your doorstep, a bit unexpectedly perhaps."

Bobby laughed. The man didn't waste any time getting to it.

"I can't argue with that, Sam. Race has never been a big topic here, at least among the majority of the people who have grown up in this small town. If you've read much about the case, you know Leon and I played football together in high school. We were friends, and still are. That's why he asked me to be his lawyer. But to be honest, I'm not sure I understand what he has stirred up or why. There was a demonstration, a march maybe, a few days ago. It was not just about race. Some of those folks were out to threaten Leon."

Madison nodded, the smile gone, and placed both of his palms on the table. His hands appeared to be those of a young man despite his age. "The relationship between white people and black people in the US has been shaped by history, Bobby. It runs deep, and it is changing. Some think it is changing too slowly, and some think it is changing too fast. And from the black man's standpoint, it is most always quite personal." The hands on the table turned and moved in chorus with the words.

Bobby sat quietly, nodding only to encourage Sam.

"What Leon has written goes to the very essence of the dichotomy we find on that issue in this country. The US was founded on the principle of freedom—freedom from an oppressive, dominating government and, therefore, freedom of the individual in society. It is that principle which has attracted immigrants from around the world for 250 years. But many black men and women came to these shores not because they sought freedom but because they were in chains and had no hope of freedom."

Madison took a sip of the coffee which was before him, carefully eyeing Bobby to discern his reaction. He continued, "I don't intend to sound as if I am lecturing at the university, but it is all part of trying to explain why I think Leon has been sued by another black man and why that demonstration happened at the courthouse."

"No, no. I understand," Bobby demurred.

The smile returned as Sam continued, "The clash between ideal and fact was not lost on the founders of the country, but it was not resolved. Slaves constituted such a potent economic factor in many of the states, the authors of the Constitution tacitly avoided addressing the issue for fear that it would disrupt the unity of the states necessary to establish a central government. Maybe that was one of the first efforts to, as we say, kick the can down the road. And so came the Civil War and then the Great Emancipation. But even that trauma did not put all square with the freedom tenet. Then moving another one hundred years, there was the Civil Rights Act, under President Johnson, not an act to declare black men free, but an act hopefully to prohibit citizens from treating black men as if they were not free. And that act has generally worked well. So what is the problem?" Madison raised his eyebrows, wearing a Socratic facade of a professor.

Bobby smiled and answered, "Ah, so you're going to tell me, right?"

With a deep chuckle, Sam responded, "No, I'm going to let Leon tell you. In fact, I suspect he has already told you. Am I right?"

Bobby shook his head. "I have a lot to learn, Sam. We've got to be ready for trial in six weeks. I have to understand the issues, the questions the jury must answer, and then I've got to select a jury. How are black jurors going to view this case and the same for white jurors?"

Nodding, Sam said, "Right. So can we meet tomorrow with Leon? He needs to be a part of the discussion."

"You bet. He is coming at nine in the morning. Let's do this. Why don't we get you checked in at the hotel and then come and have dinner with Becky and me? She may have more questions about all this than I do."

SIXTY-SEVEN

The eggs and toast were finished when Becky leaned toward Bobby, putting her hand over his.

He looked at her somber face and put his other hand on hers. "What is it?"

"When I was in Fort Worth on Monday, I had lunch with Libby. You know, that student hangout on University Drive. She was chatting about her classes, and somehow she began talking about Josh. You know, I told you she mentioned him several weeks ago."

His attention was quickened. "And so?"

"You won't believe this, but she was complaining that he always seemed kind of distant, as if he didn't find her company, I guess, enticing was the word she used. Anyhow, I asked her why she was talking about Josh again. It's been almost six months since he died. She said she just missed him so much but could not understand his attitude. Then she said, 'I know he was older than I am, but sometimes he would just kiss me on my cheek, like a little sister.' Well, I almost fell off my seat."

"Oh boy, what does that mean, Becky?"

"Bobby, maybe I shouldn't have, but I asked her if she meant that their relationship had been totally platonic. She said yes and asked me if she was so unattractive that maybe she would never get married. She was downright miserable. I put my arms around her and told her she had nothing to worry about."

"Well, that answers a lot of questions. That's a lot off my mind."

"Okay. What a day this will be. I'm meeting at the office with Oliver, Leon, and Sam. By the way, what did you think of the professor?"

"He is very charming. He ought to be a real help. When you called about supper yesterday, I googled him. He has a PhD and taught at Howard University for more than twenty-five years. It's probably the premier black university in the country."

"It's in DC, isn't it?" Bobby asked.

"Yes, it was founded in 1867."

"Then I suppose Sam knows what he is talking about when it comes to race in America."

SIXTY-EIGHT

Karen had arranged coffee, tea, and a large display of toast, doughnuts, and pastries on the sideboard, which stood just below the *Federal Reporters*, on the only side of the room that was not totally covered by bookshelves.

"Help yourselves, gentlemen," Bobby invited, pointing to the sideboard. I've also got lunch coming in later, so we can have a full day's work."

Leon turned toward Bobby with a blank look. "And you're charging by the hour, all day?"

Sam laughed loudly, "What, is this your first venture with the world of lawyers, Leon?"

"No. But I've got a business to run. So I hope I won't be here too long, right, Bobby?"

Well before noon, much of the sideboard spread was depleted as Bobby looked at Sam. "We've covered the pleadings, the defamation issue, the judge's declarations, and where we go from here to get ready for trial. I think you have the complete picture, Sam, and now we would like your input on the overhanging race questions. Like it or not, Oliver and I will have to deal with that the minute we walk into the courtroom."

Sam turned to the other three.

"Much of the issue lies in the fact that times have changed, much for the better I say. Leon has read my book, so he understands what I am saying. He has lived a great deal of it. I'm confident that you and Oliver will read it also, so I won't summarize all of it.

"But with twenty years of teaching the subject to young black students and learning a great deal from them, I have had the chance to view this country and race relations from a historical perspective. A perspective, I'm sorry to say, which is unknown to many people who are content to treat this problem with blinders on. Yesterday, Bobby, I mentioned the Civil Rights Act and what strides we have made, but the country is still struggling. Why?"

Leon listened intently, rocking back in his chair, glancing at Bobby and Oliver as Sam continued, "I think it is because, in spite of all the progress, too many black people have yet to find, have yet to understand, and have yet to enjoy what I call the dignity of freedom. Freedom is the very bedrock of this country. No one can live here and be a full member of US society if they do not carry the dignity that is the basis of freedom. When I say dignity, I mean the pride and self-respect of achieving, or failing, by one's own effort. When you achieve, or fail, because of the effort of another, you have earned no self-respect, you have no dignity. And you are not free because you must depend upon someone else to achieve a goal, and maybe you even must depend upon someone else to set those goals."

Sam looked straight at Leon. "This young man knows exactly what I'm saying. Hell, this is what he wrote. This is what he meant when he lambasted the Reverend Benjamin."

Leon, face beaming, nodded vigorously.

Sam spoke again, "Leon may have difficulty explaining all this to his eighteen-year-old daughter because she hasn't studied American history like her father, and she has not lived in the outside world like her father. But bless you, Leon, she has a father who can teach her."

"But, Sam, UT is only is only trying to help Dee," Bobby interjected. "They want her to come to the university. What's wrong with that?"

"That's what they say, Bobby. Their last brief to the Supreme Court and the many amicus briefs supporting the university all declared how beneficial a holistic view is in creating a diverse student body, a diverse society. That is the mantra of the affirmative action movement. But it is founded upon one's membership in a class, a class of black people, or a class of some minority. Affirmative action does not look at the individual. It does not cater to individual dignity. Once classified as slaves, black people are now classified merely as victims, a class which must be given jobs, must be given economic advantages not earned by the individual's own effort, but only by the person's race. Forever classified but never honored for individual achievement.

"Political correctness demands affirmative action, but who is benefited? What is affirmative about it? The only affirmation is the washing of the guilt which PC seeks to place upon white citizens. It affirms nothing for the black man, except affirm his place as a nameless member of a pitied group."

Leon interrupted with an applause of his large hands.

Sam donned his professorial gaze and brought a quick halt to the show of approval. He continued, "Affirmative action has seduced not only those who seek resolution of white guilt, but it has also seduced a large segment of the country's black citizens. They applaud the unearned benefits which they too often demand with loud grievances. It is welcomed by those blacks who trade on white guilt and affirmative action in order to line their own pockets. Need I mention the Reverend Benjamin again? Where do Al Sharpton, Jesse Jackson, and others seek their daily bread?"

"Are you beginning to understand, Bobby, why you are witnessing demonstrations at the courthouse? Do you see why the NAACP spends thousands of dollars for attorneys to write amicus briefs to the Supreme Court?

"And what happens to the recipients of affirmative action? At some point, deep inside, they see the loss of their dignity and they are left to trade on political correctness, they clamor for it. I call PC personal cowardice. They have no individual stature, so they embrace the political correctness of race, the glory of ethnicity, afraid to offer their own self-worth. Instead, they demand respect, solely because of race. How often do you read about a person of color being criticized, and their only response is a claim of racial discrimination. Rather than competing in the give-and-take of the real world, they hide behind their color and claim immunity from criticism, immunity from their personal faults. They don't want equality. They want special treatment. But everyone knows you cannot demand respect. You must earn it."

"Okay, Sam. But surely not all black people are reduced to economic dependency, who trade on affirmative action programs and government benefits."

"No, or course not. I don't, Leon doesn't, but we are, unfortunately, a small minority. There is one exception. Blacks in the entertainment business. I mean acting, singing, dancing, professional sports, any area where the public recognizes and wants to pay for talented performance. But where are the blacks who are creating services, medical treatments, education, and all the other needs in society beyond mere entertainment? People like Dr. Carson. He worked, he achieved, and he understood the dignity of freedom. So I hope I have answered why."

A silence filled the room. Then Oliver, for the first time, joined into the conversation, "What you are saying, Sam, is that political correctness, affirmative action, welfare programs, and so forth are denying blacks the dignity of freedom?"

"Exactly, Oliver. You've got it."

"But who will buy that? Most of the Democrats and maybe half of the Republicans either preach political correctness or cringe for fear that they will run afoul of it. And people like Al Sharpton show up on every corner or TV to remind everyone what is politically correct. It is so prevalent no one is allowed to dissent even on a college campus."

"That's a question I ask myself every day," Sam replied. "Where are we if the country is so lost in seeking absolution from slavery? Will it end up, as Leon puts it, reslaving black people? Maybe Leon's trial is one arena where individual dignity can be discussed."

Oliver's face contorted as he responded, "Wow, sounds good, but Judge Welton won't sit still while we put race relations on the right track. He is going to ask the jury only a few simple questions. Did Leon publish his writing to anyone? Did Leon's writing defame

Benjamin? Did the writing damage Benjamin's reputation? And what amount of money would compensate for that damage?"

"I'm no lawyer, Oliver, but isn't the jury going to read what Leon wrote?"

"Sure, you bet Benjamin's lawyer is going to wave it in front of the jurors' eyes all day and talk about slave master."

"But what about Leon? Can't he explain the rest of it to the jurors why he wrote it, what he meant?"

Oliver replied guardedly, "Yeah, he can, to a certain extent, but the judge won't allow any speeches. He is even going to limit the number of press corps in the courtroom. He was not happy about the demonstration the other day."

"Ah, Oliver, then you will have to make sure that all the jurors are open-minded people, willing to listen to reason." Sam laughed and glanced at Bobby with a broad smile.

Bobby returned the smile and said, "Exactly what we do in every trial, Professor."

SIXTY-NINE

On the twenty-fifth floor of a new office tower in North Dallas, Malcom Colter's law office displayed an expensive decor of black leather and chrome, all capped by an impressive vista of the downtown Dallas skyline to the south. Jeremiah Benjamin was not impressed.

"Damn it, Malcolm. It's not the fees I'm mad about. The coalition has voted to spend whatever it takes, and we've got plenty of support from the Rainbow Push folks and the National Action Network. But how am I goin' to tell our friends that the judge thinks black folks should shut up and sit in the back, that he's goin' throw 'em in jail if they speak out for their rights? Who does he think he is?"

"Calm down, Benjamin. He's not goin' to throw anyone in jail. But you can't try a lawsuit in front of a judge that is mad at you. He's called us lawyers in twice. I told you the first time to stay away from the courthouse."

"Yeah, and I told you I'm not goin' to give up my right to walk down a public street. I've worked goddamn hard to be the president of the coalition, and I ain't about to let that Leon the Loper wreck that work with his talk about our brothers bein' responsible for discrimination. He's goin' pay me $2 million!"

Benjamin ceased his angry pacing and slumped into one of the chrome and leather chairs.

Colter sighed, adding, "Look, we've got a lot of work to get ready for trial. If we do it right, we'll put Leon in his place even if we don't get as much as $2 million."

"What? That's what I'm askin'."

"Yes, but it's up to the jury. And don't forget, our research shows he doesn't have that much. Nice cars, a big house, a business. But I'm tellin' you, a lot of it is mortgaged. He probably doesn't have $100,000 clear in the business."

"Maybe so, but I'm tellin' you, Mr. Lawyer, he is goin' to pay. Nobody is goin' to call me names and get by with it."

"All right, all right. Enough! Just make sure your people keep quiet until we get closer to the trial date. I may have another case someday in Judge Welton's court. I have to make a living too."

"I hope the trial is soon. That lawyer Sanford's got a lesson comin' too. Sittin' up in the council seat like some potentate when I was down there in Lamar. Alece says he won't help us."

SEVENTY

It was a small book, slightly more than two hundred pages, that fleshed out many of the thoughts which Sam Madison had expressed the prior week. Bobby glanced again at the inscription inside the front cover: "With admiration to a fellow colleague, Sam Madison."

"Oliver, have you read the book we got from Sam? I sat up most of the night, reading my copy."

"Only part of it, Bobby. He was nice to send it. His visit was very helpful. At least I think I grasp now what Leon was trying to say. But it's goin' be a tough job to get the story to the jury. I'll finish the book and use what I can to outline the voir dire questions."

"Good idea. When do you believe we will get the jury list?"

"I talked to the judge's clerk yesterday. She said she will have it to us by next week. That'll give us two weeks to prepare."

Bobby chuckled. "Still think we should have turned down the case?"

"Come on, Bobby, that's a moot point now. We've had tough ones before, but this may take the prize. One way or another, we will have an answer in a few weeks."

"Okay, I'll get off. I've got to get ready for council tomorrow night."

He looked one more time at the inscription. Was Sam suggesting that Bobby was worthy to be considered a "Fellow" at the

American Policy Institution? He smiled, remembering the intensity Sam had displayed amid the doughnut and pastry wreckage. Small wonder he had traveled to Lamar to meet Leon. That same ardor permeated *Where We Are*, especially in the opening chapters which ascribed racial tensions as a part of, and a result of, a national schism between modern-day conservative and liberal political camps. His illustrations were difficult to refute, given the pervasive political correctness which lay on the country like a sickening miasma. Madison's conclusion was that the rift was so ingrained in America the nation was in deep peril, with little hope of reaching common ground. The thought left Bobby sorely shaken.

He pondered again the recurring thesis of the book. Liberal depiction of a debt owed the black race, a guilt borne by all present-day whites, which was now embedded in the War on Poverty and the Great Society and enforced by the polemic of political correctness. He likened PC as a sword which quickly condemned any other view as racism. As the theme unfolded, Sam had opined that such a mind-set had largely replaced the malevolent paternalism of slavery with a benevolent paternalism of white guilt, a paternalism that benefitted whites, but resulted in pervasive damage to the nation's black families. He described it as both a denigration of the black's self-esteem (the dignity of freedom?) and a siren song leading blacks to identify themselves as a class of grievance and inferiority.

Bobby viewed with a new clarity the words of Leon's manifesto, which had addressed the same issues in only a few statements, concluding that Benjamin epitomized the protest politics seeking to cash in on the grievance mantra. He also realized how the term *racism* had been redefined by liberals to mean the use of race to harm a person of color, whereas the use of race as a factor to benefit a person was no longer racism but a laudable tool of affirmative action. That twist of the English language had ignited the fire in Leon.

In short, Sam believed the paternalistic condensation of white guilt and governmental social programs were causing infinitely more harm than good to blacks in America. Oliver was on the right track. How were they going to get that message across to the people in the jury? If they failed, it would be an easy step for the jury to award big money to Benjamin.

Yet stirred by the powerful words in the small book, he stared out the window, watching the few cars which slowly circled the square. Were Sam and Leon the only black citizens in the country who cried out for the dignity of freedom? Then he recalled the many appearances on TV of Dr. Carson and the response his story had elicited from a host of primary voters. Had the election of a black president awakened people to a new view, a view that judged people by their personal performance, not their color? Sam had not answered that question; he only offered the fervent hope that America would never abandon its touchstone of freedom.

SEVENTY-ONE

At supper, Becky, Libby, and Bobby reveled in the ease and joy of a quiet family dinner, knowing that the unanswered questions about Libby's relationship with Josh were behind them, and together they could now recall with love and fondness the tall young man they had known so briefly. Libby was relentless, however, in her newfound comradeship with Bobby, no longer just a loving, and sometimes stern, father. Bobby withstood it for a brief while before reminding her that she still could not escape his duty to oversee her actions, a duty born of his love for her. She simply smiled in delight.

Finishing the last bite of apple pie, Bobby spoke, "Before I forget, I got a call from Dave Mellon. He's that reporter from the *Star Telegram*. He's writing an editorial about Leon and he wants me to, as he says, put a face on it and fact-check a first draft he has completed. He's coming down in the morning."

Becky replied, "But, Bobby, I thought the judge was leaning on you to stay away from the press?"

"Yeah, well, Dave said he was not going to comment about the issues in the case, so we'll see."

* * *

Karen ushered Mellon into Bobby's office and quietly closed the door.

"Let's both of us sit in the armchairs, Dave. I don't want to talk across my desk like a lawyer," Bobby intoned, walking around his desk. "I guess your editor is finding Lamar a hotbed of news these days. Seems all the media is fascinated with Leon's lawsuit. The judge has certainly noticed that the press is interested."

"I understand, Bobby. We in the press are very much aware of Judge Welton's admonishment. That editorial in the *Times* awhile back caused a stir, but from what I can see, it has slowed down a bit."

"I hope you're correct. But I won't be surprised if we see some more demonstrations soon around the courthouse. The judge can't stop that."

* * *

Friday morning Bobby was finishing breakfast before going to the office. Becky closed the kitchen door as she stepped to her car in the garage, list in hand for the usual Friday-morning grocery trek.

Bobby mentally listed the tasks he needed to complete at the office. Time devoted to Leon's case was pushing more of the other files to the weekend.

The front door suddenly opened with a shattering slam against the doorstop.

"Bobby, Bobby, come here! Oh my god!" Becky cried in a high, shrill voice.

He bolted out the open door as Becky raced to the front of her idling car, the driver's side door still hanging open.

"What's wrong, Becky?" He saw nothing amiss with the car, and all was calm out on the street.

"Look at that," she demanded, pointing to the closed door on the front of the garage. Bobby gasped: "Nigger Lover."

It was scrawled obscenely in black paint across the door, underpinned with centipede legs, where some of the wet paint had run down before drying. The epithet, applied in haste during the night, seemed to scream at him.

"What in holy hell is this about, Bobby? I can't believe this."

"I don't know, honey, I don't know."

Bobby pulled out his cell phone and hit one of the buttons.

The patrol car arrived in less than five minutes, and two of the city's policemen clambered out to view the spectacle.

"When did this happen, Mr. Sanford?" the sergeant asked, walking up for a closer look.

"We just found it. Someone must have done this last night. We just found it."

"We'll take a look around and see if other paint, brushes, or something was left." He and his partner scanned the drive and the lawn, welcoming the chance to avoid any further conversation with the councilman.

Finding nothing, the sergeant returned to his car and began speaking into his radio mike.

Watching near the front door, Becky began trembling, clutching her hands, her knuckles white. Putting his arm around her shoulder, Bobby pulled her to her car. "Turn off the engine and let's go inside. Looking at this crap won't do any good."

They walked to the kitchen and slumped into the seats near Bobby's unfinished food.

"Who would do something like this, and why?" Becky wailed, staring at him.

With his head shaking, he blurted, "It must be that article Dave wrote, the one in yesterday's paper. Remember he went on and on about my friendship with Leon and my defense of the lawsuit."

"But we've never had any racial problems here. It must be some crazy people from Fort Worth or someplace."

"Who knows, honey. The suit has created a lot of publicity. I just don't know."

Rising from his seat, he took a step toward the door leading to the garage, glancing back at Becky. "I'm going to open the garage door so people can't see that stuff." He was quickly back in the kitchen.

"The policemen said they have finished the search and they left. The door is up. The sergeant said they may be back to do more. Maybe take an ink sample. I doubt—"

The sound of the telephone startled him in midsentence. He paused and put the receiver to his ear.

"Hello? Oh yeah, Dub, it's a mess. Yes, they were here but said they may come back for another look. What? You told them to forget it? Okay, I understand. Right, I will."

As he put down the phone, Becky asked, "Was that the mayor?"

"It was. Apparently, the sergeant called him from the patrol car. Dub is really concerned. He told the police to ignore it. He warned that we don't need any publicity about this. He asked that we keep the door up so it won't be seen. He is going to get someone over here to remove the sign or repaint the door. Whatever it takes."

Silently, they cleared the dishes and loaded the dishwasher.

"I'll forget about the office this morning, hon. Dub thought he could get someone here pretty quick."

She turned, and he was surprised to see a tear run down her cheek.

Less than an hour later, he responded to the front door bell and was surprised to see Estella Jiminez, a tiny grin on her bronze face.

"Bobby, we understand you have a paint problem." She stood, partially blocking the view of the man standing behind her.

"Estella. Yeah, but what—"

"The mayor called, asked if we could help." Turning her head over her shoulder, she nodded and added, "This is my husband, Jorge. He's a painting contractor. He's gonna fix your problem, okay?"

With several drop cloths hung strategically to block any view from the street, Jorge completed the painting of the entire door in an hour, and he and Estella departed, with profuse expressions of gratitude from Bobby and Becky. Jorge declined their offer of payment. "Mr. Sanford, we love Lamar as much as you, and we understand how painful this has been. Some people are no good."

In the house once more, Becky sat at the kitchen table, holding her head in her hands. Bobby came in and sat next to her.

"What a morning! I hope no one drove by earlier and viewed that junk. I suppose there are people who believe they have a dog in the hunt."

Becky looked up, her eyes red from the earlier tears. "While you were watching the paint repair, I called Ray. I wanted to check on Mom's condition, and I told him about that awful sign on our door. I'm scared. What if they come back? All they have to do is come up our driveway. They could come in the house and attack us!"

"I don't think so. Nothing like that is going to happen, hon. Whoever did this is a coward."

"Ray is concerned, Bobby. He asked me if I still own that pistol I had. I'm going to get it out and load it. We can't live like this, with people getting upset because of some lawsuit. Why don't you just get out and let Oliver and the other lawyers in the office handle it? Why do we care about a fight between two black people? It's not our fight." She began trembling once again.

"It's going to be okay, I promise you, Becky."

"But the mayor told the police to ignore it. No one is even going to be looking for them." She threw up her hands in despair. "Ray and Darla asked me to come and spend a few days with them in Muleshoe. I'm going to do it. Just drop the case. No one expects us to put up with these threats."

"Becky, your brother has got you overreacting. I'm not about to quit the case. Leon is relying on me. I can't just walk off and leave a client."

SEVENTY-TWO

Becky's departure for Muleshoe weighed heavily on Bobby. It was a five-hour drive, and she was noncommittal when he asked when she would return. He remained surprised at her reaction. She was tough and not easily disturbed by unexpected events.

Pulling into his parking space, he resolved not to mention the garage door incident to Oliver. The mayor was probably correct. The event didn't need any publicity, and Oliver's knowledge of the sordid affair would not add anything to their effort to complete the trial preparations.

He looked at Oliver, seated across the table. "Do we have enough from our investigator to analyze this jury panel?"

"I think so. There are always a few that don't leave much of a trail. But he has searched the Fort Worth City records, the county records, the criminal records, the school records, birth records, state drivers records, the internet, available credit records, and, where possible, he has talked to employers. He has even spoken to some relatives he was able to trace, but as you know, that is always a little dicey. It was a lot of work. Seventy on the panel. The most I have ever seen. I'm worried that may not be enough, given the publicity we've seen. I know the judge is worried about that too."

Bobby replied, "Could be, but half the time they say they've heard nothing about the case when they have, and the other half say yes, they have, in hopes they won't be picked for the jury. Picking a jury is an art, not a science. I guess an ugly art at that."

"You're right. But let's get to it. The selection starts a week from Wednesday."

A 4:00 PM call from Becky confirmed her safe arrival in Muleshoe. She seemed more at peace and told him she had spoken with Libby, who was going to join him for supper if he would call her as soon as he left the office. Relieved by her tone, Bobby spent the afternoon with Oliver, identifying sixteen panel members who, for various reasons, appeared likely to sympathize or lean toward Benjamin. If Colter's review tracked theirs, he was going to want to seat them. Each was marked with a red symbol, significant only to Bobby and Oliver. Special questioning would be called for to disqualify them, if possible, or to raise sufficient doubt of their neutrality to get the judge to sustain a motion to dismiss. As a last resort, they would have to use one of the five preemptive strikes the judge was allowing each side.

Next, they culled out the members whom they felt were likely to lean toward Leon. Again, various reasons, employment history, schooling, family history, and on and on provided a slim guide.

"How many times have you been wrong, Bobby?" Oliver asked as they put a young black college graduate in Leon's camp.

"I don't want to know. I tried several years ago based on how my picks voted in the jury room, and it was either too depressing or my lessons learned never seemed to work on the next case. Like I said, it's a dark art."

Finally, fifteen names were marked with a green symbol, leaving nine names which they called a crapshoot. It was clear that the voir dire process, the question-and-answer session with the panel in the courtroom, was going to be crucial and hopefully produce twelve jurors who were attentive and believed Leon's side of the story.

Assembling all the jury notes, lists, and reports into their respective files, they turned to the last topic of the day. "Oliver, if you've finished our proposal for jury questions and instructions, I've got to go to Fort Worth on Tuesday to meet with Leon, so I'll just drop them at the clerk's office."

"Yeah, all done. I'll be anxious to see what Colter comes up with. I still think only four issues are necessary. More than that and our friends in the box might get confused."

SEVENTY-THREE

Climbing into the Jeep, Bobby placed the folder on the passenger seat. Would the judge agree with the jury issues and instructions which they were presenting? Words and phrases were parsed for hours in many cases, with the plaintiff and the defendant adamant in arguing that their version of the jury questions was correctly supported by many prior court opinions. Bobby knew however, that all too often, the trial judge harbored a personal view of the crucial questions which ought to go to the jury box, questions that would determine the winner and the loser. Whatever Judge Welton determined, he and Oliver would be saddled with the task of molding the evidence to support the answers which could work a judgement in Leon's favor.

The ping sounded on his smartphone before he started the engine. A short message from Alece simply stated, "Hey, Bobby. Let's talk. I'll buy you a beer at Mac's in five."

Bobby swiveled his head, glancing around the square. Surely Alece must have him in view and know he was preparing to drive away. But he could not see Alece, and he texted, "Okay."

The early evening crowd was yet sparse, and he had no difficulty in spotting Alece, sitting alone in a rear booth.

"What's up, Bobby?" Alece greeted, nodding toward the seat on the opposite bench.

"I was just goin' to ask you the same thing, Alece. We've not shared a beer since you and Carl and I were here a couple of months ago."

"Yeah, that's been too long. We never get a chance to talk much at the hall. I just want to see how life's treatin' you these days."

"Busy, busy. But say, I did get a chance to meet a nephew of yours the other day. Elisha."

"Oh yeah, where was that?"

"I almost ran over him in the Walmart parking lot. He seems a nice kid."

"He's okay. But he's got a lot to learn, that boy. His mama is hidin' him from the real world." Alece's face wore a disdainful expression.

"He told me he is going to college soon," Bobby replied, puzzled by Alece's remark.

Alece smiled and then said, "Say, I bet that suit with Leon has been keepin' you on the move."

Bobby started as a warning flag arose in the back of his head. Why would Alece be concerned about the Harris case?

"Well, as you've probably seen, the case is getting a lot of publicity. But it's like any case, a ton of work to get ready for trial."

Alece leaned forward, warming to the subject. "That's just a few weeks down the road, right? The trial I mean." He turned to wave the waitress over to take their order.

Waiting for their beers to arrive, they chatted about some of the issues the council confronted at the last meeting. But after the waitress placed the schooners on the table, Alece returned to the impending trial.

"Bobby, seein' as how Leon grew up here, his suit is causin' a lot of talk over in the Camp. I think most of the folks are disappointed that Leon is sayin' such bad things about Reverend Benjamin. Some are talkin' about puttin' together a march. You know that kinda thing right here in Lamar would not be good."

"Alece, is that why you wanted to meet? To talk about Leon and Benjamin?"

"I'm just tryin' to help out, Bobby. That lawsuit ain't goin' to help anyone. I know Jeremiah was upset, but I see him at the coalition in Dallas, and I can tell you, he wants to get all this behind him. He and the coalition don't need a long fight in the courthouse. They are busy people."

Bobby's eyes bore into Alece as he took a long pull from his schooner. He firmly set it on the table before he spoke, "I'm not goin' to talk about Leon's case, Alece. That's his business, and it is not your business."

"Hold on, Bobby. I understand. I'm just sayin' that there ought to be a way to settle it where both sides can come out ahead."

"Has Benjamin appointed you to speak for him, Alece? Does he know we are meeting?"

"No, no, but he has said some things. I know he would he would like to get this over with—and the sooner the better."

"Is that so? And why should you care, Alece? You don't have a dog in this hunt, or do you?"

"Well, I don't like seein' a brother fight a brother."

"Okay, tell me how you can help."

Alece took a slow draw on his beer and again leaned toward Bobby as though launching into a conspiracy.

"I know Leon. He has done right well in his business. A couple of friends of mine work for him. But Leon can't stand to lose $2 million. Who can, right? It would kill his business and him and his family. And why should he take that risk? He and Jeremiah should work this out."

"Very good, Alece, but I don't think the Reverend Benjamin is goin' to dismiss his lawsuit," Bobby replied with a wry smile.

"I agree, but here's my idea. I believe I can talk him into dropping the suit for, say, $200,000, just a tenth of what he is asking for. He was really insulted by Leon. It's not just money he wants."

"Oh, just a $200,000 apology from Leon, is that it?" Bobby made no effort to hide the scorn in his voice.

"No, but I think he would consider it if he got two more things."

"And what is that?" Bobby asked, wishing he had a recording device with him.

"Okay, you know our council could be of help here. Jeremiah believes he was not treated with respect the last time he came to the council to offer his help for the folks in the Camp. Some of his programs have been received in other cities, and they are backed by federal grants. It's like the amendment we have proposed for the city's financial policy. Help for the disadvantaged will be a benefit for the whole city." Alece paused for another drink as Bobby sat silently.

"You carry a lot of influence on the council, Bobby. You could get both of these items approved. Carl and Leech and Paula would listen to you. That's all it would take."

Bobby simply stared ahead, his face impassive.

"And it's no secret that Fanning will step down before too long. You could be the next mayor, Bobby. Benjamin and the coalition would be happy to speak for you, to support you for your help in getting the financial policy changed."

Alece stopped, his eyes concentrating on Bobby.

A long tremulous sigh escaped Bobby's lips before he replied, "Alece, as Leon's lawyer, I have a duty to uphold, a duty that requires me to do several things. First, I am bound to report this settlement offer, if that is what it is, to Leon before I make any comment. Second, it would be a huge conflict of interest, a betrayal of Leon, for me to even consider trading Leon's interests for a promise of personal support for me if I were ever to run for mayor. I'm in the case to serve Leon, not me. Even beyond that, as an elected member of the city council, I owe a duty to the citizens of this city to vote for what is in their best interest, not what would be in my personal best interest. You are a council member. I hope you understand that."

As Alece started to reply to Bobby's last comment, he was halted as Bobby continued, "I'm not done, Alece. Let me give you some advice. You say Benjamin has not sent you here with this proposal, but if I were you, I would let him know what you have done. He strikes me as a man who prefers to speak for himself, and he and his lawyer may not be too happy with you appointing yourself as a mediator. And finally, I better not hear anything from anyone about this conversation we've had unless it comes from Mr. Colter, Benjamin's lawyer. I don't want to be accused of trading my client behind his back. You understand what I'm sayin', Alece?"

"Yeah, Bobby. Have it your way. But I'm tellin' you, some people here are gettin' riled up about this case and the things Leon has said. It could spill over if you're not careful."

"I hope that's not a threat, Alece. The judge in Fort Worth is keeping a close eye out for anyone who wants to move the lawsuit out of the courtroom. You don't need to get on his radar."

The tension was palpable as they parted company at the front door. Bobby's last remark rang in Alece's head: "I better not hear any more unless it comes to me direct from Colter. If so, I will tell him what my client thinks about any settlement offer, if there is one."

SEVENTY-FOUR

O n the drive home, Bobby related the strange meeting over his smartphone, picturing Oliver's face as he listened to the story.

"Jackson must be crazy or stupid, Bobby!"

"Maybe so, but Alece always thinks first about Alece. I would like to be in the room when he tells Benjamin about our meeting. That is, if Alece was truthful when he said Benjamin did not ask him to speak with me."

"I think you handled it well, Bobby. I'll be interested in hearing about Leon's reaction."

"Sure. I'd be surprised if he even gives two seconds to consider a settlement, regardless of the terms. I'll discuss it with him first thing in the morning, and then we will get on with trial preparation."

* * *

Bobby again traced the story as he and Becky ate supper. Her return from Muleshoe was the one bright spot of the day. Her equilibrium seemed to be restored by her short family visit. She listened silently until Bobby mentioned Alece's words about tensions spilling over in Lamar.

"You don't think Alece had something to do with the paint on our door, do you?"

"Oh, I doubt it. But it's possible that he heard about it. Whoever did it was probably upset that it got removed so quickly. Maybe they were eager to tell some people about it."

"When you meet with Leon, are you going to tell him what was on the door?" she asked with growing tension in her eyes.

"Sure. I believe it's part of the lawsuit, and he should know. But like I told Oliver, I'd be surprised if he gives any thought to the ideas Alece was tossing around. Leon is dead set on telling his story at the courthouse."

SEVENTY-FIVE

The drive to Oak Cliff in the gathering dusk provided time—too much time—for Alece to contemplate Benjamin's reaction to the high-handed rebuff from Sanford. It was a surprise. He had at least expected an agreement that Sanford and his client would consider the offer. Even Benjamin had said that the meeting would open the door. Alece only hoped he would not receive another ranting session like the one following Benjamin's earlier episode before the Lamar Council.

In Benjamin's large office at the coalition headquarters, Alece reported the session at Mac's, word for word, as best he could remember.

"Is that all? That Sanford man didn't say what he thought?" Benjamin grumbled.

"No. He just lectured about his duty. But, Jeremiah, don't forget he said he would tell Harris about everything that came through Colter. Let's get Colter to talk to him."

Benjamin laughed loudly and then stared at Jackson. "Alece, sometimes I think you were born with no brain. Didn't yo mama teach you anythin'? Hell, Lawyer Colter don't know nothin' about that."

"You mean he don't know you want to settle it?" Alece's eyes widened in disbelief.

"Man, I don't want to settle it! That damn Harris is bad news, but there are some people who hate him more than I do, and the last thing they want is for him to get on that witness stand and talk about that trash he wrote."

Alece worked his jaw, but no words came out. Finally he said, "I don't understand. Who are you talking about?"

"I'm talkin' about the folks who are bankrollin' the suit. They don't like what Harris said, but now that it's gettin' so much publicity around the country, they just want him to shut up and go away. They got too much invested in the way things are goin', and they don't want anyone stirrin' up a lot of nonsense."

"Well, I'm sure surprised, Jeremiah. I thought you wanted to wring him dry."

"You got that right. But I got to look at the big picture, long time. The coalition counts on those folks for support, and we can't afford to get them upset."

Alece sat upright in his chair, pleased that he was being taken into Benjamin's confidence. Bolstered by that, he ventured, "How do we get to Stanford then? Are you goin' to have Colter take a settlement offer to them?"

"I don't know. I'll have to think about it. I'll need to talk to our supporters. They're pullin' the strings, and I ain't goin' to do anything without talkin' to them."

Alece was soon on the road back to Lamar, smiling now that he was privy to the inner workings of the Fort Worth litigation. The only sour note was Benjamin's parting comment. "You know more than what's good for you, Jackson. Keep your mouth shut or you may wish you were someplace else."

SEVENTY-SIX

"I really appreciate your coming in this morning," the mayor said as Bobby settled into the chair across from Dub Fanning's desk.

"I know how busy you must be, with Leon's trial starting soon, but I want to discuss some things with you before our next council meeting."

"Sure, Dub, not a problem. The suit has kept me away from the hall more than I would like," Bobby responded, quietly noting the strained demeanor which cloaked the mayor's face. Aside from a few brief greetings, they had not spoken at length for several weeks. Even the phone conversation about the garage door lasted only a few minutes. Dub's secretary had almost pleaded when she called Bobby the evening before and requested that Bobby drop by.

"You know, Bobby, I have sat in this chair for a lot of years, even when Lamar was just a small sleepy town. Now it seems like we're having to contend with all the world's problems, budgets, pensions plans, etc. We've seen all the slaughter in Paris, San Berdardino, and other places. Who knows, maybe we'll get a riot here."

Bobby grimaced, wondering what had caused Dub to ramble so. But the mayor was not done.

"And we still don't have a way to fix the damn pension shortfall. The fire and police won't even accept my invitation to hold a meeting about it. They keep talkin' about the Texas law."

Booby frowned. The mayor was usually more taciturn, dealing with the city's problems in a few words. Bobby nodded, but remained silent.

"There was a time when the council would pull together and find a solution to these things. You know how much I have relied on you, Bobby, and Carl and even Estella. But lately, I don't know. The whole country is boiling. and it's spilling into Lamar."

"What do you mean, Dub," Bobby interjected.

"Well, all these marches and riots, like in Chicago and Ferguson. Everyone is getting restless. And that dirty sign on your garage. I don't know why you let them publish that article in the *Star Telegram.*"

The mayor stopped, looking at Bobby's face, which had suddenly reddened.

"Dub, that had nothing to do with Lamar. Leon's case is in Fort Worth!" Bobby was shocked at the suggestion that his defense of Leon was somehow detrimental to Lamar.

"Leon used to live here, Bobby. Now he has accused a man of being a slave master, and it gets spread all over the *New York Times.* You think no one here ever reads the national news? You made a mistake when you agreed to take on the case."

Bobby could only look upon the mayor in disbelief, stunned by the last statement.

"Well, I'll tell you someone who is very aware of the Harris case. Alece Jackson was in two days ago with a list of what he called grievances. I think he and that Benjamin fella have concocted an agenda, aimed squarely at Lamar."

Rocking back in his seat, Bobby's mind flashed to the strange meeting with Alece at Mac's. Was that just a continuation of a confrontation between Alece and Dub?

They both sat mutely for a long moment, then the mayor proceeded, "I've asked you to come in because I need your help. I'm going to visit with Carl and Estella today. I've asked the city secretary to include on our next council agenda the proposal to amend our financial policy, to require future budgets to review and consider more expenditures in the city's underserved areas. Jackson says that people in the Camp are getting stirred up by those things in Ferguson and Chicago, and he believes there is a group getting ready to organize a march on city hall."

"What? He can't be serious," Bobby blurted.

"I thought so too. But he then pulled out his next complaint about our police department with only one black police officer. He said that would not look good if a march in the square got out of hand. Those were his exact words."

"But, Dub, we've only had three black people apply for the department, and two of those didn't come close to the listed qualifications."

"Yes, but I don't want to get into that argument with some newspaper reporter, Bobby. We are going to continue to grow, and we can't look like some backwater village that doesn't belong in the modern world. I told Jackson we would hire at least two more black officers in our next class."

Bobby could only shake his head. The words *entitlement* and *affirmative action* raced through his brain, stifling any thought of replying to the stunning remarks from the mayor. Had political correctness now become the watchword in Lamar?

The mayor lowered his eyes and mumbled, "I know, I know, Bobby, but this is not a lawsuit. We are running a democracy here, and we've got to listen to the citizens."

"Okay, Dub, I understand. But what about leadership? Do we just let threats and terrorism guide our future?" The temptation to tell the mayor about Jackson's plan to settle the Harris case welled up but was quickly suppressed. The pressure on the mayor could be part of a scheme by Jackson and Benjamin, but he could not let it influence Leon's case.

The mayor went on. "So I hope I can count on you when we discuss the financial policy next time. If we make the change, we can simply address the matter once again each year as we put the budget together."

"It's a mistake, Dub. Let me think about it," Bobby replied, rising from his seat.

The mayor nodded and silently watched Bobby depart. He shook his head, taking little comfort in the knowledge that he would not be running for mayor again next year.

SEVENTY-SEVEN

Before returning to the parking lot, Bobby stopped briefly in his council office to check for any mail which needed attention. He felt conflicted after the session in the mayor's office. The words of Sam Madison and Leon's case stood in contrast to the accommodations which the mayor was proposing. Who was correct? Could he advocate a position in the courthouse and then cast a contrary vote at the council? His duty as an attorney mandated advocacy in behalf of a client, without regard to his personal beliefs, but an opponent in a political race would never hesitate to highlight what might appear to the voters as insincerity.

He could recall no case in which his role on the council had seemed to clash with his role as an attorney. And now, the mayor had actually condemned his decision to defend Leon. Was it only a coincidence that both Alece and Dub were using Leon's case as a tool to influence action at city hall? The mayor had not hesitated to cite the garage door graffiti as a cause for his unrest. Did Alece know about that event, or had he even caused it?

Walking across the parking lot, he wondered if he would be hearing from Colter about the supposed settlement outlined by Alece.

* * *

"I'm worried about Dub Fanning," Bobby remarked, pushing back from the supper table.

"Really? Why do you say that?" Becky responded as she began to clear the dishes.

"He doesn't look good. Pale and wan. He says that the world is closing in on Lamar, and he rambled on and on when I met with him this morning."

"Maybe he is just concerned about Sue Lynn. I heard that her cancer is not going so well."

"Could be, but he has changed his position on a couple of things that are very important to the city. I mean he is doing an about-face and wants Carl and me to support him. I'm worried about it."

"Well, isn't he still hoping you will be the next mayor? Can't you just change things later?"

"It just doesn't work that way, hon. The changes are not that simple. I'm not too sure I will run for mayor anyhow. The job has not treated Dub very well—at least it is beginning to look that way. That sign on our door has really affected him. I think he believes we are about to have race riots on the town square."

"Are you serious?"

"I don't know. Dub has been here a long time, and he doesn't scare easily. But I'm not sure now. He even got riled up about the *New York Times* article that came out about Leon's case a couple of months ago. Why is a mayor in Lamar, Texas, worried about that?"

Later in bed, Bobby reviewed the bizarre meeting at city hall and how it might affect his next session with Leon. The far-ranging impact of a defamation suit was becoming more apparent each day.

SEVENTY-EIGHT

Bobby arrived early the next morning at the law office and was surprised to find Carl Jeffers sitting in one of the visitors' chairs, staring through the window at the people hurrying across the square to begin the workday. He gruffly responded to Bobby's good morning with a deep grunt and waved aside the offer of coffee.

"This is not a social visit, Bobby," he said, brows creased above his dark eyes.

"I got a call last night from Dub. I think he has lost his mind! He wants you and me to vote for that change in the financial policy. He said the time has come."

Bobby eased into the chair behind his desk and replied, "I know. He told me the same thing yesterday afternoon. I was surprised too."

"What's happened to him? Something's goin' on, and it can't be good."

"Yeah. I was awake most of the night trying to answer that question myself. Dub even said I should have never taken Leon's case." Bobby grimaced, his eyes on Carl, who was rubbing a hand over his hair.

Carl rose, paced slowly toward the door, and returned to his seat.

"Do you remember our conversation at Mac's the other day when I told you about the New Orleans train song? How the country is goin' to hell?"

Bobby nodded as Carl continued, "Well, it looks to me like it's now come here. A terrorist bomb in Lamar of all places! And why? That guy had a truck and apartment and a job right here. He must have had help from someone around here. But even the FBI, DHS, and CIA say they don't have a clue. Policemen being shot down like dogs a few miles from here, Alece Jackson serving demands on Dub." His head shook in disbelief.

"There are people just looking for an excuse to riot in the streets like in Baltimore, Baton Rouge, Minneapolis, and Milwaukee. And on TV last night, they showed an American flag burning in the street. People were walking by just looking."

"Oh, where was that?"

"In San Francisco. You might expect that in Iran, but right here? No one has any respect anymore. Everyone wants to express outrage by killing and burning. And we had two people running for the White House that sowed vile discord every day with name-calling and outlandish promises to buy every vote they could find. People who voted for the loser feel duty bound to continue their diatribe, and the media has encouraged it. Hell, I won't be surprised if someone in power will be shot in a year. If you could burn the flag, why not kill a human symbol of the country to make your point?"

"Come on, Carl. That's a little far-fetched."

"Really? What if I had told you a year ago that over 50 percent of all voters had to hold their noses to vote for either candidate. Unbelievable, right?"

Carl paused, his breath expelling before he went on.

"What has anyone done to stop all this? The rioters and criminals are spoon-fed pity and excuses. Washington has made it clear that our border restrictions are just a bad joke, that people who ignore our laws deserve only our sympathy for their personal problems that supposedly drive them over the edge. People in Central America don't have jobs, so it's okay to just walk over to the US. Blacks that don't have jobs can kill and riot because society has failed them.

"Do you remember the oath we took when we were sworn into the council, the same oath taken by almost every elected official in America? Well, it went like this, "I solemnly swear that I will preserve, protect, and defend the Constitution and laws of the United States and this state, so help me God." In San Francisco, Los Angeles, Chicago, Houston, Dallas, and San Antonio, those officials have declared their cities to be sanctuary cities which will not enforce and defend the immigration laws of our country. They have violated their oath and openly encourage their citizens to do the same. Hypocrisy doesn't begin to describe it.

"You know, when people are told they have the right to accept or reject the law you' re only a step away from anarchy. You can't hire enough policemen to keep order when people decide they will not voluntarily respect the rules.

"But it is worse than that! Did you hear about that pro football player who refused to stand during the national anthem? He said he was protesting the way people of color are treated in the US."

"I saw it on the sports news. You wonder what he thinks he will accomplish."

Carl laughed. "I hope it will be ignored. Where does that guy get off, deliberately disrespecting our country? My uncle practically gave his life for the country. I fought for it, and so did Jim Grant. It's because of all our dead soldiers that this guy was born in a country where he can earn millions by playing a game six months out of the year. This is a democracy. People can act as they wish even if you disagree. You can't blame the country for the action of other people exercising their free speech." Jeffers finally stopped.

"I agree, Carl, trashing the US solves nothing. John Kennedy was right when he said, 'Ask not what your country could do for you.' No one seems to remember that. Leon told me the same thing a couple of months ago. He said the more the government does for you, the less freedom you have. I'm afraid these things are what have upset Dub. He's letting fear replace his common sense. He told me not long ago that people look to government—even our council—to maintain stability. Maybe he believes we are failing."

Carl sat up in his chair. "Well, you tell me if you can detect any stability in Washington. The president issues regulations every day to promote his agenda while Congress sits on one hand and points a finger with the other hand."

"But you and I have a vote, Carl. What did you tell Dub about the financial policy?"

"I told him any change would be a big mistake. What about you?"

"I said I would think about it, but unless someone comes up with an argument that makes sense, I can't vote for it."

With that, Carl rose slowly to his feet, taking a final glance at the bustle on the square, and growled.

"I suppose Dub will want to punt again on the pension question too. It's not good. Thanks for hearing me out, Bobby."

The door closed quietly behind Jeffers as he headed toward his car and the drive across the interstate to open the Auto Zone store. In the quiet, his frustration and anxiety hung in the air, suppressing Bobby's intention to prepare for his next pretrial review with Leon.

SEVENTY-NINE

They did not begin until one thirty. The start was delayed because Leon had to oversee a new tenant at his business, and nothing seemed to flow smoothly that morning.

"I'm sorry, Bobby. It's been one of those days. This new tenant has more merchandise than I was led to believe. But I'm glad to have them on board. The place is almost full."

"It's okay, Leon. I had plenty to do at the office this morning. But we've got a lot to cover." Bobby reached over the table, handing Leon a small file.

"Here is your copy of our proposed jury issues and jury instructions. I hope the judge will limit it to just four questions. Benjamin will have to prove that his reputation was damaged and the amount of money he says will cover the damage. The most important question, as far as your testimony goes, is the first issue. Did you publish your writing? That is a fact question which you can provide direct evidence on, and of course, Carla will also address that issue."

Leon nodded as he thumbed through the file. "When will we know if the judge agrees with all this?"

"Well, we talked about that when Colter and I last met with him. Judge Welton usually plays it close to his chest, and he indicated he may not decide until we have picked the jury. That doesn't help either side when we question the jury panel, but it gives him the opportunity to see what kind of jury is seated before he decides. I don't like it, but he is the judge."

"He has ordered the trial to begin on Wednesday, the twentieth. That's only twelve days away, so we have a lot of work to do. He is going to be at a judicial conference on Monday and Tuesday, so he is starting us midweek. It means we will probably spend the rest of the week picking the jury and then begin opening arguments and the evidence the next Monday. We will need to review again the jury list before that Wednesday. Have you told your staff that you may be at the courthouse for as long as two weeks?"

"Oh sure. They can cover it. I'm ready."

Bobby laughed. "This is no football game, Leon. We've got to go over every question Colter may ask you and every question I may ask you. Remember, the jury will be hearing it all for the first time. What you wrote might be all over the internet, but some may know nothing about it. It will raise issues in their head they may never have thought about."

"Gotcha. Let's get started then," Leon responded.

"Okay. But first, I need to tell you about a settlement offer that was put in front of me. You need to know about it."

"You're kidding, right? What's Benjamin want, $1,999,999?"

"Let me explain it," Bobby said and told of Alece's visit in detail, including Alece's comment that he was acquainted with one of Leon's employees.

"I'm glad you told him to take a walk, Bobby. Sounds like Benjamin and Jackson are two animals of the same color."

"Could be, Leon, except Alece insisted that he was not sent by Benjamin. If that's true, he is playing a strange game."

"He's strange all right. One of my guys came to me a couple of weeks ago and said Jackson had been pumpin' him about the case and about our business. Say, have you heard anything from Colter since you saw Jackson?"

"No, at least not as of this morning. I don't think I will. I'll bet Alece was just trying to curry favor from Benjamin."

"It doesn't make any difference, Bobby. I won't consider any settlement that would put you in a bind as a council member. This is my fight, not yours. Besides, I've talked a lot with Sam about once a week since he left. He's encouraged me to stick with my guns. What I said is the fact, and Benjamin knows what he is doin'. His reputation stinks. Ask anyone who sits on the city councils he's tried to scam."

Bobby grinned and shrugged his shoulders. "Let's hope the jury has the same reaction. One more thing you should know. A few days ago, after that article about you and me was in the paper, someone painted graffiti on the garage door at my house. It really upset Becky and the mayor."

"Graffiti? What do you mean?"

"It said nigger lover in capital letters."

"Oh man. I don't know what to say, Bobby."

"It's not your fault, Leon. This case has brought out a lot of stuff. Seems everyone has an opinion."

"I heard plenty of talk like that before I was even in high school, but I thought things were better now."

"Things are better now, Leon."

"What did you do?"

"The mayor sent Estella Jiminez over. She is one of our council members, and her husband is a painting contractor. It was fixed before anyone saw it. At least we think so."

"Maybe Jackson or Benjamin was behind it."

"No, it was probably some bad white guy. I don't think Alece is dumb enough to pull a stunt like that in his own town."

"You know him better than me, but I've gotten some e-mails and letters that I wouldn't want Carla and the kids to see."

With nothing but speculation to feed further comment on the subject, Bobby turned the discussion to Leon's trial testimony. "Leon, your famous writing will be waved in front of the jury every time Colter gets on his feet. There's no question you wrote it, so I won't be surprised if he reads it during his opening statement to the jury. I don't like it, but there's no point in objecting about it. You need to be prepared to explain not only when and why you wrote it, but you've got to make the jury understand also what you mean. What you mean when you call people dependents and when you say they are losing their responsibility and freedom. All that can explain why you made remarks about Benjamin and will go a long way to answer his claim that he has been defamed."

Leon leaned forward and said, "Okay, it's like Sam said when he was here. It's about more black women than white living without a husband. It's about government programs paying money to them, depending on how many babies they have. It's about the black kids with no father around to guide and counsel them. It's about enticing kids like my Dee into a school where they are not ready to compete and succeed. Then when they fail, they have nothing to prop them up but the old claim of black discrimination. Look at those black students at the University of Missouri. Why do they think they are receiving no respect? They march to create their self-pride, which they feel they lack. And even at Yale, which pats itself on the back for its affirmative action program, they are unhappy."

"That's right, Leon, but you've got to make the jury understand that. It's your testimony they will hear. All I can do is ask the questions. And Colter will have plenty of questions too. So you must be ready to turn his questions against him. It won't be easy. None of the jurors will have read Madison's book. Colter will strike them from the list, if they have even heard of the book."

"Okay, Bobby, let's rehearse."

* * *

It was a long and arduous afternoon. Most of the employees had already departed when Bobby called a halt. "Enough, Leon. We could go on all night, but you've got the picture. Trial preparation can be grueling, and then you get to the courtroom and discover that much of it was irrelevant or unneeded."

"Okay, if you say so. I think I can make the jury understand where I am coming from. I guess it's just a question of whether they agree with me or not."

Bobby smiled and replied wearily, "That's the truth. The jury selection will be crucial. I hope Oliver and I can pick the right ones. That's why you've got to be ready to feel their vibes when we review the panel list."

Walking to their cars, Leon put his hand on Bobby's arm and spoke softly, "It's late. Why don't I call Clara and ask her to put another plate on the table for you? I want you to meet Dee and Leo, and I know they would like a chance to meet the Lawyer."

"Fine, a good idea. I'll call Becky and let her know I will be late getting home. I've wanted to spend a few more minutes visiting with Clara."

"Good. Follow me. I've got a quick route from here to the house."

EIGHTY

The Senator punched the numbers into his private cell phone as the grandfather clock in his DC apartment ticked quietly in the entry hall. The connection was made and the phone rang twice before the answer. "Yeah?"

"Hey, Floyd, Rick here. Where are you?"

"I'm in my car on a downtown street. No one can hear anything."

"Good, good. What is happening so far?"

"Well, the public records have been checked. It took three days. They were a dead end. Harris and his lawyer were high school football teammates, but they went their own way after graduation. Sanford is a small-town lawyer and sits on the town council in Lamar, south of Fort Worth. No criminal records for either one. Harris has a good-sized business, a warehouse in Fort Worth, and seems well respected around here. The Fort Worth paper carried a recent piece about them and the Benjamin lawsuit, talked about their friendship years ago in high school. But nothing of any use to us."

"Hell, Floyd, we've got to find a glitch," the Senator complained.

"Yeah, I know. After I read that news article, I painted a sign on Sanford's garage door in the middle of the night. It said, 'nigger lover.' Thought it might make him a little nervous about handling Harris's case."

"I'll bet that lit a fire."

"Afraid not. I cruised by the next afternoon and the door was already repainted. Not one word on the street in Lamar and apparently it was not even reported to the police. Nothing in the local paper."

"Damn it, Floyd! You've got to do something. I've had three calls this week from the coalition. I'm pushing the civil rights folks to have Benjamin drop his suit, but he says no. We can't let it go to trial. Harris will preach from the witness stand like a banshee and the newspapers will have a field day. The best Benjamin will do is make a settlement, but he still wants some money. Is there some way you can intimidate Harris? Get him to agree to pay something and settle."

"I don't know, Rick. He has a wife and two kids. Maybe I can get a message across that someone could be hurt if the case is not settled."

"Well, do it then. He has got to understand that settlement is his only choice. We have seen that work before. What about your friend in Tuscaloosa that helped you in the primary several years ago?"

"I don't know. I'll see if I can reach him and get him over."

"Yes, do that. And soon. This is important, Floyd. Call when he gets there."

EIGHTY-ONE

Leon was surprised when Bobby called late Sunday morning, and he made no effort to hide it.

"Do what? Bobby we just spent three days together, getting the jury lined up. What more can we do?"

"Yeah, I know. But, Leon, one or two more ideas have crossed my mind. We start the trial tomorrow. We've got to be ready."

The strain in his voice was apparent through the phone, and Leon acceded to the request that he meet at Bobby's office at 6:00 PM. "Okay, I've got it. Leo's baseball game will be done by three. I'll see you then."

* * *

The town square appeared deserted with empty parking spaces and only one or two people on the street. Leon turned away from the window, remembering the days years ago when he had walked around the square as a teenager. From his vantage point, it didn't appear that much had changed, except for the new city hall, which sat silently, glowering down on the square's west side.

Bobby broke the silence. "I want to thank you again for supper at your house the other night. You have married a great cook. I hope Clara didn't mind me dragging her through a rehearsal again."

"No. She has talked and talked about the trial. I think she is more eager than I am to put Benjamin down. And Dee and Leo wouldn't go to bed after you left. They think you are the greatest for inviting them to sit in the courtroom."

"They are impressive kids, Leon. I want the jury to see them. You and your family will make a nice contrast to Benjamin and his lawyer. When you talk about Dee's offer from the university, the jurors can see her and understand why you don't want her to be the recipient of a handout. Well, I'm sorry to interrupt you on a Sunday. Thank you for coming down. But I have a concern. Yesterday I read again your manifesto. I've never heard the word *reslaved*, and we've never talked about it. So I looked in the dictionary. I couldn't find it. Anyhow, the word *slave* is obviously a sensitive one in this case. So I want to be sure we are prepared to explain what you meant when you wrote it. Colter may have his own interpretation."

"What did I mean?" Leon looked puzzled, then went on, "I suppose I was feeling that the university, with its social engineering agenda, was trying to entice Dee into joining all the black people who have accepted the invitation to become no more than a symbol of incapable citizens. I don't want her, or Leo, to ever become dependent. If you are dependent upon someone else's agenda, you are not free, you have to live by their decisions, not yours."

Booby nodded. "But if the dependents have been enslaved, who did it? And why?"

"Well, I don't mean it's been like the people who put chains on the Africans. But I guess to answer your question, the people who have reslaved are the politicians who hand out public money to buy votes or people like the university who hand out admissions to prove how enlightened they are, how politically correct they are."

"But do you think they have done this on purpose to denigrate or put down black people in America? No one has to take what is offered, you know. You haven't."

"I just don't know, Bobby. There are probably some who are aware of what they are doing, who know what they are causing and are doing it deliberately, and others who pat themselves on the back for being socially conscious even if they are sending the wrong message. If I was going to point a finger to place blame, I would have to include those who think they are entitled to receive the handouts, who believe they are due something from society. But it goes far beyond a question of race, Bobby."

"What do you mean?"

"I mean that affirmative action, with respect to minorities and women, is only a symptom of how the original governmental concepts of the eighteenth century have changed in this country. As I told you, I majored in American history, but I didn't put down the books the day I left college. I read books, maybe ten or fifteen a year, about the development of America and its political system. The process is still working. So I've seen a lot of what you see on the council, what makes government work, and what is changing it."

"Hey, Leon. You're beginning to sound like Professor Madison."

"Maybe so. But his book deals only with the black man's role in the US. What I wrote is about the same thing, but if we are talking about dependency, especially dependency on the government, blacks are not the only victims."

"The trial starts tomorrow, Leon. It is one black man against another black man. Now you're telling me that this is not about race, it's something else?"

Leon smiled and rubbed his hands together, as if to clear the scene.

"I'm sayin' the whole point is about individual freedom and what government is doing to freedom. It affects everyone, including white people, even those on the jury."

"Now that's a mouthful! But how does that get Benjamin off your back?"

"Well. You're the lawyer, Bobby, and also a councilman. Your talk at the Rotary Club touched on the same thing. What I see every day in my business are government rules and regulations that tell me what I can and cannot do. Each law restricts the freedom I have to conduct my business. Some are Fort Worth ordinances, some are Texas laws, some are federal laws or regulations. You know what I'm talking about. You pass ordinances in Lamar almost every time you meet. The basic laws for Lamar, or any other city, are to provide for public health and safety, public roads, public water supply and sewers, public spaces, public schools. So you hire policemen, firemen, road workers, code enforcers, and so on. And the same basics applied at one time to the federal government, with the addition of public defense and relations with other countries. But that's not true today. Government today does more than provide for public needs—food stamps, unemployment welfare, disaster relief, retirement benefits, education grants, and the list goes on. So in addition to the basic laws which restrict an individual's freedom in a law-abiding society, we now have laws which provide and promote individual economic aids. Just as federal grants provide to unwed black mothers, they also provide to citizens who are unemployed and to those who claim they have no food. These recipients become dependent upon the government and the public treasury and lose the dignity of freedom that Sam talked about. They are not all black. They are encouraged to rely on others, not as one might rely on charity, but to clamor for an entitlement due from the mere fact that they are a citizen, a citizen armed with the power to vote, the power to elevate elected officials which control the public treasury. They claim a right to economic equality, a right to lifetime health care, and they demand that the government provide it to them simply because they live in the US with or without citizenship. But worst of all, too many of our elected officials say amen!"

"Did you learn all this from the books you've read?" Bobby asked, a bit surprised by the civics lecture.

"No, not just books. It's set out in every newspaper, every article that reports the continuing deadlock between Democrats and Republicans in Washington. The welfare state is alive and well while representatives bash one another to support their pleas for more campaign contributions. People are no longer elected to enact laws for the common good, but elected to defeat the other political party." Leon sighed in resignation.

"What you say is true," Bobby replied. "Even in Lamar, we see constant demands for money, money which people believe they are entitled to receive from their taxes or, more often, from someone else's taxes."

"Where does it all stop, Bobby? There was a schoolteachers' walk out in Chicago because of layoffs and inferior classrooms and a breakdown of public water supply in Flint, Michigan. In both cases, part of the problem was because the taxes paid by others had disappeared. The taxpayers had moved out to another state. The public treasury was bankrupted by excessive public employee pensions and other costs expenditures granted by eager politicians."

Bobby nodded, saying, "This is all very good, but we have got to find the one or two jurors whose background shows they will echo your thoughts. Direct your responses to them. If we don't win over the jury, you could lose everything you have built over the years. Your family could really suffer. Does Clara understand that?"

Leon nodded. "Clara's on board. She gets what's at stake here. But she also feels the anger that made me write it. Last night she laid it all out to Dee, so Dee and I are on good terms again. We're all in this together."

One more review of the possible issues which the judge might present to the jurors and Bobby declared the session finished. Outside the office, Bobby watched Leon open the door of his Corvette and slump into the low driver's seat. It was nearing nine thirty, and the midsummer dusk was deep, almost obscuring the black side of Leon's car. As Leon reached out to close his door, Bobby saluted and said, "You are a great man, Leon Harris!"

The reply was almost too faint to hear. "No, Bobby, I am a free man. I don't want to be kept."

The exhaust pipes emitted a throaty rumble as the Corvette accelerated and turned east toward I-35.

EIGHTY-TWO

Becky was sleeping soundly. Bobby quietly prepared for bed and slipped under the covers on the far side. He lay on his back, eyes open. The night before opening arguments was never pleasant, and his mind, unbidden, continued to roll through the points he must present to the jury in the morning so that they might follow the evidence to a favorable verdict for Leon. It was an exercise he had wrestled with before every jury trial, but he could not recall a case in which he was so emotionally bound. Leon and his family could be facing financial ruin if they did not win, and it was all too evident that the racial overtones of the case had awakened the awareness of most of Lamar's citizens, not the least of which was the mayor.

As usual, sleep overtook him at some point, but was interrupted in the midst of a dream by the repeated ringing of the telephone. Reaching out to his bedside table, he lifted the receiver, noting that the nearby digital clock read 3:47 AM.

"Hello," he answered.

"Is this Mr. Sanford?" a distant voice asked.

"Yes, it is." Bobby came awake.

"Mr. Sanford, this is Captain Bransom with the Fort Worth Police Department. I apologize for disturbing you at this hour, but I am sorry to inform you that your client, Leon Harris, has been killed in an auto accident."

"What! That can't be true. He just left my office a few hours ago." Bobby swung his feet to the floor and carried the phone into the bathroom, shutting the door with a soft click.

"Hello, are you still there, Mr. Sanford?"

"Yes, yes. Are you sure you have the right information, Captain?"

"Yes, it is true. His car, at high speed, hit the concrete overpass abutment on I-35 at Rendon Road. He was in a Corvette registered to Leon Harris and was identified by documents in his wallet. I've called you, Mr. Sanford, because we know your trial is set to begin this morning."

Stunned, Bobby managed to reply, "That's right, in Judge Welton's court."

"Yes, sir, we've just contacted the judge and he is going to call the other lawyer. And two of our officers have already gone to the Harris home."

"My god, Captain, I don't know what to say. What can I do?"

"Well, Mr. Sanford, his body was badly mangled and partly burned. The car caught fire from the impact. But, Mr. Sanford, I need your assistance. What I am about to tell you must remain confidential. Can I have your agreement on that?"

"Yes, of course. But I don't understand."

"Good, thank you. Shortly before the crash, a gentleman pulled onto I-35, also heading north. He observed the crash and called 911. When one of our officers arrived, the gentlemen said he had seen what he thought were two cars traveling about half a mile ahead of him. Both cars swerved to the right, and the one on the far right went straight into the embankment. The second car went on. Now even though Mr. Harris's car was badly damaged and burned, we've found some light-colored paint and scratches on the left side of his car, which doesn't seem to be a result of the contact with the abutment. I must tell you, Mr. Sanford, that I have assigned a homicide detective and ordered him to open a file. The wreckage of Mr. Harris's car been impounded, pending our investigation."

"Do you mean someone may have deliberately caused the wreck?" Bobby asked, making no effort to conceal his alarm.

"That's a possibility. It could have been only a simple accident, or someone could have forced Mr. Harris into the abutment. I hope you understand, Mr. Sanford, how important that these facts not be made public. If someone is culpable, we do not want him to be made aware that we are investigating. This will all be made public when we know more. We have told no one else of the investigation, not even Judge Welton and certainly not Mrs. Harris and her children."

"I appreciate what you are saying. What a tragedy."

"Yes, it is. Later today, Mr. Sanford, I hope you will come to my office at our headquarters. I will need to get a statement from you concerning Mr. Harris's visit with you, when he left and so forth."

With Bobby's assurance that he would do so, the connection was ended.

As Bobby returned to the bedroom, Becky stirred an asked, "Did I hear you talking, Bobby?"

"Yes, dear. It's terrible. Leon was killed in a car wreck just a few hours ago."

"Oh no! What happened?"

Bobby relayed the story, omitting the facts which the captain said were confidential. They soon dressed and went to the kitchen and brewed a pot of coffee.

Later, the rising sun glinted off the Jeep's windshield, slowing Bobby's drive across town to I-35. His call to Clara had been answered by Clara's sister, who lived in Fort Worth. She was gracious and welcomed Bobby's request to come and see Clara and the kids.

He grimaced as he drove past the blackened bridge abutment, now outlined by yellow police tape. The Monday morning traffic was dense and moved slowly past the scene, most oblivious to what had happened there.

The horrific news was almost unbearable. But the prospect that Leon was intentionally killed rendered the morning surreal, a nightmare which he could share with no one.

EIGHTY-THREE

"Where are you, Floyd? You haven't answered my calls."

"I'm back in DC. Got here late last night."

"My god, Floyd, every paper has an article about Harris's death. What the hell happened? Doesn't that friend of yours know what *intimidate* means? Was he crazy?"

"It's okay, Rick. He left Texas right away. Didn't even talk to anyone while in Fort Worth. He said he was just trying to put a scare into him but the Corvette went out of control."

"Floyd, now you listen to me. This cannot get back to us. That man has got to keep quiet. You got that?"

"Sure, of course. The car doesn't even exist anymore. It was stripped and crushed at a wrecking yard in Waco. I watched it myself. The plates were removed and are gone." He had never heard the Senator so agitated.

"Your friend—don't tell me his name—I don't want to hear it! He is a murderer as far as the world is concerned, and he was to stay buried now and forever or you and I both could be hunted." The Senator was gasping.

"He will be quiet, Rick. He knows he could be in the ditch too. I trust him."

"Don't forget, Floyd, your neck is on the line if he says one word. This won't blow over in a few days. Harris's suit and his death will be talked about for months, and the police in Fort Worth may be forced to pursue it. You may have to return to Texas to see what they are doing. That lawyer may start nosing around."

In a calm voice, hoping it would carry to the Senator's ears, Floyd responded, "You could be right, Rick, but I don't think I should go back for a while. Let's see if it will cool down. I'm just sorry it turned out this way."

"Now, Floyd, we've been through this before. Don't back down on me. The party has kept the blacks in our camp forever. We can't let them believe that they have a choice. That man was going to tell them they do have a choice. We can't live with that. There's too much at stake here."

EITHTY-FOUR

Two weeks after the funeral, the sun splayed across the room early Friday morning as Becky and Bobby cleared the breakfast table.

"I still can't believe what happened, Bobby. There was another article in the Dallas paper yesterday speculating about Leon. How long will it go on?"

Bobby sighed and replied, "I don't know. The captain said their investigation is continuing, but they have not found much and they really have no leads. I wanted to look at Leon's car, but they said no."

"Don't you do anything, Bobby! First that sign on the garage and now Leon's dead. Somebody may be watching us. I'm scared."

"It's okay, hon. The police now think the wreck may have been an accident."

"What? That's not what the newspapers are saying," Becky retorted.

"Yeah, but those reporters know even less than the police. They just want to sell newspapers."

Becky shook her head, unconvinced.

Bobby stood and turned toward the garage door. "I'm going to the office, and then I'm having lunch with Clara at the college cafeteria. She hasn't heard yet from the last insurance company."

"How is she doing?"

"Well, it's tough, but she is strong. I'm not too sure about Dee and Leo. They really miss their Pappa. They are back in school again."

* * *

Clara's face remained stoic, no longer creased by her warm smile. The insurance discussion completed, Bobby inquired, "Have you heard anything from the Fort Worth police?"

"Yes, a Detective Cox called. He is coming by the house tonight after Dee and Leo are in bed.

"They are following up on their look into the wreck, I guess. I think they want to ask you a few questions about Leon."

Clara nodded and said, "Not surprised," her shoulder slumped. She went on, "Bobby, I never said anything, but a few days before he died, he got a late telephone call one night. He talked to someone and kept saying, 'No, I won't do that.' When he hung up, he was angry and told me a man urged him to pay Benjamin some money and settle the case. He was very upset but told me to forget it and not tell anyone."

Bobby's eyes widened, and he replied, "Clara, Leon never said anything to me about a call. He should have told me!"

"I'm not surprised. He didn't want to stop the trial. He said he wanted to get the message out. I suppose he never told you that he sent the message to a friend?"

"No. He claimed he had no idea why it all went viral. Why wouldn't he tell his own lawyer?"

Bobby's face flushed at hearing the revelation.

Clara shrugged. "He was determined to get this viewpoint heard, Bobby. He felt very strong about it. But look what it got him!" The bitterness in her voice was a tone Bobby had not heard before.

"I agree, Clara. That's why I asked the police if I could look at Leon's car. They said no, it might be evidence."

"Well, I sure will tell the detective about the phone call. But, Bobby, please don't start your own investigation. Some bad people may still be around. I can't have them coming after the kids and me or you. Please."

"Right. I understand. Becky is concerned too. The police aren't finished, but they said it was likely an accident."

"Really! Leon was a good driver, and he knew how to handle that car. I can't believe he wrecked it. Won't they find who did it?"

"I don't think so, Clara. They said it was only an assumption that someone deliberately forced Leon off the road. They said it is only an assumption that the apparent contact with another car was caused by the other driver. They said even if it was intentional, they have found no leads to the identity of the other car or who was driving it. You can't charge anyone with a crime with no evidence."

Clara shook her head and said nothing.

Bobby rose, patted her on the shoulder and said, "Will you call me and let me know what the detective said after he leaves?"

With her affirmation resting in his ears, Bobby returned to his law office puzzled and disturbed with the information that Leon deliberately or unintentionally put his writing on the internet. He said otherwise at his deposition. Leon could have been charged with perjury had the truth come out at trial. Perhaps it only confirmed how strongly Leon felt about his plain spoken view which had put him into the courthouse. It looked as if he deliberately picked a fight with Benjamin so he could spread his message. Bobby snorted and tossed his head, as if it cleared his mind. Why was he grasping at straws to defend a client who no longer existed?

EIGHTY-FIVE

The pre-council meeting Wednesday afternoon was loaded with announcements of staff appointments, the schedule for the upcoming budget retreats, and the items which needed resolution before the end of September. It was somber. There were still no plans to address the pension shortfall, no new budget director was yet on board, and the new financial policy, opposed by Bobby and Carl, was still an unknown, weighing on the coming budget discussions. Maybe it was Bobby's imagination, but the mayor's communications seemed cold and stilted due, perhaps, to Bobby's refusal to vote for the policy changes.

His last visit with Carl ran through his thoughts, blocking his effort to concentrate on city matters, now appearing mundane.

With a rap of his gavel, Fanning dismissed the conference and Bobby returned to his office down the hall to review the evening agenda once more. A weary smile spread on his lips when he noticed that a natural gas matter on the agenda had brought no request for comment from Unsel or any other protesters.

"Good. Maybe they are finally convinced that foreign terrorists pose a greater public threat than the Barnett Shale," he murmured aloud, just as his phone rang.

"Bobby, your law office is switching over a call they received from some man who wants to visit with you."

"Okay, ring it through," he replied. He lifted the receiver on the first sound.

"This is Bobby Sanford."

"Bobby! Sam Madison here. Hope I am not interrupting."

"Sam. No problem. Good to hear from you. We've had some tough times recently."

"Yes, I'm sure," Sam replied. "What a horrible loss. I came to the funeral in Fort Worth and you were there, but I didn't want to disturb your family, so I didn't speak."

"I understand. That was a bad day. I know you were as shocked as anyone. I was going to call, but I kept putting it off."

"Well, Leon's death has raised a lot of questions, even here at the Institute. Everyone somehow knows I visited before the trial, and they expect me to have answers. I don't. Has there been an investigation?"

Bobby grimaced and said, "Yeah, in fact the Fort Worth police found strange marks on Leon's car and assigned a homicide detective to open a file. But, Sam, they have simply reached a dead end. There is no sign of the other car reported in the papers and no way to identify the driver. Do you think he was deliberately killed?"

Sam had dodged the question at the Institute but offered a thought, "After I was in Texas, Bobby, Leon and I visited several times on the phone. He was very concerned about using the trial as a platform to get his message out, as he put it. He even read to me a few of the comments he made during his deposition. Wanted to know if they were accurate, if they were strong enough. I agreed with most of them but cautioned him that they would not be well received by most people in the country and reminded him that Benjamin and his lawyers knew exactly what he was saying and that they were capable of sending the comments to others. At that point, he interrupted me and said, 'Sam, that may explain why I got a couple of phone calls saying I would regret it if I didn't pay Benjamin some money and settle the lawsuit.' It was ugly. Those were his exact words, Bobby, and I was not entirely shocked when he died!"

"You mean it was murder?"

"How could I know, Bobby? I think there may have been a motivation, but it proves nothing if the police have no evidence."

"Sam, Leon wasn't the only one who received threats. My garage door was painted with a racial epithet, and Alece Jackson, who serves on the council with me, gave me the same message about settlement. I don't think those contacts with me and Leon were because Benjamin was convinced he would lose in the courthouse."

"Interesting, Bobby. It is hard to believe, as contentious as the lawsuit was, that Benjamin would have caused Leon's death. He wanted money, not death, and in fact, Leon's death has left Benjamin without receiving a penny."

"That's probably true. Then who else?" Bobby inquired.

"Leon's viewpoint, which he hoped to express at trial, and the points I have set out in my book are anathema to the so-called civil rights crowd. As we talked about in your law office, there are many politicians and others who trade upon the racial issues in this country, some of the real issues and some which they invent. Political reputations and millions of dollars are at stake. Strong motivations without a doubt! The Black Lives Matter, kneeling at football games, and similar parades don't happen by accident. And they are aided by the media, perhaps for other reasons, and maybe not. I know since my book was published it has enjoyed a fairly wide audience, and I have received letters, texts, e-mails, and phone calls, some calling me Uncle Tom, a traitor to my race and worse. They work hard to get their threats across. So yes, I believe there are a lot of people who strongly wished Leon's message should be stifled. Settlement of the case out of court would have been one way to do it, and since Leon refused, maybe another approach was deemed necessary."

"Ah, Sam. It's awful. Not only was Leon risking perjury but he must also have known the phone calls were more than an idle threat. You know, he told me, just before he was killed, that he did not want to be kept. I guess I am finally understanding what he meant and how deeply he felt about it."

Sam released of deep sigh and said, "Amen to that. What a wonderful teacher he would have made, given the chance. Leon's kind may yet be the salvation of black people. I know the battle will go on. It's yet boiling. There is talk now of establishing a committee or conference to consider the payment of reparations to the descendants of slaves. One more scheme to remind the black man of his place and his dependency upon white government for his well-being." Sam's voice reached a rising tone with that statement.

"That's funny, Sam. Leon mentioned that to me. He said it sounded like an effort to violate the Bill of Attainder provision in the Constitution."

"That idea is so filled with quicksand I don't think Congress could ever enact it," Sam responded.

"It would only rub salt in the wound and thwart any true reconciliation."

Both sat silently, cogitating the future course of the subject which was lodged in their consciousness.

Finally, Sam opined, "Bobby, I believe in time it will all come good for the blacks and the whites in this country. The freedom and opportunities are here for the taking, and someday everyone will realize that and move on to a better future. Leon won't be here and perhaps you and I won't, but it will come to pass."

Sam signaled his readiness to end the call, and Bobby said, "Thank you, Sam. I've needed an encouraging word. Please call again anytime and come see me if you get to Texas again."

He hung up, picked up the agenda book, and walked slowly toward the council chamber.

EPILOGUE

With the fiscal year drawing to a close, the city council put the finishing touches on the new budget. It included a revolving account for economic incentives in the underserved areas of Lamar, adopted by a split council. The no votes by Councilmen Jeffers and Sanford were summarily dismissed by the *Tribune* editor as an outdated matter of principle.

The talk about Leon Harris's death had faded, replaced by the more current news of interest in Lamar, and Bobby was surprised when Dave Mellon called, asking him for a meeting to discuss an article he was writing for the *Star Telegram*, a retrospective concerning racial unrest that had arisen around the country in the last five years.

Dave Mellon looked apologetic, sitting in Bobby's law office.

"I really do appreciate your visiting with me again, Bobby. As I explained on the phone, our editor has assigned me and two other writers to put together a series of articles about our country's race relations. The killings of those five Dallas police officers in July has brought the whole crazy issue to our doorstep."

"Yeah, it sure has," Bobby nodded.

"Well, that's why I wanted to visit. Our first article is going to focus on the reaction of typical people to what happened in Dallas— what do they think about it and so forth. You know, how has it affected Lamar?"

"The murder of five policemen? Well, it sent a chill down the spine around here. We were almost recovered from the suicide bomber, and now just forty miles away, another suicide killer. It has put everyone on edge, for sure. There is a fear hanging in the air."

Dave began scribbling quickly and looked up.

"Why do you say it was suicide in Dallas?"

"I mean that here and in Dallas, both killers surely knew they were going to die. The shooter in Dallas had no plan to escape and even refused to surrender. But he was determined to kill others before he was done. Out of vengeance, he said. FBI said the man here appeared to be an avowed Islamic terrorist, but they still don't know why he decided to blow up a gas well instead of trying to kill people."

"Has anyone here actually said they were now in fear because of the Dallas shootings?"

"Yes, but not in so many words. Just last week, our council approved next year's budget. It established a revolving account for economic incentives in the so-called underserved areas of Lamar. The mayor has resisted that for years, but this time he pushed it through the council. Only Carl Jeffers and I opposed it because we think it makes no economic sense and because it won't really help the black people in Lamar. It's just part of the push from Reverend Benjamin and his kind. But I think the mayor and the other council members are nervous about all the marches and riots around the country and now Dallas."

The reporter shifted in his chair and looked across at Bobby.

"I'm not surprised. People just don't know how to react to all this. It seems to intrude on their lives even when it doesn't directly impact them. No one I've talked to can explain why that man, Johnson, was so angry he was willing to die if he could kill a few white policemen."

Bobby frowned and hesitantly replied, "Well, maybe Leon had it figured out, Dave. He would have said Johnson was reslaved. You remember that thing he wrote about black people becoming part of a dependent culture?"

"Yeah, that was something. But what made Johnson so crazy?"

"I'm not sure. I guess you should have met Sam Madison, a black professor who helped us prepare for Leon's trial. Madison said that affirmative action and government policies have deprived many black people of what he called the dignity of freedom. Maybe Johnson felt that loss and had to blame someone. I think that shooting of black men in Minnesota and Baton Rouge gave him the excuse in his mind to act. If you think about it, Johnson and the Afghan here in Lamar were not too different. They both seemingly vowed to kill themselves for the sake of avenging a wrong they believed they and their people had suffered. What I can't understand is why they thought their actions would solve anything. The desperation must be deep to cause that kind of rationale. It's senseless. Martyrdom is the only explanation anyone has offered, to glorify, I suppose."

Dave's writing paused again, and a weak smile flickered on his lips.

"It's unreal, Bobby, sitting with you here again and remembering the talk we had only months ago about you and Leon. You know, I went to his funeral. The church couldn't hold all the people."

"That's right. Maybe that was due to the article you wrote about Leon and me."

"Oh yeah. The two lifelong friends."

"That's not entirely true, Dave. We were teammates, but we didn't cross paths after that for years. He had changed, grown up I guess, when he came looking for a lawyer. Not the same one I knew in school."

"Say, did they ever find out what happened? You know, Leon was a good driver."

"No. I mean the police have never found the other car that man talked about. Maybe they are still looking. I don't know.

"Well, Leon's lawsuit made quite a splash in Fort Worth. The thing Leon wrote, it seems like he was really angry."

"I suppose so. But he was not mad at Benjamin. Not personally. I don't believe he ever met him before the suit was filed. Leon was upset about what was happening in this country."

"He wasn't alone, Bobby. All these racial marches and movements have everyone on edge. It's one of the reasons my editor suggested I do this piece."

"All that stuff was just the catalyst for Leon. He deeply appreciated the fact that the US stands for freedom and the opportunity that is created by freedom. He made good use of his opportunities, but his observations were telling him that today's society might be infringing on those opportunities, not just for his children but for everyone, black or white. It was what he referred to as his point."

"It's a shame his case never got to be heard. It might have answered a lot of questions, don't you think?"

"Maybe, but Judge Welton made it clear that only the elements of defamation were going into the jury room. The jury would have given a verdict, but who can say what it would have been or what it would have meant? Anyhow, the questions of race are not going to be resolved by twelve people in a jury room."

"That's probably true, Bobby. But how did you view the piece that Leon wrote, the one that got Benjamin so upset?"

"Dave, I've asked myself that question every day since Leon was killed. Getting ready for trial, Oliver and I were focused on the strategy and tactics needed in the courtroom to block Benjamin's money claims. Judge Welton instructed us to keep all debate about race relations out of the courtroom, so we didn't dwell on Leon's statement outside the legal elements which form a defamation claim.

"But it's clear to me now that Leon had other interests. In high school, he was always intense in preparing for a game and then almost hyper once we kicked off. He brought that same intensity to form his successful business. After his death, I discovered that he put his statement on the internet or directly caused someone else to do it, so he could publicize his manifesto, as he called it. He was a student of US history and felt the country was in deep trouble on several fronts not just race relations, and he could not understand how the values of opportunity and freedom were being ignored and abused. I believe he felt so strongly about it he was willing to risk his bank account and maybe his life to make his points. He adamantly refused to consider any kind of settlement of the lawsuit, even when he got threatening phone calls."

"Are you serious, Bobby? He was threatened?"

"Yes. But he told me nothing about that. Clara told me after he died."

"Won't that information help the police investigation?" Dave asked, leaning forward in his chair.

"Sure, it might confirm their decision to open the investigation, but it won't identify who made the call or that car or the car's driver," Bobby replied in desperation.

"Well then, where does it go from here? Will Leon's statement just fade away? The newspapers have quit writing about Leon and his manifesto."

"I know. It's a shame. There are others, even among the black people, who share his views. But look, it gets little attention in all the media uproar and the constant reminder of slavery, Jim Crow, and sympathy for the cop killer in Dallas. You know, African Americans make up about 15 percent of our population. If the majority of them continue to hold out for entitlements and restitution, we will end up with 9 or 10 percent of our citizens permanently abandoning the opportunity which freedom offers in America. We have the rest of the world clamoring to come here to enjoy that freedom while we teach our own to sell it for empty promises. That will lead to no good—maybe to the end of our country."

Dave chuckled. "Well, now I know what you think about Leon's statement. You have just outlined for me the content of my first draft."

"Whoa, Dave. That was off the record. Please don't quote me in that paper."

"Okay, okay. I won't cite you or your name. But Leon's lawsuit has really added an important viewpoint to the whole subject."

"Before I go, one last question. What is your opinion of Leon now that he is gone?"

"Leon? Well, Texas high school football produces a new crop of sports heroes every season, briefly praised and then gone the next year. Even in Lamar, few people remembered Leon the Loper after he left and few read about his lawsuit. But I will never forget Leon. He forever changed my view of our country."

ABOUT THE AUTHOR

Holding a degree from Harvard Law School, the author practiced law in Texas for more than forty years before retiring. Writing under the pen name Brad Flint, he calls upon his experience as a former city council member to explore many of the issues confronting elected officials and citizens in our democratic republic.